"What the hell w— creeping around in the dark?"

His tone raised her hackles. She lifted her chin and gave him a look guaranteed to freeze lava. "I was *not* creeping."

"Oh, yeah? Well, I don't know what else you'd call it. What were you doing, tiptoeing in here like that?"

"If you must know, I came in here to seduce you," she snapped.

"Well, that was a damned stupid thing to do!" he roared.

"Obviously, if I'd known you had a gun, I wouldn't have done it," she responded primly.

"That's beside the—" He stopped, his face going blank. His voice changed from a shout to a croak. "Wait a minute. Did you say...? You mean...? You came in here to...*seduce* me?"

Abigail sniffed and lifted her chin a notch higher. "Yes. But I've changed my mind."

* * *

Dashing David Blaine came to the rescue of his sisters, saucy Erin and sweet Elise, in Ginna Gray's "twin" Silhouette **Special Edition** novels, *Fools Rush In* (#416) and *Where Angels Fear* (#468). But for *Once in a Lifetime* (#661), *he's* in more than double trouble now....

Dear Reader,

From a most traditional marriage of convenience to a futuristic matchmaking robot, from a dusty dude ranch to glistening Pearl Harbor, from international adventure to an inner struggle with disturbing memories, this month's sensational Silhouette **Special Edition** authors pull out all the stops to honor your quest for a range of deeply satisfying novels of living and loving in today's world.

Those of you who've written in requesting that Ginna Gray tell dashing David Blaine's story, and those of you who waved the flag for Debbie Macomber's "Navy" novels, please take note that your patience is finally being rewarded with *Once in a Lifetime* and *Navy Brat*. For the rest of you, now's the time to discover what all the excitement is about! Naturally, each novel stands solidly alone as, you might say, an extra special Silhouette **Special Edition**.

Don't miss the other special offerings in store for you: four more wonderful novels by talented, talked about writers Nikki Benjamin, Arlene James, Bevlyn Marshall and Christina Dair. Each author brings you a memorable novel packed with stirring emotions and the riches of love: in the tradition of Silhouette **Special Edition**, romance to believe in . . . and to remember.

From all the authors and editors of Silhouette **Special Edition**,

Warmest wishes.

GINNA GRAY
Once in a Lifetime

Published by Silhouette Books New York

America's Publisher of Contemporary Romance

For a very special friend
and super bookseller,
Linda Wright. Dusty, too.

SILHOUETTE BOOKS
300 East 42nd St., New York, N.Y. 10017

ONCE IN A LIFETIME

ISBN: 0-373-09661-5

First Silhouette Books printing April 1991

Printed in the U.S.A.

GINNA GRAY

A native Houstonian, Ginna Gray admits that since childhood, she has been a compulsive reader as well as a head-in-the-clouds dreamer. Long accustomed to expressing her creativity in tangible ways (Ginna also enjoys painting and needlework), she finally decided to try putting her fantasies and wild imaginings down on paper. The result? The mother of two now spends eight hours a day as a full-time writer.

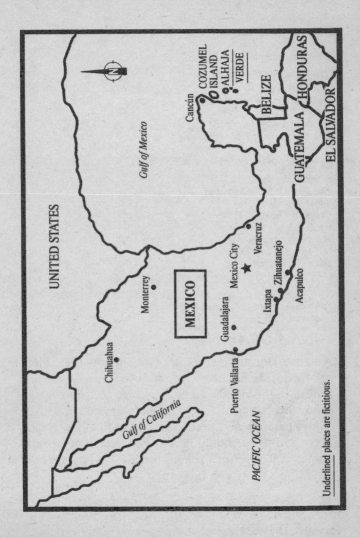

Underlined places are fictitious.

Chapter One

The last thing Abigail Stewart expected to find in her hotel room was a man. The sight of two of them pawing through her things jerked her to a halt in the doorway, the plastic key card still clutched between her fingers.

They apparently hadn't expected to see her, either, for at the sound of the door opening both men spun around. Their expressions mirrored the shock she felt.

For the space of perhaps four heartbeats no one moved. Then Chelsea, Abigail's three-pound Yorkshire terrier, poked her golden head out of the side pocket of her mistress's purse and growled.

The sound shattered the frozen tableau.

The man farthest from Abigail, an ugly brute with a broad flat face, reached inside his suit coat and pulled out a gun. Abigail's eyes widened, and her heart lurched. "Get her," Shovel-face snapped out, and the other man hurried forward, drawing a gun from inside his coat as well.

Abigail hadn't the slightest idea what was going on, but she wasn't fool enough to stick around and find out. Giving a squeaky yelp, she spun on her heel and ran.

Ingrained habit made her pull the door shut behind her. Almost immediately something hit the other side with a solid thump. A growl of pain followed, then grumbled words in a foreign language, and the doorknob rattled under fumbling hands.

Fright lent wings to Abigail's feet, but she'd barely covered a dozen yards when the door flew open and the two men came barreling after her.

She let out another squeak and pelted down the hallway as fast as her long legs would carry her, her canvas shoulder bag bouncing against her hip. Chelsea hung over the top of the side pocket, bristling at their pursuers and making a tremendous racket. Her agitated barks ran together like the choppy wail of a high-pitched siren.

One of the other hotel guests stuck his head out, scowling, but one look at the two men and he withdrew and shut his door.

Abigail reached the elevators and punched the Down button, but nothing happened. She glanced over her shoulder, gave a panicked groan and snatched open the stairwell door.

On the dimly lit landing she paused just long enough to flip the lock before pounding down the stairs. Her leather sandals clanged against the metal treads, and Chelsea's sharp barks echoed off the walls, reaching ear-splitting intensity in the confined space. Adding to the din were the unconscious, desperate whimpers issuing from Abigail with each gasp of breath. They were making enough racket for a deaf man to follow their progress, but she was too intent on escape to notice.

She tore down the three flights of stairs in seconds, praying all the while that the elevator would prove as poky as it had a few hours earlier when she'd checked in. She was so panicked, she galloped right past the ground-floor exit and descended three more steps before realizing that she was heading for the basement. With a groan she raced back up and burst through the door into the lobby at a dead run.

Skidding to a halt by the tiled fountain in the center of the lobby, Abigail looked around desperately. The desk clerk was busy talking on the telephone. Abigail doubted the young woman would be of any help against the two brutes in any case. And there wasn't a bellman or security guard in sight.

Gnawing her lower lip, Abigail made a frustrated sound. Where was everyone? When she had returned from sightseeing, just minutes before, there had been three men reading newspapers in the lobby. Now all the chairs were empty.

In the quiet stillness, her pet's barking finally registered. "Quiet, Chelsea. Hush now," Abigail commanded. The tiny dog gave her an offended look but she reluctantly obeyed after one last growl.

Abigail wrung her hands and turned around in a circle. Oh, Lord. What was she going to do? She cast a worried glance at the floor indicator above the elevator. The light blinked out on number four and a second later the number three lit up.

Abigail sucked in her breath and bolted for the front entrance.

She shoved open the heavy glass doors and ran pell-mell down the sidewalk, arms and legs pumping, every muscle in her body straining. The thick brown braid coiled at her nape escaped its pins and lashed out behind her like a whip. Her canvas purse bumped and bounced against her hip. The oversize shirt she wore over her walking shorts molded the front of her body and billowed out in the back like a sail that had caught the wind.

Just short of the corner Chelsea started barking again. Abigail darted a look over her shoulder. "Ooohh noooo!"

A block or so behind, the two men raced after her.

She turned on more steam and skidded around the corner.

"Quiet, Chelsea." The gasped command silenced the dog's furious yapping but earned Abigail another wounded look. The little Yorkie seemed to have no concept of her diminutive size. Nothing intimidated her—not German shepherds nor Dobermans nor two-hundred-pound men. When it came to defending her mistress, Chelsea was a holy terror. Abigail appreciated her loyalty and protectiveness, but the shrill barks were a beacon for the two thugs.

Instinctively Abigail headed for the market with its throngs of people and maze of streets and alleyways.

By the time she'd covered the six-block distance, her lungs were on fire and her legs were aching. She plunged into the crowd, running full tilt, darting and dodging her way through strolling tourists, brightly dressed natives and street vendors.

The scent of spices and tortillas and frying meat hung in the air, along with the smell of animals, straw, dust, leather and humans. Blending with the pungent aromas came an occasional whiff of heady perfume from the island's profusion of wildflowers. When Abigail had visited the market earlier she had been enchanted and intrigued by the varied sights, sounds and odors. Now she was oblivious to it all.

Expecting to be grabbed from behind at any moment, almost sobbing with frustration and fear, she shoved and twisted and bumped her way through a crowd gathered around a Mariachi band. Move! Get out of my way! Oh, please, she begged silently. Please!

She glanced over her shoulder and whimpered when she spotted her pursuers. They were a couple of blocks behind, but it appeared that they had lost sight of her. Their pace had slowed to a fast walk and both were searching the crowds around them and peering into the shops as they hurried by. Among the casually dressed tourists and Mexican islanders, the gray-suited men stood out like sore thumbs.

A painful stitch grabbed at Abigail's side. She tried to ignore it but couldn't, and her headlong pace slowed to a halting stumble. She sucked in great gulps of air, but her tortured lungs screamed for more. Oh, God, what was she going to do?

Clutching her side, Abigail hobbled into a shadowed alley between two buildings and flattened herself against the wall behind a stack of empty wooden crates. The coolness of the adobe penetrated her sweat-soaked cotton shirt, and the rough plaster scraped against her palms and her calves below her walking shorts. Through an opening in the narrow slats of the crates, Abigail watched the street.

Her heart boomed and her lungs burned. A muscle in her right calf began to cramp. She gritted her teeth, and on either side of her hips her splayed fingers clutched the rough adobe wall. But she didn't move.

Seconds ticked by. Minutes. Out in the sunlit street, people meandered by in a constant stream, amid a babble of Spanish and English voices, distant strains of Latin music, the occasional bray of a donkey and rattle of a vendor's cart. Abigail's chest heaved. The rasp of her labored breathing sounded so loud to her ears, she was terrified that everyone could hear it above the drone of activity.

She waited, motionless.

Her heart leaped when the pair stepped into her narrow line of vision. Abigail pressed back harder against the wall and held her breath.

Chelsea growled low in her throat.

"Shhh." Abigail clamped her hand around the dog's muzzle. Her eyes never left the two men.

One had his head turned away, searching the other side of the street. The man nearest to Abigail peered into the alley as he went by, but his steps barely slowed. They moved on, disappearing from sight as quickly as they had materialized.

Closing her eyes, Abigail released her breath and slid down the wall. Her bottom hit the ground with a jarring bump, and she collapsed, knees bent, her head tipped back against the rough adobe. Her hands lay limp at her sides, palms up. She breathed deeply, her galloping heartbeat gradually tapering off.

Some great vacation this was turning out to be, she thought, on the verge of hysteria. She'd been on the island less than five hours and already her room had been ransacked and she'd been chased by armed bandits.

She had known when she booked the trip that Alhaja Verde was just beginning to develop as a vacation spot so she'd been prepared for the local customs and conditions to be a bit behind the times. But she certainly hadn't expected such uncivilized behavior!

What did those awful men want with her, anyway?

In those first few seconds it had flashed through her mind that she had walked in on a burglary. Now, given their determined pursuit, she wasn't sure. Surely common thieves would have run away when they had the chance—not given chase.

It didn't make any sense, but they appeared to be after her. Why?

Oh, why had she let her friends talk her into making this stupid trip? she lamented, swiping at her sweaty brow with the back of her hand. Normally she would never have come to such an exotic place. Especially not alone.

But turning thirty and receiving the inheritance her parents had left her had seemed to call for a celebration of some sort.

Do something wild! her customers at the bookstore had urged. *Something you wouldn't ordinarily dream of doing. Live a little, Abigail!*

Deep down, she had craved a little excitement, and the trip had seemed like a harmless adventure. So she had let herself be persuaded.

And look what it had gotten her. Here she was, all alone, sitting in a filthy alley on a remote foreign island, hiding from two thugs who wanted God knew what from her, fearing for her very life.

Unbidden, all of her late Aunt Harriet's dire warnings about white slavers and unscrupulous men who prey on unprotected women flashed through her mind. Abigail shuddered.

Aunt Harriet had never held with foreign travel. Of course, to her that had meant anything outside the Texas state line.

Abigail could just imagine what her aunt would have had to say about this mess. She could almost hear her.

"Humph! I could have told you no good would come from traipsing off to some heathen place. Excitement is for fools and sinners. You, my girl, are getting no more than you deserve."

And she would be right, Abigail silently wailed. If she had stayed home in Waco, none of this would have happened.

Exhaling a weary sigh, she looped her arms around her updrawn legs and let her head droop forward, resting her forehead on her knees. At once something cold and wet nudged her elbow.

"Oh, Chelsea." Abigail straightened and picked up the little dog, who was trying to burrow her way onto her mistress's lap. "What are we going to do?"

Cuddled close against Abigail's chest, the tiny animal answered with a soft whine and offered comfort in the only way she knew how—licking Abigail's chin and gazing up at her, her button eyes concerned and adoring.

"We don't dare go back to the hotel," she murmured, stroking Chelsea's long coat. "Those two men might be watching it. And there isn't an American embassy or consulate office on Alhaja Verde that we could go to for help." Abigail thought longingly of the airline ticket in her purse, but she couldn't risk going to the airport, either. They might be watching it as well.

One thing was certain, she couldn't stay there. She'd already wasted too much time feeling sorry for herself as it was. Those two thugs might decide at any moment to double back for a more thorough search.

She got to her feet and brushed off the seat of her walking shorts. Still holding Chelsea close against her bosom, she edged to the alley entrance and peered out into the street.

It was getting late. Soon the market would close. Already the crowds were thinning. She had to do something, and soon.

The logical thing would be to report the incident. But to whom? Abigail hadn't seen anyone who even resembled a policeman since arriving. Alhaja Verde was the largest in the chain of small, underdeveloped islands off Mexico's eastern shores, but even so, San Cristobal was its only town. But surely there had to be some sort of local law enforcement?

What she needed was some help. The problem was she didn't know anyone on the island ... except ...

Abigail's expression grew thoughtful as she recalled the nice couple who owned the cantina where she'd had lunch. Pepe and Constanza Morales had been about to close for the afternoon siesta and the cantina had been deserted when she'd walked in, but they had graciously served her anyway. While she'd eaten, the friendly couple, along with several of their relatives who worked for them, had sat at her table and chatted.

It was presumptuous of her, Abigail knew, but she had to ask them for help. She had no other choice.

Gathering her courage, Abigail deposited Chelsea in the side pocket of her purse and eased out into the street, looking cautiously in every direction.

The shadows were lengthening, and already some of the vendors were packing away their wares and closing their shops and stalls. Abigail hurried over to one who was still open and purchased a floppy brimmed straw hat and a large embroidered shawl. As a disguise, it wasn't much, but it was the best she could do.

Her whole body quivered as she made her way back toward the waterfront. Pepe's Cantina was on the beach road a block from San Cristobal's harbor. Clutching the shawl around her so that it covered her purse and Chelsea, and most of her body as well, Abigail kept her head lowered and peered out from beneath the floppy hat brim.

With every step she expected to be accosted. By the time she reached the cantina her nerves were so taut, her breath was coming in choppy little sobs.

Abigail slipped inside and stood against the wall, letting her eyes adjust to the dim interior.

It was early yet for the evening crowd. There were a few customers at the bar, but only a couple of tables and one booth were occupied by diners. Two of Pepe's cousins were playing the guitar and mariachi in the far corner, and other relatives scurried around, setting up tables.

As Abigail removed her hat, Pepe looked up from drying glasses and spotted her. His mustachioed face lit up in a beaming smile.

"Señorita Stewart. How nice to see you again so soon. Mama! Señorita Stewart, she has come back to see us," he called over his shoulder to his wife as he came around the end of the bar. "Come. Come sit. We will have a little wine, a little talk, and then my Constanza, she will cook something special for you. *¿Sí?*"

"Pepe, I—"

"Ah, *señorita,* so you are back." Constanza bustled out of the kitchen, wiping her hands on her apron. *"Muy bien. We are most pleased to see you again."*

"Th-thank you. I hope you will still be when I tell you why I've come."

Constanza's black eyes narrowed with concern on Abigail's pale face. "You have troubles, *señorita?*" At Abigail's nod Constanza guided her toward the corner booth. "Come. Tell us. Pepe, bring some wine. *¡Pronto! ¡Pronto!*" she snapped at her spouse, and rattled off a string of Spanish that sent the little man scurrying.

In moments he returned with the wine and three glasses. "Here, *señorita,* you drink this. Then you tell Pepe and Constanza why you tremble so. You see. Even the little one, she is worried about you," he said when Chelsea climbed into Abigail's lab, whining.

Abigail stroked her pet, and with a shaking hand she lifted the glass of red wine and gulped it down. The Mexican couple exchanged a concerned glance. In a halting voice that shook with nerves, Abigail explained what had happened.

"¡Pobrecita!" Constanza commiserated when she'd finished. "Such a terrible thing. No wonder you are upset."

"I . . . I was hoping that you could tell me what to do. I know I should report the incident, but to whom? Is there a local police force?"

"Sí. But if I were you, *señorita,* I would stay away from the *policía,"* Pepe advised gravely, and Constanza nodded her agreement. "They are *muy* bad."

"Bad?"

"*Sí.* The *policía,* they are mixed up in everything crooked on Alhaja Verde. On all the islands."

"Then . . . what can I do?"

Pepe's mouth pursed as he considered the matter, his narrow, debonair mustache turning down at the ends. After a moment he sent a furtive look around the cantina, then leaned across the table toward Abigail. "Go to Señor David Blaine," he whispered. "He can help you."

"Who is David Blaine?"

Another furtive look, and Pepe's voice dropped another notch. "If I tell you, you must promise not repeat it to anyone. Ever. You understand?"

"Yes, of course," Abigail agreed, wide-eyed.

"Señor Blaine, he owns a boat, which he keeps here. He comes to Alhaja Verde four, maybe five times a year. For the deep-sea fishing, he says. He also claims to be the, uh . . . how do you say . . . the head of security for Telecom International, but it is all just a cover."

"A cover?"

"*Sí.* You see, *señorita* . . ." Pepe paused and cut his eyes around once again before continuing the hush-hush conversation in a dramatic whisper. "Señor Blaine, he is really a G-man."

"You mean . . ."

"*¡Ai yi yi!*" Constanza threw up her hands. "Spies and secret missions! That's all this hombre ever thinks about." She shook her fist at her husband. "Pepe, how many times I tell you—you read too many books! See too many movies!" Her mouth twisted. "James Band! Ha!"

Pepe drew himself up. "Bond, Mama. The name is James Bond. And it is true about Señor Blaine. He told me himself."

"You mean he really is a government agent?" Abigail asked hopefully.

"*Sí.* He is with the CIA, and he is here working on a top-secret mission. So you must be very careful not to blow his cover," he cautioned, smugly pleased at his knowledge of the slang term.

"Oh, I won't. I promise. How do I find this David Blaine?"

Pepe sprang to his feet, his eyes alight with excitement. "Come. I will take you to him."

Immediately Constanza jumped up as well. She jabbed her husband's chest with a plump finger. "Oh, no, *mi esposo*. You are going nowhere."

"But, *querida*—"

"Don't *querida* me. We have a cantina to run, and you are staying here." She looked at Abigail and rolled her eyes. "This one, he is worse than a *niño*, always running off looking for adventure."

Pepe tried to argue, but Constanza jabbed his chest again and launched into a rapid-fire tirade in Spanish, cutting him off.

Pepe was a small, wiry man, not much taller than Abigail's five foot four inches. Constanza stood three inches taller than her excitable husband and outweighed him by a good seventy-five pounds, a circumstance for which Pepe apparently had a healthy respect. When Constanza, in the midst of the heated exchange, snatched up a weighty glass ashtray and brandished it at her husband's head, he threw up both hands in surrender.

"I am sorry, *señorita*," he said sheepishly to Abigail. "But Constanza is right. Saturday, she is our busiest night. I am afraid I cannot leave."

Constanza added her apologies, patting Abigail's hand. "*Señorita*, please believe me. If I thought you were in danger I would insist that my Pepe go with you. Those two men, they are probably just thieves who mistook you for a rich American tourist. You go see Señor Blaine. I'm sure he will tell you the same."

Only about an hour of daylight remained by the time Abigail reached the docks. A broad, picturesque bay formed the island's natural deep-water harbor. Fishing boats and pleasure craft of all sizes and types lined the piers jutting out into the turquoise water. A moderate size cruise ship, heading out to sea through the narrow inlet, gave a farewell blast of its horn, making Abigail jump.

She located pier four and started down it. Pepe had said that David Blaine's boat was a thirty-five-foot power cruiser, but Abigail didn't know a sloop from a battleship, and she peered at the prow of each vessel she passed. The smell of salt air, fish, wet hemp and diesel oil assailed her. Overhead, sea gulls swooped and squawked their demanding cry. Ropes creaked, and water slapped the pilings beneath the pier and the hulls of the moored crafts. At last, almost at the end of the dock Abigail spotted the name she'd been searching for.

She hurried toward the boat, only to pull up short, the relief she felt turning to shock.

Abigail had expected David Blaine to be an average-looking man—a conservatively dressed, clean-cut, all-American type. He was, after all, a government agent. But there was nothing average about the man on the deck of the *Freewind*. Nothing conservative, either.

Big and powerfully built, he stood with his legs braced arrogantly wide, his head thrown back, guzzling beer straight out of a can. To Abigail's dismay, the man looked like a street tough—lean and mean with a battered face. Even from where she stood, she sensed a dangerous, uncompromising air about him.

And all he wore was an almost obscenely brief pair of ragged cutoffs and a three-day growth of beard!

David chugalugged the last of the beer, making an appreciative sound as the cold brew slid down his throat. He swiped the back of his hand across his mouth, crushed the can and tossed it down through the companionway into the galley, hitting the trash container dead center. He stretched and scratched his furry chest. Damn, he felt good.

There was nothing like a few days of fishing to unwind. It didn't even matter whether or not he caught anything. Just being out on the water seemed to take the kinks out.

He gazed at the peaceful bay. The low-hanging sun splashed the rippling surface with rose and gold. David sighed. Life had been good to him lately. Good, hell. He had it made. He had a great-paying job he liked that afforded him a few of the things he'd always wanted and the time off to enjoy them as well.

Not for a minute did he regret leaving that stuffy law firm. Or even the Bureau, for that matter. No, sir, no more long hours of boring office work for him. No more risking his hide on dicey assignments, either. He'd leave that to reckless young studs like Travis McCall.

At the thought of his cousin, David grinned. Travis was due to join him and his sisters over at their place on Rincon Island next week. Man, he was going to flip when he saw the *Freewind*.

David rubbed his hand over a shiny metal fitting, a look of satisfaction on his hard face. God, he loved this boat. Owning it was a dream come true.

He still couldn't believe his luck. He'd purchased the craft the year before from the widow of a wealthy sportsman who had kept it in pristine condition. It wasn't one of those new jobs made of fiberglass and chrome with a fru-fru designer interior. No, sir, this was a man's boat, a quality craft made the way a boat ought to be, of wood with brass fittings and real teak decking. The interior had been refitted and modernized with an eye to comfort and convenience, but without, thank God, the fancy-schmancy frills so popular with today's yuppie boaters and fishermen.

Yessir, life was sweet.

Hell, he'd even gotten his two sisters married off to men who might—just might—be able to handle them. Now he could quit worrying about Erin and Elise and just enjoy life's pleasures.

A ghost of a smile twitched his hard mouth. And if you expect to sample some of that pleasure tonight you'd better get your butt in gear, Blaine. Maxine would be there soon, he reminded himself, loping down the companionway steps.

In the galley he lifted the wine bottle from the bucket of ice in the sink and felt the frosty glass. Perfect.

As soon as Maxine arrived they'd head out. His smile twitched again, and a lecherous gleam entered his brown eyes. A sunset cruise, dinner on deck by moonlight, a little wine...and a hot blonde. What more could a man ask for?

He ran a hand over his stubbled jaw. Maybe he ought to shave. He hadn't bothered the last few days while he'd been out fishing. He thought it over for a second and shook his head. Naw. Last night, when he'd met her in Pepe's Cantina, Maxine had seemed to think the three-day growth was sexy.

David took the steaks from the refrigerator and placed them on the broiler pan. As he rummaged through the small pantry for seasoning, he felt the boat rock. He glanced over his shoulder through the companionway and spotted the lower half of a female body. "Make yourself at home," he called out. "I'll be right up."

About to turn back to the steaks, he paused for a more leisurely perusal, a roguish look on his face. Damn, the woman had fantastic legs. Even in those godawful walking shorts. He thought about how she'd look, skinny-dipping in the moonlight, and the gleam in his eyes grew wicked.

Whistling, he seasoned the steaks, slid the pan under the broiler and bounded up the steps.

At the top, he paused, but Maxine made no move toward him. She stood at the side, watching the sea gulls riding the air currents. David's puzzled gaze ran over her back. He'd expected a warmer greeting. Last night at Pepe's she'd been all over him. If she hadn't been stewed to the gills, he would have invited her back to the boat with him then. He liked his women eager, but he also liked them sober.

David took in her attire and frowned. He'd expected Maxine to show up wearing something with a bit more pizzazz—something skimpier. Sexier. He sure hadn't figured her for the type to go in for baggy walking shorts and an oversize shirt. Or for that matter, to wear her hair tucked up under that ugly straw hat.

Women. Who could figure them?

Shrugging away the vagaries of the female sex, David cast off the lines and climbed the ladder to the bridge. "I'm glad you came early," he called down to her, taking his position at the control console. "This will give us plenty of time before sunset to reach that romantic little island I told you about.''

Abigail spun around, her eyes wide.

Romantic island? Oh, dear Lord. He thought... "Mr. Blaine, I'm afraid there's been a mista—''

The deck vibrated beneath her feet as the boat's engines rumbled to life, drowning out her words. "Wait! Mr. Blaine, wait!''

She started for the bridge but lurched and grabbed the side when the boat pulled away from the pier. Horrified, Abigail stared at the receding structure, her mouth open. Oh, good grief. This was ridiculous! Bracing against the rocking motion, she started once again for the ladder. At the same instant she spotted the long black car with two men inside, cruising slowly along the quayside road.

Abigail gasped and ducked out of sight. Her heart began to pound. She couldn't be sure it was the same two men, but she wasn't taking any chances.

Suddenly, putting a few miles between herself and the island didn't seen like such a bad idea. Of course, under normal circumstances she wouldn't dream of putting out to sea with a stranger, especially not one who looked as disreputable and rough around the edges as David Blaine, but at the moment she couldn't be choosy. After all, the man *did* work for the U.S. government.

They cleared the harbor, and David opened up the throttle. From her crouched position at the rear of the boat, Abigail eased up just enough to peek over the stern. There was no sign of the black car, but she ducked back down and remained out of sight. For all she knew they could be watching through binoculars.

Besides, at the moment, she wasn't in any rush to introduce herself to Mr. Blaine.

"Hey, Maxine!'' he yelled from the bridge, and Abigail jumped. "Why don't you grab a cold one and join me up here?''

She grimaced and took another peek at the island. "Very well. But first I've got to go below for a minute,'' she called back, and crossed her fingers that between the wind, the roar of the engines and the pounding waves he wouldn't question the difference in her voice.

She still didn't feel safe revealing herself. Squatting on her haunches, dragging her purse along the deck and ignoring Chelsea's worried whines and licks on her arm, Abigail ducked into the companionway and scrambled down the steps to the cabin.

She huddled on the bottom step, too nervous to even notice her surroundings. Gnawing her bottom lip and absently scratching Chelsea's tiny head, she wondered how long she could stall before facing Mr. Blaine.

Five minutes later she had her answer.

"Hey, Maxine! What's taking so long? Come on up!"

Abigail grimaced. She had a hunch he wasn't going to be pleased when he discovered his mistake. Taking a fortifying breath, she went back up on deck and climbed the ladder to the bridge. At least they were so far from shore that the island was just a speck on the horizon.

David stood before the control console, gripping the wheel, his powerful legs braced wide against the boat's motion. Abigail swallowed hard and approached him cautiously, her eyes riveted on his broad back, watching the play of muscles beneath his tanned skin.

A step behind him she hesitated. There was no reason to be nervous, she told herself. No doubt he'd be surprised, maybe even a bit annoyed, but he wouldn't kill her. After all, it was just an honest mix-up. And once he heard her story, he'd understand.

The quivering in her stomach continued unabated.

Gathering her courage, Abigail drew a deep breath and moved to his side.

"There you are. It's about ti—" David Blaine glanced her way, then did a double take. His rugged face registered shocked disbelief for a full five seconds . . . then hardened.

"Who the *hell* are you?" he bellowed over the roar of wind and engines.

Chapter Two

The barked question made Abigail jump. Her eyes widened, and her quivering stomach started playing a game of leapfrog. The fierce-looking man scared the pants off her but, as always, she quickly sought to cover her disquiet.

Assuming a haughty expression, she drew herself up. "When you, sir, have the common decency to ask in a civil manner, I shall tell you," she shouted back in her starchiest tone. "Not a moment sooner."

David Blaine stared, thunderstruck.

Abigail's prickly defenses wavered under that piercing glare, but she swallowed hard and jutted out her chin.

He cut the engines, and as the boat slowed to a drifting stop in the sudden silence he swung to face her.

He took a menacing step forward. Abigail gulped and took one backward.

Up close, he was even more intimidating than she had first thought. He towered over her, topping her height by almost a foot, and the close proximity of that powerful, nearly naked body sent prickles of alarm up her spine. She could smell his masculine scent, feel his heat.

"All right. I'm going to ask you one more time. Who the hell are you?"

A low growl rumbled from the pocket of Abigail's purse, but he either didn't notice or didn't care.

"I told you. I have no inten—"

"Lady, you got five seconds to start talking."

"Oh, really? And if I don't?"

"Then you're outta here. And I gotta warn you, it's a helluva long swim back to Alhaja Verde."

"You . . . you wouldn't dare!"

"In a New York second. So don't push it, lady."

Abigail's eyes grew as round as saucers. He meant it!

The man was a barbarian. There wasn't an ounce of softness in him. Whiskey-brown eyes glinted with anger in a tough, lived-in face that looked carved out of granite. The only things about him that even hinted of warmth were the red highlights in his dark brown hair and the deep bronze tone of his skin, of which, to Abigail's way of thinking, far too much was exposed at the moment.

Inside, she quailed, but that only made her respond with even greater prickliness. "Very well, I will tell you," she sniffed. "But only because it's obvious that you are no gentleman and would no doubt use your superior strength against a woman. My name is Abigail Stewart."

"A tourist, right?" He looked her over from her head to her toes. His expression didn't change, but Abigail thought she saw a flicker of disdain in his eyes. She lifted her chin.

"Yes. I arrived on the island just before noon."

"So why did you stow away on my boat?"

"I did *not* stow away."

"Oh, yeah? What do you call it?" He darted a puzzled frown toward her purse as the soft rumble issuing from it increased in volume. "And what the hell is that noise?"

"I came to your boat to talk to you about a matter of importance," she informed him, ignoring the last. "It's hardly my fault that you assumed I was your girlfriend. Before I even knew what was happening, you were heading out to sea."

"So why didn't you stop me? You could've said something."

Her righteous indignation faltered at that. "I . . . well . . . that is . . . you see, there were these two men . . ."

Their clash had temporarily made her forget her fright, but as she haltingly began her story it all came back, and by the time she'd finished the words were tumbling out one on top of the other. Through it all, David scowled and maintained a stony silence—until she got to the end.

" . . . And so, Pepe sent me to you for help."

"Why in hell would he do that?"

Taken aback, Abigail blinked. "Well, I . . . I assume because you work for the government."

"*Worked* for the government, lady. *Worked*. Past tense. I left all that behind more than two years ago. It's over. Kaput. Finis. You got that?"

He bit off each word, his big forefinger jabbing the air just inches from the end of her nose. Abigail flinched at each explosive syllable but fought the urge to back away. She would not let this boorish bully intimidate her. She was a taxpayer, after all. That entitled her to his protection.

"Mr. Blaine, you don't have to pretend with me. Pepe explained that your position with Telecom is just a cover for your spy activities."

"He *what?* Why that . . ." Abigail jumped when he punched one palm with his balled fist. "Just wait until I get my hands on that little tortilla. I'll strangle him with my bare hands!"

"Please, Mr. Blaine. There's no need to shout. I assure you I won't . . ." Abigail paused and frowned. "How did Pepe put it? Oh, yes. I remember. I won't blow your cover."

"Dammit! There *is no cover!*"

Chelsea's growl grew louder. David glanced at the furry head sticking up over the edge of the purse, and his mouth twisted.

Abigail sniffed. "My stars. Such an atrocious temper. I thought secret agents were supposed to be cool and unflappable."

Jaw working, David looked heavenward. Through clenched teeth, he ground out a long and colorful string of obscenities. Abigail took immediate offense.

"Mr. Blaine! Really! I must insist that you watch your language. Not only is cursing low and vulgar, Aunt Harriet always said it revealed a distasteful lack of self-control. To say nothing of a poor vocabulary."

The growl that rumbled from him put Chelsea's to shame. Planting his balled fists on his hipbones, he bent from the waist until they were nose to nose.

"All right, lady, listen up!" he snarled. "First of all, I'll cuss anytime I damned well please. And second, I am not now, nor have I even been, a damned CIA spook. I was with the FBI. And the operative word there is *was*. Understand?"

"Oh, my." The words came out on a weak puff of breath. "Are . . . are you saying that you really *aren't* with the government anymore?"

"Bingo! Give the lady a prize."

"There's no need to be sarcastic. At any rate, under the circumstances, I would think that even a former FBI agent would feel a certain sense of responsibility for a fellow American."

"Well, there's where you're wrong, lady. I'm just a businessman, here for a few days of R and R. I have no intention of wasting my vacation nursemaiding some hysterical female."

"I am *not* hysterical!"

"Ha! What else would you call a woman who jumps at her own shadow and sees a rapist behind every bush? I bet those men you *think* you saw ransacking your room were just part of the hotel housekeeping staff."

"They *chased* me! With guns!"

"Uh-huh. Yeah, sure, lady. You probably set up such a racket they were running for their lives."

Throughout the tirade he stomped back and forth across the bridge, gesturing with both hands. When his gaze happened to again fall on her purse he jerked to a halt and pointed to the furry face sticking out of the side pocket. "There! You see? That just proves my point. What kind of woman but a repressed old maid carries a stuffed animal around in her purse!"

"Stuffed an—?" Perplexed, Abigail followed the direction of his accusing finger. "For your information, that is *not* a stuffed toy. That happens to be my dog."

"You're kidding! That's a real dog?" He leaned in for a closer look.

Chelsea growled and lifted her lip.

"Aw, jeez, it is alive." The look he sent Abigail reeked disgust. "You call this a dog? Shoot, this is just a rat with long hair— Ow!"

He jumped back, rubbing the end of his nose, and glaring at Abigail. "Dammit to hell! He bit me! That damned little fur ball bit me!"

"*Her* name is Chelsea. And she only nipped you. She didn't even break the skin. Anyway, it's your own fault. You shouldn't have insulted her."

For an instant Abigail thought he might explode right before her eyes. His jaw bulged, and a tick appeared at the corner of his upper lip. A vein in his temple wriggled and pulsed like a tiny blue snake just beneath the surface of his tanned skin.

"All right, that does it!" he shouted, throwing up his hands. Abigail shrank back. "I'm taking you and that vicious wad of fluff back to port right now. I'm not about to get sucked into your problems, lady, so you can just take your sad tale somewhere else. Besides, I don't have time for this nonsense. Dammit, I've got a hot date tonight with a very sexy lady."

"You mean . . . y-you really aren't going to help me?"

He stomped to the control console and started the engines. With his hands on the wheel he shot her a hard look. "That's right. Once I dump you on the dock at San Cristobal, you're on your own."

"Well!" She huffed to cover the surge of terror that tightened her chest. "You're certainly no knight in shining armor, are you?"

"Nope." He raked her from head to toe with a dismissive look that made Abigail squirm. "But then, you're not exactly a fairytale princess, either."

Opening the throttle, he gave the wheel a hard spin. With a roar of engines, the boat heeled to starboard and cut through the turquoise waters in a tight arc, the hull thumping and bouncing over the waves as they raced back toward San Cristobal.

Not so much as a word passed between them on the trip back to the dock.

Abigail's prickly defenses crumbled under a renewed rush of fear. Quaking, she gripped the rail and watched the island grow steadily larger. Despite David Blaine's rough manner and cantankerous disposition, she hadn't expected him to refuse her. What was she going to do now?

Abigail considered pleading with him, but his rigid posture and tight-jawed expression were not encouraging. Oh, Lord, how could this be happening to her? She wished she'd never come on this trip!

David tried his best to ignore the woman. Scowling, he steered a straight course for San Cristobal's harbor, but over and over again his eyes strayed her way. He noted her white-knuckled grip on the rail and the tense set of her shoulders and gritted his teeth.

Damn silly female. Just his luck to get tangled up with a skittish old maid! What the hell was she doing vacationing alone, anyway? She wasn't worldly enough to be traipsing around in a foreign country on her own. Didn't she have any family to look after her? A brother? Or a male cousin, at least?

David ground his teeth and flexed his hands around the wheel. He fantasized about having them around Pepe Morales's scrawny neck. He ought to choke the man for siccing this drab little mouse on him.

Not for a minute did David believe that she was in danger. The fool woman probably got hysterical and bolted over nothing. He glanced her way again and sighed.

Foolish or not, her fear was genuine. Beneath the minimum of makeup she wore, her face was pale, and her eyes were clouded with apprehension.

Dammit, she looked like an abandoned waif in that hideous big shirt and baggy shorts.

The wind molded the garments to her slight body and whipped the ridiculous sombrero and her long braid out behind her. Shooting her another sour look, David grudgingly admitted that she wasn't all that bad looking. She was no great beauty, and she certainly wasn't his type, but she wasn't a dog, either. And dammit! She did have fantastic legs.

He felt his anger fading and gritted his teeth. Hell, Blaine, don't go getting soft. The woman's not your problem.

A buxom blond woman wearing an outlandish low-cut sundress was pacing up and down the pier by the *Freewind*'s empty berth when they entered the harbor. Easing the boat into the dock in reverse, David waved and called out a warm greeting that caused Abigail's jaw to drop.

My stars. Why...he was almost handsome when he smiled!

The blonde tapped her foot. Hands on her hips, she bristled with anger. When her eyes switched to Abigail they shot sparks.

"You rat!" she shrieked the instant David jumped to the pier to secure a mooring line. "How dare you leave me standing here twiddling my thumbs while you're out romancing someone else!" She gestured toward Abigail and shot her a venomous glare. "What is she? The early shift?"

"Maxine, I can explain—"

"Don't bother! If you think you can sandwich me in between your other women, you're nuts. You can take your sunset cruise and your romantic dinner and stick it, buster!"

"No, Maxine, wait! I..."

But the blonde was already stomping away, her stiletto heels hammering the wooden planks of the pier.

Frustrated, David stared after her and swore.

From the corner of his eye he caught a movement as Abigail descended the ladder from the bridge, and he swung on her, his anger finding a target.

"All right! That's it! You're outta here!" He jumped back aboard and jerked his thumb toward the pier. "Take that excuse for a dog and your sad tale and hit the road, lady. Now!"

Abigail flinched. Swallowing hard, she nodded and scrambled past him.

On the pier she smoothed her clothing and patted a stray wisp of hair back into place while her eyes made a quick inspection of the docks.

Casting a wary look at David, she began to edge away. "I, uh...I'm sorry I troubled you, Mr. Blaine. And for, uh..." She glanced in the direction Maxine had taken and grimaced. "Well...the misunderstanding. I...I hope you can patch things up with your girlfriend."

His expression didn't alter by so much as a flick of an eyelid. With a grimace and a feeble wave, Abigail turned away.

David clenched his jaw tighter and watched her creep toward quayside, her gaze darting all around as if she expected a bogeyman to jump out at her any second. After a few yards she stopped and shifted from one foot to the other, absently stroking her little dog's head with one hand, the other twisting the tail of her shirt.

Aw, for crying out loud! Did she have to stand there looking like a frightened little mouse?

Ignore her, David told himself. She was not his problem. Anyway, she was making way too much of the incident. Jeez. Getting all bent out of shape over a simple little burglary.

But it simply wasn't in him to turn his back on a woman in distress. For over thirty years, from the time he was seven and they were born, he had looked after his twin sisters, protected them. They had both married recently, and he had gladly turned the job over to their husbands, but the habit was ingrained.

Cursing a blue streak and calling himself a sap and a sucker and worse, he leaped onto the pier and stalked after her. "Damned silly woman. Nothing but a damned nuisance."

Well, he'd give her a choice; he'd take her back to her hotel and prove to her that she had nothing to fear, or he'd put her on a plane for home. But that was all the help she'd get out of him. He sure as hell wasn't going to spend his precious time off hand-holding some neurotic female. And he intended to make that clear to Miss Prim-and-Proper Abigail Stewart!

His long angry strides quickly narrowed the gap between them. Abigail had almost reached the end of the pier and he was only a dozen or so yards behind her when two gray-suited men jumped from a car parked along the quayside and grabbed her.

A hand clamped over Abigail's mouth cut off her startled yelp, but she struggled wildly, bucking and kicking as the pair dragged her toward the long black car. Chelsea set up a terrible racket, lunging and snapping at the pair, her shrill barks an assault on the ears.

For a second, David's steps faltered, and he stared, astonished. "Hey! Hey, stop that!" he yelled, breaking into a run. "What the hell do you think you're doing! Let her go!"

The two shot annoyed glances over their shoulders and tried to hustle Abigail toward the car, but David was on them in seconds.

He rammed one man with his shoulder and sent him sprawling, a big brute with a face that looked like someone had bashed it in with a shovel. In one continuous motion, he spun, grabbed the other man from behind in a choking hammerlock and wrenched him away from Abigail.

The sudden release caught her off balance. She staggered backward and went down hard on her rear end, making jarring contact with the pier as the first man scrambled to his feet.

He lunged toward David, but before he could reach him, Chelsea leaped from her perch in Abigail's purse and sank her needlelike teeth into the back of his ankle.

The brutish man let out a blood-curdling howl and hopped around the pier, kicking his leg out to the side every other step. The little dog flopped and swung from his ankle like a fish on a hook, but his efforts to shake her loose were wasted; Chelsea hung on tenaciously.

Abigail scrambled to her feet. Pale and shaken, she clutched her purse to her with both arms and gaped, unable to move. This couldn't be happening! Not to her! Things like this simply did not happen to Abigail Mary Stewart of Waco, Texas.

But it was. Right before her eyes there was her beloved Chelsea being shaken like a rag doll. And David Blaine was slugging it out in a dirty, no-holds-barred fight that appalled her, leaving her torn between gratitude and revulsion.

Barefoot and wearing only the brief pair of horrid cutoffs, his dark brown hair disheveled around his bristly face, he looked more like a thug than his opponent.

Both men landed some solid blows. David had a cut above one eye that was bleeding, but even as inexperienced as Abigail was in such matters, it was clear to her that the stranger was getting the worst of it.

She winced as David drove his fist into his opponent's stomach. The man doubled over, and David followed up with an upward jerk of his knee, catching him in the chin. As he began to crumple, David clasped his hands together and slammed them down hard across the side of the man's neck, finishing him off.

Immediately he whirled on the other man. The expression on his bleeding, battered face shocked Abigail out of her trance. He looked lethal. Murderous.

Fear for her pet's safety shot through her as David advanced on his new opponent. She didn't think he was even aware of the little dog hanging on valiantly to the man's ankle.

"Chelsea, come!" she called. "Come here at once!"

Chelsea's growl changed to a pleading whine, but after one more sharp command from Abigail, she released her hold and scampered to her mistress's side.

Braced in a crouch, David moved in. "All right, you ugly gorilla. You wanna take me on? Huh? C'mon," he taunted, motioning the man closer. "Let's see if you're as tough when you're fighting a man. Or do you only fight with women?"

His opponent gave a guttural growl and lunged, throwing a wild punch. David ducked it, countered with a vicious two-handed swing that caught him in the midsection and followed up with a swift kick to the groin.

Clutching the injured part of his anatomy, the brute collapsed in a groaning heap.

David grabbed Abigail's hand. "C'mon! Let's get the hell out of here!"

He hauled her back down the pier toward his boat at a dead run, jerking on her arm so hard he almost pulled it from its socket. Stumbling after him, Abigail looked back over her shoulder and saw Chelsea, still dancing around the men, snarling and barking.

"C'mon! Run, dammit! Run!" David snarled when she dug in her heels.

"Wait! My dog!"

"What! Are you nuts? You can't— Hey! What're you doing?" he yelped when she broke loose and raced back.

"Chelsea, come! Come on, girl, run!"

She ran halfway back before the little dog gave up her assault and raced to meet her.

Abigail scooped up the animal just as David skidded to a halt behind her, cursing a blue streak. Once again he grabbed her arm. "Of all the stupid, harebrained... C'mon, will you! Those two goons are coming around!"

Yanking her along with him, he pounded down the pier. They were only a few yards from the boat when something hit a piling just ahead of them with a dull *thunk*. David glanced back over his shoulder. One man had struggled to his knees and was taking aim with the gun he held in a two-fisted grip.

"Damn! They're shooting at us!"

Abigail squawked like a chicken and tried to hunch over in a ball.

David gave her arm another yank and turned on more speed. "C'mon, Legs! Move it!"

A splinter of wood shot off the side of the *Freewind* as they reached it, leaving a long raw gouge in the pristine white paint. Immediately a rapid *splat, splat, splat* sounded, and miniature geysers went up in the water off the starboard side.

Cursing, David grasped Abigail's waist and tossed her into the boat. She landed facedown in an ungainly sprawl. He cast off and leaped in after her. Abigail was struggling to regain her feet, but he shoved her down again.

"Get below! And stay there!" he hollered as a bullet ricocheted off a brass fitting and two more hit the stern with a sickening *Whomp! Whomp!*

Grabbing the rails of the ladder, David gained the bridge in two leaps, while she scooted across the deck on her belly and slithered headfirst down the stairs into the cabin, dragging her purse and Chelsea along with her and letting out a shriek each time a bullet struck the boat.

A barrage peppered the craft at the same instant the powerful engines sprang to life.

"Oh, God. Oh, God. Oh, God," Abigail whimpered, scrambling on her hands and knees toward the tiny stateroom in the bow.

David opened the throttle, and the engine sounds changed from a rumble to a roar, sending the boat surging forward. Abigail shrieked again, and went somersaulting backward like a rolled-up hedgehog. She slammed into the companionway steps and ended up head down, her legs sticking up in the air.

Her oversize shirt fell around her armpits and bunched over her face and neck, nearly suffocating her.

"Help! Help!"

She fought the smothering confinement, yelling and sputtering and flailing her arms, but her cries were lost in the powerful engines' roar.

By the time she fought her way free and regained an upright position, the gunfire had stopped and the boat ride had changed from smooth to rough. Abigail realized that they had cleared the harbor.

The cabin cruiser bucked and bounced over the waves at an alarming speed. She grabbed the pedestal leg of the small banquet table and held on for dear life. Each jarring bump shot her several inches up in the air, striking the top of her head on the underside of the table, then slammed her bottom down against the deck.

She had expected David to slow down once they left the island behind, but he continued the breakneck pace without letup. After a while, Abigail struggled to her feet. Holding on to anything within reach, she made her way unsteadily topside.

The first thing she saw was the dense green mountainous terrain of Alhaja Verde. They were not in open waters as she had expected, but running parallel to the island.

She lurched to the ladder and climbed up to the bridge. "Mr. Blaine! What are we doing here? Where are we going?" she yelled over the noise of the wind and engines.

David glared at her. "I told you to stay below!"

"What for? Those men are miles away back on the docks."

"Oh, yeah? Then who do you suppose that is behind us?"

Abigail turned toward the stern. The sun had just sunk below the horizon. In the fading light she could barely make out a small boat, several hundred yards to the rear. It bounced over the waves at high speed, following their course.

"They commandeered a speedboat," he shouted. "That's why I didn't head out to sea."

"Wh-what are we going to do?"

"Lose 'em—if we can. There's a string of small islands and atolls off the north shore of Alhaja Verde that's like a maze. If we can get there before they overtake us, we may be able to give them the slip."

"And if we can't?"

"Then we'll—"

Abruptly one of the engines began to sputter, cutting him off.

"What the..." Muttering under his breath, David jiggled the throttle and checked the gauges on the control console.

"What is it? What's the matter?"

"I'm not sure. But she's overheating and we're losing speed fast."

Abigail wrung her hands and glanced over her shoulder, but they were rounding a curve and for the moment their pursuers were out of sight. "Wh-what are we going to do?"

Jaw clenched, David tried to coax more speed out of the boat, but it was hopeless. The craft coughed and wheezed like an asthmatic in pollen season. "We're going to take advantage of the failing light while we've got this shoreline for cover," he shouted, and the boat veered sharply landward as he spun the wheel.

"There's a little hidden cove just ahead. The entrance to it is almost impossible to spot from the water. You have to know it's there to find it. Keep your fingers crossed that we make it before they round that last bend."

"But...but what if they know about the cove, too?"

"In that case, Legs, we're in big trouble."

Abigail's heart jerked as David gave the wheel another sharp spin and headed for the island. For a moment she was sure they would run aground, but he nosed the sputtering craft between two spits of land, and they passed through an inlet so narrow she could almost touch the lush vegetation on either side.

Inside the small cove he cut the engines. In the sudden quiet they could hear the water slapping against the hull and the faint whisper of the surf. From the distance came the buzz of a speedboat's motor.

The sound grew louder. They waited, not moving. With every second dusk deepened into darkness. Their eyes strained through the gloom, trained on the opening of the narrow inlet.

The distant buzz became a drone, then a high-pitched rumble.

David stood motionless; his tough face looked carved of stone. Abigail held her breath, one hand clamped over her mouth, the other over Chelsea's muzzle.

The rumble of the speedboat engine reached a nerve-wracking zenith . . . and then began to fade.

Chapter Three

"It worked," came Abigail's surprised whisper. Then, jubilantly, "It really worked! They passed us by!"

She turned to David, but her smile faded when she encountered his fierce scowl. The words of gratitude she had been about to utter immediately slipped from her mind.

"Who the hell are you?" he snarled.

"I . . . I told you. M-my name is Abigail Stewart."

"All right, Abigail Stewart. I want some answers, and I want them fast. What have you done to get those two after you?"

"Nothing! It's true, I swear it!" she added in a rush when his mouth twisted. "I'm just here on vacation. Honest!"

"A tourist, huh? Where are you from? What do you do for a living?"

She blinked at the rapid-fire questions.

Chelsea growled.

"I . . . I'm in the book business. That is . . . I own a small bookstore in Waco, Texas. It's a moderate-size town about ninety miles south of Fort Wor—"

"I know where it is. How long have you lived there?"

"A-all my life."

"How long have you owned the store?"

"A couple of years."

"And before that?"

"I was a librarian."

Even in the near darkness she saw the disdainful twist of his mouth and the way he rolled his eyes. "Figures," he muttered.

"Now, see here—"

"Tell me about this business of yours," he ordered, ignoring her budding indignation. "Do you handle rare books? First editions? Manuscripts?"

"N-no, not at all. I...I carry mostly popular fiction. You know..." Her hands fluttered in a vague, nervous gesture. "Mysteries, westerns, sci-fi, romances...that sort of thing. And most of those are paperbacks. I sell both new and used books, but nothing of great monetary value."

"I see. So, if what you say is true, then whatever's behind all this isn't connected with your business?"

"Certainly not. How could it—?" She stopped, her eyes widening. "Oh, my stars! You're not suggesting that I deal in anything illegal?" she demanded huffily.

"I'm not suggesting anything. Just exploring possibilities."

"Well, that isn't one, so you can just forget it! I am not a criminal! I lead a quiet, simple, law-abiding life. For heaven's sake, *I'm* the victim here!"

Disturbed by her agitated tone, Chelsea whined and licked Abigail's elbow, then bristled at David. He glanced at the tiny dog, snorted and returned his attention to her mistress.

"You can save your outrage, Legs. Those wide-eyed looks, too. They don't cut any ice with me. When I was with the Bureau I came across a sweet little old lady who was a rabid terrorist. And angelic choirboys who worked as runners for drug dealers. So until I know for certain that you're what you claim, I'll reserve judgment."

"Of all the...I refuse to stand here and be insulted li—"

"You're right. We'll go below where we can get comfortable. This is liable to take a while."

Ignoring Abigail's outraged sputters, he grasped her arm and propelled her down the steps. Chelsea snarled and would have jumped from the purse and attacked him, but a command from Abigail checked the action and silenced her.

Below, David shoved Abigail down onto one of the bench seats that enclosed the table. Once the curtains were drawn over the windows and the doors closed, he turned on a light and joined her, sliding in on the opposite seat and bracing his back against the bulkhead.

In the small confines of the cabin Abigail was uncomfortably aware of him—his size, his overwhelming masculinity. His near-naked body.

It struck her that they were alone together on a boat, miles from anything or anyone. All she knew about the man was that he was rude and overbearing and and ex-FBI agent. Abigail grew still, the word '*ex*-FBI' echoing in her mind. For the first time it occurred to her to wonder why he had left the Bureau.

Abigail wasn't accustomed to being alone with a man—any man—especially not a tough-as-nails specimen like David Blaine.

No one would ever describe him as handsome, she realized. His features were too strong, his face too harsh and etched with experience. He exuded a raw maleness, an aura of leashed power that unnerved her.

She had never seen shoulders that wide or that muscled—except maybe on a movie screen. A purple bruise the size of a saucer marred the bronze skin covering his left shoulder. Another created a darker shadow through the whisker stubble along his jaw. A line of dried blood marked the cut above his left eyebrow, and his knuckles were scraped, beginning to puff. David appeared oblivious to his injuries. He just sat there, studying her.

His scent drifted to her, musky and virile and not at all unpleasant, a heady combination of soap and sweat and man. The simple act of breathing took on an unsettling intimacy as, with each breath, Abigail inhaled that masculine aroma. Every nerve in her body hummed. With an effort, she fought the urge to squirm and returned his stare with a haughty self-assurance she was far from feeling.

Considering her though narrowed eyes, David absently scratched his furry chest. Abigail's jaws clenched. The man was an uncouth savage. And did he have to flaunt himself that way?

Her heart began to thud, and her mouth went dry. Folding her hands together on top of the table, she set her face primly and struggled to hide the foolish reactions.

Her glare hadn't the slightest effect on David. He continued his interrogation as though the interruption hadn't occurred.

"You say you're here on vacation. Do you take these kinds of trips often?"

Her wintry expression slipped. "Well...no. Actually this is my first. You see, I recently came into a substantial sum of money, and—"

"How? And how much?" he demanded, pinning her with that unnerving steady stare.

Oh, Lord. If only he weren't so...big, so...so masculine. If only he had on more clothes.

To cover her unease, she glared back and snapped, "If you *must* know, by turning thirty. That's when I received the inheritance left me by my parents. And the amount is none of your concern. Suffice it to say that I'm far from wealthy, but the trust fund does insure that I'll never go hungry."

"How long ago did your parents die?"

"When I was a child. I was raised by my Aunt Harriet."

"The one who disapproved of cussing, I take it. I'll lay odds she was a straitlaced spinster, too."

Abigail couldn't be sure, but she thought she saw his cynical mouth twitch. Rude, sarcastic brute. Folding her lips in a tight line, she gave him a censorious look but refused to confirm or deny his statement. It galled her to admit, even to herself, just how accurate his assessment was.

"Anyway," she continued with a sniff. "Most of my customers seemed to think the occasion called for some kind of celebration, and they all urged me to take an exotic trip. So I came here.''

''What made you pick Alhaja Verde? There are dozens of better-known island vacation spots you could have chosen.''

''One of my regular romance readers, Edna Mae Polson, recommended it. Her husband's second cousin had been here. She'd won the trip on a television game show. Anyway, it sounded perfect, since I didn't want to go to a trendy spot. I . . . I'm not comfortable in those kinds of places.''

The long steady look he gave her said he wasn't at all surprised. Again fighting the urge to squirm, Abigail lowered her gaze and focused on her laced fingers. Anything was better than staring at that brawny chest.

For a few moments neither spoke. Just when she thought the questions were over, David asked, ''So tell me about your social life. Are you seeing anyone on a regular basis? Sleeping with anyone?''

Abigail's head shot up. Her face couldn't have registered more shock if he had thrown a bucket of water in it. ''That is none of your business!''

He leaned forward, his whiskey-brown eyes narrowed and hard. Emitting a low growl, Chelsea propped her tiny snout on the edge of the table and lifted her lip. David ignored her.

''Now you listen up, Legs, and listen good. I don't like getting shot at. Not one damned bit. In fact, when it happens I get downright nasty.''

''So I noticed.'' Her cool tones dripped contempt. ''You behaved like a savage back on the pier.''

''*What!*'' He jerked forward on the seat. His jaw dropped, and his eyes bulged. ''Jeez, I don't believe this! Lady, in case it didn't register, I saved your butt on that pier! And if you'll recall, *you* came to me!'' he shouted with righteous ire, jabbing his chest with his thumb. ''I didn't ask to be dragged into your troubles! And while we're on the subject, why the hell didn't you lend a hand instead of standing there like a stump?''

''*Me!* What could I do?''

"I don't know...kick...bite...scratch. When some-one attacks you, you hurt him any way you can. Hell, you could have hit him with your purse. From the looks of that thing, it would've coldcocked the guy."

Abigail's stiff spine grew even stiffer. She lifted her chin, her mouth pinching as though pulled by a drawstring. "For your information, I abhor violence," she said in her best starchy librarian voice. "I find it repugnant, demeaning and crude, as well as unnerving." Plus, she'd been scared wit-less back on that pier, but she wasn't about to admit that to this Neanderthal. "I came to you for help, hoping to avoid violence. I thought our government hired civilized men. Obviously I was wrong."

"So, what did you expect? Robert Stack in a three-piece suit?"

"Certainly not a barbarian! You, sir, are nothing but a...an uncouth hooligan!" she sputtered.

"Oh, yeah. Well let me tell you something, Legs. You'd better thank your lucky stars that you stumbled across this hooligan," he snarled, thumbing his chest again. "Instead of some pencil-pushing cerebral type. And believe me, the Bureau's got its share of those jerks. If you hadn't, you'd be enjoying the hospitality of your two ugly friends right now, experiencing the pleasure of having your toenails pulled out."

Abigail's face paled. Her spine lost its starch, and she sagged back against the bench seat, her indignant bravado whooshing out of her like air from a pricked balloon. "You...you..." She paused and tried to swallow, but her mouth was as dry as dust. "You think they would have tor-tured me?"

David shrugged and resumed his casual slump against the bulkhead. "That or worse."

"Worse?" she croaked. "What could be worse?"

"Several possibilities spring to mind," he replied dryly, giving her an under-the-brow look that made her breath catch.

"Oh."

The shaky one-word reply in no way softened his demeanor. He continued to regard her through narrowed eyes, his harsh face like granite. "If I'm going to keep that from happening, I've got to know what's going on. Which means you'll damned well answer any question I ask you. You dragged me into this mess, don't forget."

Guilt mingled with fear and anger, creating a tight knot in Abigail's chest. "I...I'm sorry," she said as crisply as she could manage. "I shouldn't have involved you. I realize that now. If you'll kindly take me back to San Cristobal I'll get the next flight home and we'll both be out of it."

He stared at her and shook his head. "Are you really that naive? Or just plain stupid? You don't seriously think I can just drop you off and go on my merry way, do you? Or that you can just toddle back to Waco and leave all this behind?

"First of all, I may not be Sir Galahad, but I sure as hell don't go around leaving helpless women to fend for themselves. And second, even if I tried, I'd still be up shi... uh...the creek." Her uncomprehending expression drew a burst of muttered profanity from him. He raked a hand through his unruly hair. "Look, Legs, don't you see? Those guys are after something. They're not going to give up until they get it. Or we get them."

She flinched. The picture of that violent encounter on the pier was still fresh in her mind. The thought of going through something like that again made her stomach queasy.

"They aren't going to forget my face. Or my boat. Like it or not, I'm involved. If I'm going to get both of us through this in one piece, I'll need all the information I can get. You never know what might give you the answers you need. So start talking."

Abigail still didn't like it, but she felt too guilty to refuse. "There's no man in my life. Not at the present, anyway," she added quickly. The last thing she wanted was for David Blaine to find out that her social life was a big fat zero. She hadn't gone out with a man in years. Not since Ted had...

Abigail caught herself and firmed her lips, refusing to even complete the thought.

"How about friends? Tell me about those. Especially these customers of yours. The ones who urged you to take this trip."

She almost laughed out loud. The people he referred to were all women, avid romance readers who came into her shop to pick up the latest books and talk. It was ludicrous to suspect any of them of some nefarious plot.

Abigail told David so, but he kept hammering away. He questioned her about every facet of her life, about every move she'd made and every person with whom she'd spoken or come into contact since leaving her home the day before.

Throughout the grilling, David's face remained impassive, his stony expression and cold eyes giving nothing away. Not until she told him about the woman who had been her seat mate on the plane trip to Alhaja Verde did he show a reaction.

"When you say this Patrice Johnson had to get off the plane in Mexico City, what do you mean?" he asked with sudden interest, sitting forward and bracing his forearms on the table. "Are you saying it was an unscheduled departure? She wasn't ticketed for Mexico City?"

"That's right. She became ill—quite suddenly, actually—and the minute we landed, she hurried off the plane. I tried to get her to ask the stewardess for assistance, but she refused."

"And you're sure she was a passenger on the plane before it got to the Dallas-Fort Worth airport? She didn't perhaps go on board a few minutes before you?"

"Yes, I'm sure. She told me she was from Alexandria, Virginia, and had caught the flight in Washington, D.C. Why? Do you think she's connected with all this somehow?"

"I'd say there's a strong possibility. The men who ransacked your hotel room obviously didn't find what they were searching for. That's why they're after you now. They think you have it with you."

"Have *what* with me? I don't understand any of this."

"My guess is that the Johnson woman was a courier. She probably spotted someone on that flight who spooked her, so she planted whatever she was carrying on you and cut out. I'd guess, too, that she phoned her contact in Alhaja Verde the minute she deplaned in Mexico City and told them where they could find the goods."

"Ma-maybe she's one of our agents," Abigail stammered hopefully.

"Not a chance. Those two had KGB written all over them. And didn't you notice? After I kicked him, that ugly bast . . . uh, brute was moaning something in what sounded like Russian. No, if the Johnson woman is part of this she's either a mole or she sold out."

"A mole?"

"A plant." Her face remained blank, and he rolled his eyes. "You know—a foreign agent in a sensitive position within our government."

"But she seemed so nice," Abigail protested.

"Oh, brother." Looking the classic picture of a thoroughly exasperated male, David slowly pulled his palm down over his whisker-stubbled face. "Jeez, if you're that gullible, it's a wonder you manage to survive from day to day. Lady, you need a keeper."

"Oh, *really?* A male, I suppose? No doubt some unkempt ruffian like you?" She looked him over, the coolness in her eyes not betraying the wild fluttering in her stomach. "I don't think so, Mr. Blaine. I've been looking after myself just fine for quite some time now, thank you very much."

"I wasn't offering."

"Good!" she said haughtily.

"Fine!" he snapped back.

Scowling, he reached across the aisle and extracted a cigarette from a partial pack on the counter. Abigail wrinkled her nose.

"That is a disgusting habit, you know."

"Oh, yeah?" David lit up and squinted at her through the spiral of smoke. "Well, it so happens I'd almost kicked it, but after being around you, I need a cigarette. Bad."

Abigail could think of no reply, so she sniffed and folded her arms.

They regarded each other in hostile silence for several minutes. Abigail sat ramrod straight, her chin in the air. David puffed on his cigarette, inhaling deeply and blowing a lazy stream of smoke at the ceiling, his look daring her to object.

After a while his eyes narrowed. He sat forward and stubbed out the butt in the ashtray. "Gimme your purse."

"What!" She clutched it closer. "I most certainly will not!"

"Give me the damned purse," he demanded. "I want to see if I can find whatever it is those two gorillas are after."

"No! I won't have you pawing through my things!" she replied indignantly, jumping to her feet. "I'll look myself."

"Oh, hell!" With lightning speed his hand shot across the table, grasped the tail of her shirt and jerked her close.

"Wha—? Here now! Stop that!" Abigail gasped, but before she could stop him, he snatched the purse from her arm.

"You give that back, you . . . you . . . ruffian!"

She struggled with him for possession of the voluminous shoulder bag, but it was a hopeless quest from the start.

"Back off, Legs, and let me handle this," he ordered. "Believe me, you wouldn't have the slightest idea what to look for or how to find it."

David fended her off with one arm, and after a moment Abigail gave up, unwilling to continue such an undignified tussle.

He upended the bag, and Chelsea leaped from the side pocket onto the opposite bench seat, carrying in her mouth a three-inch toy dog. She deposited the stuffed animal in the corner of the seat and took up a bristling stance in front of it, growling at David and baring her little needle teeth.

"What the hell's wrong with that dog? And what's that she's got over there?" he asked, craning his neck.

"Nothing," Abigail snapped. She was shaking with anger. Her lips were pinched so tight, a white line encircled them. "It's just a stuffed toy. She thinks it's her puppy."

"Puppy? Huh! Neurotic little wad of fluff." He dismissed the dog with a disparaging glance and turned his attention to the items covering the table.

A look of astonishment came over his face as he sifted through the pile. In addition to wallet, passport, keys, brush, comb and the usual assortment of feminine cosmetics, there was a miniature first-aid kit, a tiny stapler, scissors, a collapsible toothbrush, a tube of toothpaste the size of his little finger, a compact sewing kit, a plastic bag filled with some sort of pellets, which, from the smell, he assumed to be dry dog food, and a small compartmentalized case containing an assortment of vitamins. David shook his head and picked up a plastic box the size of a cigarette pack. It held a set of miniature screwdrivers.

Even empty the purse still felt weighty. He spread the top wide and peered inside, and his jaw dropped. "Good God! I don't believe this!" Stitched to the lining of the voluminous canvas bag were at least twenty small overlapping flap pockets with zipper closures.

Muttering to himself, David went through them one by one. From the first he pulled a sample of laundry detergent, from another a pack of seasick tablets. Still another pocket yielded a sack of raisins, another a penlight and spare batteries and another a full-size rain poncho folded into a two-inch square.

Abigail gasped and turned tomato red when he extracted an unadorned pair of ladies' cotton panties. He held them up for inspection, and those whiskey eyes slid over her. "Very... practical," he said, his mouth twitching.

"Give me those!" Abigail snapped, and snatched them out of his hand. She stuffed the undies into the pocket of her shorts and glared at him, but her ire was wasted. David was digging in her purse again and didn't even notice.

He pulled out a hotel-size bar of soap, a tiny bottle of shampoo, Scotch tape, hand lotion, a Boy Scout knife and numerous sealed packets of snack food. The stunning variety of items, many of them sample packages, piled higher and higher on the table as he systematically emptied every pocket and compartment.

When at last finished, he stared at the conglomeration. He pinned Abigail with a perplexed frown. "What in the name of hell are you doing carrying around all this junk? This stuff must weigh a ton!"

Abigail snatched the purse from his hand. "It never hurts to be prepared," she replied tartly, shooting him a withering glare. "Now, if you're through pawing through my things, I'll put them back. That is, if that's all right with you, of course."

He ignored her sarcasm and picked up a tin of throat lozenges from the top of the pile. "Not until I have a look at everything."

One by one, he subjected each item to a minute inspection before handing it back to her. From the corner of his eye he watched Abigail return everything to its precise location within her bag and felt a mixture of pity and irritation.

God, he thought. The woman wasn't only a pack rat, she was one of those compulsively neat types. A place for everything and everything in its place, he silently recited in a nasty singsong. Hell, he could almost hear her saying it in that snooty tone she used.

Why me? What the hell have I done to get stuck with a repressed, prissy old maid?

The search proved fruitless. "Nothing. Not a damned thing," he muttered when he had finished.

He snatched up another smoke. With quick, angry movements he lit up and flung the spent match into the sink. Leaning back against the counter, he puffed on the cigarette and regarded Abigail moodily as she returned the last item to its proper place.

"You say you arrived here today?"

"Yes. Around noon," she replied shortly. "As soon as I arrived, I unpacked. Then I went sight-seeing."

"Did you change clothes?"

"No."

"Okay, take them off."

She spun around. *"What?"* Abigail clutched the collar of her shirt, holding the edges together.

"Strip off those clothes," he repeated impatiently. Pushing away from the counter, he flicked the cigarette butt into the sink where it sizzled in a puddle of water.

She backed up. "I'll do no such thing! Now... now, you stay away from me you... you masher! Pervert!" She clutched the collar of her shirt tighter and held the other hand up, palm out, but he kept coming. "Do-don't you touch me!"

"Oh, for crying out... Look, I just want to see if she planted anything on you."

"Well, I'm not taking my clothes off, and that's final, so just stay away from me."

David sighed. "All right, Legs, if that's the way you're gonna be, we'll do this the hard way."

Abigail's pounding heart jumped right up into her throat when he made a lunge for her. She let out a squawk and made a break for the steps, but he snagged her arm, spun her around and shoved her face-first against the door to the shower stall. With two quick thrusts of his foot he had her legs spread wide.

"Oh! Wha—! Stop that! How dare—! Oh! *Oh!*" she gasped when his hand cupped her breast.

With his forearm braced across her shoulder blades, he held her pinned spread-eagle to the door and subjected her to a thorough and shockingly intimate frisk. Beneath the loose folds of her shirt his free hand roamed her body, circling each breast, probing the cleavage between, sliding over her rib cage and abdomen. He patted her bottom, her back and sides and explored each armpit.

From head to toe, Abigail's body pulsed with embarrassed heat. She bucked and squirmed and squawked, but to no avail. "Stop it, you beast! Stop that I sa—! Oh! Oh! *No!* Don't you da—!"

She sucked in her breath, her gasp of outrage becoming a strangled moan as his fingers insinuated themselves between her legs.

With maddening indifference he ignored her indignant yelps and the snarling warning from behind and ran his hands down the inside of her thighs.

Chelsea growled again. When he paid her no mind, the tiny animal launched herself at him with all the ferocity of an attack Doberman.

Three pounds of furry, snarling fury slammed into the back of David's legs, buckling his knees.

"What the hell!"

He toppled forward and crashed into Abigail, flattening her against the wall. For an instant she was squeezed between the door and David's body like the cream center of an Oreo cookie.

David scrabbled for balance as he clung to the wall, but before he could steady himself he felt a stinging nip on the back of one foot.

"Ow! *Ow!* Dammit to hell!" he raged, glancing over his shoulder. He kicked out at the little dog. "Get away from me, you bloodthirsty mutt! Get!"

At first, regarding the animal as merely a nuisance, David tried to shove her aside, but Chelsea proved quick and agile and easily avoided his flailing foot. When she zeroed in on his unprotected ankles, he realized that he was under serious attack.

Relentless, the little terrier kept up the furious assault, keeping him off balance and on the defensive, charging his unprotected ankles, darting in and out, barking and snapping.

As David scrambled to fend her off, a sharp mental image flashed through his mind of the dog flopping at the end of the shovel-faced thug's leg, hanging on tenaciously, her needle teeth sunk into the back of his ankle.

Holy hell! She was going for his Achilles tendon!

He kicked out with more force. "Stop it! Get away! Heel, you miserable little dust mop! Heel!"

Chelsea scampered out of range, then zipped back. David felt another sting and yelped. Cursing, he twisted around until his back was to the wall, and jerked Abigail against his chest. "Get back! Back! Shoo!"

With his elbows he levered himself upright. Chelsea charged again. Holding Abigail in front of him like a shield, David hopped around the cabin as though the deck were covered with hot coals, trying desperately to keep the woman between him and those snapping teeth. But the ferocious little dog was too quick.

"Ow! Ow! Dammit! Can't you do something?" he yelled in Abigail's ear. "That little beast is worse than a Tasmanian Devil."

Abigail shot a triumphant glance over her shoulder. "Good girl, Chels!" she praised, egging the dog on. "Get him! Get him, girl!"

"Ah, hell."

David backed to the steps. Bending to maintain his hold on Abigail, he eased up onto the first, then the second, keeping his eye on Chelsea. As his foot reached for the third step he had to release his hostage.

David leaped up onto the deck and made for the bridge. The dog was after him in a flash.

By the time Abigail made it topside, Chelsea had David backed up the bridge ladder.

He stood on the fourth rung, holding on to the side rails, and glared down at his tiny attacker. Almost hysterical with victory, Chelsea jumped and leaped around the base, yapping her head off. Only the perpendicular angle of the ladder prevented her from continuing the pursuit.

"Call her off," David yelled, scowling down at Abigail.

In the light spilling from the cabin she could see that he was furious. Under normal circumstances Abigail would have quailed under that dark glare, but at the moment she was impervious; she had been pushed too far.

She folded her arms across her midriff and regarded him with a smug lift of her eyebrows. "Not until you apologize."

"*What!* Lady, are you nuts! Don't forget, you need me! Besides, what have I got to apologize for?"

"For being a rude, boorish oaf and for using your superior strength against a woman, that's what. As for the other—you need me, too. I would advise you to forget your bruised male pride and say you're sorry, because I assure you Chelsea won't budge from here until I command it."

Even in the dim light she could see his jaws clench. His chest rose and fell with each harsh breath as the ominous silence stretched out. "Oh, all right! I'm sorry I man-handled you," he snapped with decided bad grace. "Now will you call off the damned dog!"

"You call *that* an apology?"

"It's the best I can do. Take it or leave it."

Abigail rolled her eyes, but she ordered Chelsea to de-sist. Reluctantly the dog obeyed, lifting her lip at David as he edged down the ladder. When he reached the deck, she gave one last little "ruff" and trotted off, disappearing be-low, returning to her "puppy." Chelsea was never parted from the toy for long if she could help it.

The two humans eyed each other in wary silence. Under his steady appraisal Abigail's prickly defenses crumbled to dust.

Horrified, she met that piercing stare and wondered where she'd gotten the nerve to oppose a tough customer like Da-vid Blaine. She wanted to run. If they hadn't been on a boat, she would have. Left with no choice, she hugged her arms around her and tried not to fidget.

"You surprise me, Legs," he finally said. "Somehow I didn't think you had that kind of gumption."

She didn't. But as always, Abigail's first instinct was to try to hide her discomfort. "For heaven's sake!" she snapped. "Why do you keep calling me that? My name, as you perfectly well know, is Abigail, not Legs."

David shrugged. "It fits. You may not be a raving beauty, but you've got the most fantastic pair of legs I've ever clapped eyes on."

Chapter Four

The matter-of-fact statement robbed Abigail of the powers of speech and movement. She stood with her face comically slack and watched him lope down the steps and disappear below deck.

She didn't know whether to be outraged or flattered. As compliments went, it was hardly grand. Certainly nothing to get excited about. Even so... a fiery tingle rippled over her skin, just as though he had caressed her with his fingertips.

Shivering, Abigail rubbed her arms. Stop it, she scolded, shaking off the delicious feeling. So you received a left-handed compliment from a vulgar ruffian? So what? That's certainly no reason to get all weak and wobbly. The man's a barbarian.

No raving beauty, indeed! She deliberately whipped up her wrath by focusing on the negative part of his comment. As if she needed *him* to tell her that.

Abigail had no illusions about her looks. No, she wasn't gorgeous. Her mouth was too wide and her nose was a tad too short for any claim to true beauty. Her only outstanding feature was her eyes. They were pale blue—aquamarine, some said—and surrounded by long dark lashes. She supposed that at best, she was passably attractive in a wholesome sort of way, but she'd learned years ago that wasn't enough to interest most men.

Not that she cared. Certainly she didn't want to attract a hard case like David Blaine. Anyway, just because the man thought she had nice legs didn't mean he was interested.

He'd just said that to rattle her, to get even for Chelsea's attack and restore his colossal male ego. So don't make a big deal of it. You've got more important things to worry about than David Blaine's opinion of your legs.

Below, Abigail found Chelsea asleep on the banquette seat, curled around her toy puppy. David was in the tiny forward cabin, rummaging through the built-in dresser.

She paused in the doorway. In the quiet she could hear the soft buzz of Chelsea's snores and the creak of the boat, feel it rock beneath her feet. She waited for David to say something, but he just continued to paw through the drawers, making a mess of the contents and offending Abigail's sense of order and neatness.

"Uh . . . what are we going to do now?"

He glanced her way and resumed digging. "Eat dinner and get some shut-eye. That's all we can do for now."

"You mean . . . spend the night here? On this boat?" Abigail's voice rose with each word and ended on a squeak.

"What did you expect? That we would go back to San Cristobal and check into a hotel?"

"Well . . . yes. I did, actually. Not the same hotel I was in, of course. Or maybe . . . maybe Pepe and Constanza could—"

"Forget it. We can't risk being spotted. And haven't you forgotten something? We've got engine problems."

"But it was still running when we entered the cove."

"Barely. I'm not going to take the chance of doing more damage. Your friends did enough when they fired on us. Until I can check things out, this boat isn't budging from this spot."

He straightened, holding a yellow T-shirt. "Here, you can use this to sleep in. Unless, of course, you've got a nightie stashed in that grab bag of yours."

Battling panic, Abigail barely registered his sarcasm. "Look, I ... I can't stay here. It's out of the question."

"Fine. You can swim ashore and either sleep on the beach or hike back to town. Suit yourself. But I'm not moving my boat." He tossed the T-shirt onto the dresser and pushed past her into the galley.

Shaken, Abigail sank onto the edge of the bed that nearly filled the cabin, her heart pounding. Darn him. He knew perfectly well that was no choice at all. She doubted she could swim well enough to make it to shore. Even if she could, she certainly couldn't spend the night on the beach—with crabs and turtles and no telling what other creatures. She shuddered and rubbed the gooseflesh on her arms. As for hiking back to town in the dark—why, that was out of the question. The coastline on this side of the island was mostly rugged cliffs with very few beaches, and a good six or seven miles of wooded, mountainous terrain lay between them and San Cristobal.

She couldn't believe it. All of her life Aunt Harriet had drilled into her the importance of being prepared and approaching life cautiously.

An ounce of prevention is worth a pound of cure, my dear. Always remember—live circumspectly, don't take risks and be ready for any eventuality. That way you won't get hurt.

Growing up, Abigail had heard those words and others like them thousands of times. She had tried hard to heed her aunt's advice, especially since that debacle with Ted, but nothing could have prepared her for this.

Of course, if she hadn't given in to that niggling restlessness and come here, if she had suppressed those vague stirrings as she'd always done in the past, none of this would have happened.

With a shaking hand she tucked a loose tendril of hair behind her ear and looked around the cabin. This was supposed to be her dream vacation, and here she was, spending her first night stranded miles from nowhere on a disabled boat with a disagreeable man she barely knew.

Under different circumstances—with the right man—the situation might even be romantic. But she was stuck with a big, tough, ill-tempered, ill-mannered hooligan!

Oh, she supposed he was attractive—if you liked the dangerous type. Which, of course, she didn't, Abigail assured herself. The quivery sensation in the pit of her stomach was caused by apprehension.

Gathering her courage, Abigail rose. She stepped into the galley to the hum of the microwave and found David hunkered down before the stove, lighting the broiler. When done, he stood and cupped the match to the cigarette hanging from the corner of his mouth. Unable to help herself, Abigail made a face. "You really should quit, you know."

Shaking out the flame, David squinted at her through the smoke. "You staying?"

Beast. He knew perfectly well she was.

"It appears I have little choice." Nervously she glanced around. "Uh...can I help with dinner?"

"No, everything is already done. I had a different evening in mind when I planned this dinner, but what the hell. No point in letting good steaks go to waste."

Noting the wine chilling in a bucket in the sink and the two salads on the table, Abigail realized that he had prepared the meal for Maxine. No doubt it had been intended as a prelude to seduction, she thought, flushing.

The microwave beeped as David pronounced the steaks done. He forked up the meat, added the potatoes and slapped both plates onto the table. "Might as well drink the wine, too," he said with an insulting lack of enthusiasm, and popped the cork from the bottle. He splashed the wine into two squat jelly glasses and thumped them down on the table beside the plates.

Abigail gritted her teeth. No doubt Maxine would have been served the wine up on deck. By candlelight. At sunset. In real wineglasses.

The silence that accompanied the meal would have made Abigail uncomfortable if she hadn't been so irked. It was hardly her fault his plans had gone awry.

Well . . . all right. Maybe it was.

But he didn't have to be such a sorehead about it. The way he was acting, you'd think she had set out to spoil his evening of debauchery with the blond hussy. Lord, was there anything crankier than a sexually frustrated male?

After the silent meal Abigail did the dishes while David showered. She was just finishing when he stepped from the cubicle.

"It's all yours," he announced.

She glanced over her shoulder, and almost dropped the dish she was returning to the cabinet.

There he stood, as bold as brass, wearing only a skimpy towel knotted low on his hips and using another to dry his hair, which hung in wet ringlets over his forehead.

Abigail sucked in her breath, and at once her senses were assaulted by the heady smell of soap and clean male. He still hadn't bothered to shave. The shadowy stubble should have been revolting; instead it added to his strange, disreputable allure.

Like a magnet, Abigail's gaze was drawn to the brawny chest she'd been trying so hard to avoid staring at all evening. Droplets of water still clung to the reddish-brown hair that ran in a wedge from just below his collarbone to his diaphragm. From there it arrowed downward in a thin line that swirled around his navel before dropping lower and disappearing beneath the edge of the towel. Below the swatch of terry cloth his thighs were long and lean and ridged with muscles.

He raised both arms and rubbed the crown of his head with the towel. The stretching action rippled muscles and drew his abdomen in until it was concave, causing the cloth draped across his hipbones to slip perilously lower.

Abigail swallowed hard and shifted her gaze. It homed in on the dark tufts of hair beneath his arms, and her stomach went woozy. Never in her life had she encountered such a blatantly masculine man. Or one with so little modesty.

"There should be enough hot water left for you to shower, if you don't dawdle."

Abigail whirled around, shoved the plate into the cabinet and slammed the door. "Th-thank you," she croaked.

Tossing aside the dish towel, she dashed into the forward cabin, snatched up the yellow T-shirt and hurried out again. Keeping her eyes averted, she sidestepped David. She was careful not to touch him, but the cabin was small, and as she squeezed past she felt his heat through every pore in her body.

Long after the supply of hot water had been exhausted, Abigail stood under the shower spray and let the cool liquid sluice down her overheated skin. When she emerged, her composure once more intact, she found David stretched out in the bed.

Abigail stopped dead in the doorway. "What are you doing?"

"What does it look like? I'm trying to get some sleep." He tossed back one corner of the sheet. "C'mon, climb in, will ya. I want to get an early start on those repairs in the morning."

"You...you surely don't expect me to sleep in that bed?"

"Sure I do. In case you didn't notice, it's the only one on board."

"But . . . you're in it."

"Yeah. So?"

Abigail stared at him, not sure if he was really that obtuse or if he was taunting her. Either way, she found his attitude exasperating. "So I will not sleep with you. That's what's so," she snapped. "Furthermore, if you were any kind of gentleman you wouldn't expect me to."

"Oh, yeah? And I suppose a gentleman would let you have the bed all to yourself and sleep up on deck. Right?"

"Yes. As a matter of fact, he would."

"Well forget it, Legs. I'm not sleeping on any hard deck. Not when there's a comfortable bed right here that's plenty big enough for two. And if you're worried that I'm lusting after your bod, forget it. Believe me, you're not my type. Skinny librarians just don't turn me on."

"I can't tell you how relieved I am to hear it," she said in her most supercilious voice. "But I still won't sleep in that bed with you in it."

"Fine. Then *you* sleep up on deck."

"Very well, I will."

"Great!"

"Fine!"

Her chin shot up at a haughty angle, but she didn't move.

David sat up in the bed and glared at her. "So, what are you waiting for?"

"I need a pillow. And a blanket." Her icy tone implied that if he had the manners of a slug she wouldn't have had to ask.

"Oh, for crying out—!" David snatched up the extra pillow and flung it at her. Abigail caught it reflexively as he tossed back the covering sheet and shot from the bed.

Her eyes grew wide. She clutched the pillow to her chest. "Oh . . . my . . . stars!"

At the shocked exclamation David straightened from pawing through the storage drawer beneath the bed and whirled around, his body braced, as though expecting to face an enemy attack. "What is it? What's the matter?" he demanded, his gaze darting around the cabin.

"You're wearing *purple* underwear," Abigail exclaimed. She goggled at the strip of cotton knit that hugged his hips. "Purple *bikini* underwear."

"That's it? *That's* what you're carrying on about?" His shoulders slumped, and he let out a gusty sigh, rolling his eyes. "Jeez, woman. What the hell are you getting so bent out of shape about? You're thirty years old. Surely you've seen a man in his underwear before?" He propped his fists on his hipbones and narrowed his eyes. "Or have you?"

Blinking, Abigail strove to clear her head and imbue her words with brisk worldliness, but they came out sounding breathy and a bit dazed. "O-of course I have. I . . . I just haven't seen purple ones before. That's all."

"Well, don't get your panties in a wad over it. Lots of men wear colored skivvies these days."

Abigail blinked again. *Panties in a wad?* She opened her mouth to give him a set down, but David bent over the storage drawer again and the scathing words flitted right out of her mind as her gaze followed the bowed line of his spine down to the purple scrap of cloth.

"Anyway it's not as though they're indecent or anything. They cover as much as a bathing suit."

Some bathing suits. Maybe. In the south of France, perhaps. But none that Abigail had ever seen. And she doubted that many men looked quite the way David did in them. The garment was little more than two small triangles, joined front to back at the hips with narrow bands of elastic. The bright material skimmed over tight buttocks and cupped his sex like a lover's hand. And, heaven help her, the snug fit of the stretchy knit left no doubt whatever of his maleness.

Abigail's gaze slid along his thigh up to his hip, bare but for the narrow band of elastic. Her heartbeat accelerated as she realized that his skin was that deep bronze color all over. Oh, God. When he was alone out at sea he must walk around stark naked.

Her mouth went dry at the mental image that formed in her mind, and a quivering began deep in her belly. Her heart beat with a slow heaviness that made her chest ache.

The foolish reactions so unsettled Abigail, when David straightened and held out a blanket, she snatched it from his grasp and scurried topside without so much as a thank-you.

Flustered, she stood in the middle of the deck for several minutes before she realized there wasn't a single lounger on board. The helm seat and narrow bench up on the bridge and the cockpit chair bolted to the deck at the stern, which she assumed he used when fishing, where the only concessions to comfort, and none would do for sleeping.

Disgusted, Abigail flung the pillow into a corner, wrapped the blanket around herself and flopped down on the hard deck. Just her luck—to get stuck on a fishing boat with a mannerless oaf. Panties in a wad, indeed!

For the next half hour she twisted and squirmed, trying to find a comfortable position, but the task proved impossible. No matter which way she turned, some part of her frame ground painfully against the teak decking—hip-bone, shoulder, knee, ankle, even a few bones she hadn't known she had. She tried bunching the blanket up under her, but that didn't help. The darned deck was as hard as a marble slab—and just about as warm.

It was so dark, Abigail could barely see her hand in front of her face. From the island came strange rustling noises and animal sounds. To top it off, the wind had kicked up and the breeze off the ocean held a definite chill.

Pulling the blanket tighter around her, Abigail wiggled and flopped and called David names that would have caused Aunt Harriet to have an apoplectic fit. At last she fell into a fitful doze out of sheer exhaustion.

Ten minutes later she came wide-awake when the sky opened up.

The deluge hit her full force without warning. At first she thought someone had doused her with a bucket of water. She jackknifed to a sitting position, coughing and sputtering, her arms clamped at her sides beneath the blanket that was wrapped, mummy fashion, around her body. By the time she untangled herself and scrambled to her feet, she was drenched.

David came awake to the sound of rain striking the bulkhead. An instant later he heard Abigail clamber down the steps. Sighing, he turned on the bedside light and rolled out of bed. The woman was nothing but trouble.

She stood in the middle of the cabin, drenched, bedraggled and dripping. Strings of wet hair clung to her face like seaweed, and that damned T-shirt plastered to her body. She stared at him with mute appeal, her big aquamarine eyes wide and confused, those ridiculously long lashes spiked with rainwater.

She looked pathetic. And defenseless. And, to his sorrow, sexy as hell.

Stretching, Chelsea sat up and yawned and regarded her mistress with sleepy adoration.

"It's raining," Abigail said unnecessarily in an unsteady voice.

David saw her chin quiver and knew that tears threatened, but she fought against them, folding her lips into a tight line.

"No shi— Uh, no kidding," he quipped with deliberate nastiness. He was fighting battles of his own. If she started crying, he wasn't sure he could keep his distance; a woman's tears turned him to mush every time.

The insult worked; Abigail swallowed a sniff and tilted her chin, her eyes narrowing on him with dislike.

Without thinking, David dropped his gaze to the wet T-shirt. It was a mistake. Soaked, the garment was semitransparent and molded every dip and curve of her body. Her small, perfect breasts thrust out impudently, the rose nipples visible through the wet fabric, the tips hardened into tight nubs by the chill rain.

David jerked his gaze lower, only to encounter the shadowy indentation that marked her navel and the darker triangle below. The delectable sight brought an immediate, unwanted tightening to his loins.

Angry with himself, he perversely took his bad temper out on Abigail. "Well, don't just stand there! You're dripping water all over the floor. Get in the shower, for Pete's sake."

Abigail jumped and scurried into the cubicle.

Chelsea lifted her lip at David and gave a low growl.

"Oh, shut up, mutt!"

He grumbled then, stepping back into the bedroom. "Darned skittish old maid acts like I'm gonna jump her bones any second. Ha! Lotsa luck, lady," he snarled at the closed shower door. "You should be so lucky."

That his body didn't agree did nothing to improve his mood. "Damnation, Blaine," he muttered, pawing through the drawers for another T-shirt like a dog digging for a bone. "You've either been celibate too damned long or you're slipping your grip if you get hot and bothered over a persnickety spinster like Abigail Stewart."

A look of grim satisfaction entered his eyes when his search turned up a black T-shirt. He stomped back into the main cabin and hung it on the door handle with a terse, "Here's another shirt. See if you can keep this one dry."

The only answer was the sound of water running, and the erotic image that created sent him searching through the cabinets for another pack of cigarettes, his muttered curses turning the air blue.

By the time the shower door opened, David had his wayward thoughts and body under control. He sat at the table across from the sleeping dog, smoking, his hard face impassive.

Abigail stepped from the cubicle amid a roiling cloud of moist air, warm and redolent with the smells of feminine soap, lotion and talc, and he realized that she'd dipped into the stash of toiletries in her purse. Except for the few curling wisps that straggled around her face, her wet hair hung in a thick braid over one shoulder. Her face was scrubbed free of makeup, rosy and shining.

David took one look at her in the too-large, thigh-skimming T-shirt and felt lust slam into him with the force of a Mack truck.

Oh, yeah. He was definitely losing it.

"I'll, uh...I'll just hang these wet things in the shower," Abigail stammered, avoiding his gaze. She bent over and scooped up the soggy pillow and blanket, and the back of the T-shirt hiked up several tantalizing inches. David's gaze zeroed in on her gorgeous legs with the quickness and accuracy of a heat-seeking missile.

Aw, hell.

His heart began to pump double time, and to his disgust, all the blood seemed to flow straight to his groin.

Grinding his teeth, he watched her step back into the shower. Through the open door he saw the hem of the shirt shoot upward to an even more dangerous level as she stood on tiptoe and pinned the pillow and the blanket to the retractable line she'd already stretched across the stall. Beside the bedding hung a pair of practical white cotton panties and a bra.

David shot out of the booth as if it were on fire and stalked into the bedroom. "Hurry it up, willya," he snapped. "I'd like to get at least a little sleep before this night's over."

Several seconds of taut silence followed. He looked back to see Abigail standing beside the table, watching him warily. "Well? What're you waiting for? C'mon."

"Mr. Blaine—"

"For crying out loud, will you knock off the Mr. Blaine nonsense. My name is David."

"Very well...David. We've been through this already. I'm not going to—"

"Don't say it," he warned, jabbing the air with his fore-finger.

"But—"

"All right! That's it!" he bellowed, and Abigail jumped. "I've had all of this damned foolishness I'm going to take!"

Stalking toward her like a rampaging bull, he covered the distance between them in three long steps. Abigail's eyes widened and she let out a squawk of alarm, but before she could unstick her feet from the floor, he scooped her up in his arms and swung back toward the forward cabin.

"Oh! Stop this! You can't— Oh!"

Chelsea awoke with a start and scrabbled to the edge of the vinyl seat, snarling.

"Aw, shut up, you little fur ball."

Stomping past the agitated animal, David marched into the bedroom, shoved the folding door shut with his foot and tossed Abigail onto the bed.

She bounced twice. By the time her backside struck the mattress the second time, he had stretched out beside her and whipped the cover up over them both.

"Why, you—"

Abigail popped up like a jack-in-the-box, but he shoved her back down and rolled half on top of her. Grabbing her wrists, he pinned them to the mattress on either side of her head. She tried to knee him, but David grunted and jumped back, evading the blow.

"Hey! Watch it!" He clamped his muscular leg over both of hers, holding her immobile. "Dammit. For a woman who claims to hate violence, you got a vicious streak in you, Legs."

The folding door rattled and shook as Chelsea launched herself against it time and time again, her shrill barks running together, choppy and ear piercing. The sounds barely registered on the pair locked together in a silent struggle on the bed. Nose to nose they glared at each other.

"Good! It's no more than you deserve! Just because I asked for your help doesn't give you any rights to my body. I told you I wouldn't sleep with you and I meant it! Now *let me go!*"

"Aw, hell. We're back to that, are we?" She bucked and pitched beneath him, but he held her easily, his hard eyes narrowing on her mutinous face. "I told you, you're not my type. But since you've obviously been waiting for this to happen, why don't we just get it out of the way," he said, and lowered his mouth to hers.

Deliberately he kept the kiss hard, a rough ravishment, devoid of emotion or tenderness. He pushed her deeper into the mattress, his lips rocking over hers with a bored detachment that was insulting. Desire streaked through him, but he held himself rigid. He fought to ignore the wonderful sensations ignited by her taste, her smell, the delicious rub of her breasts against his chest. Not by the slightest softening of his lips or touch of his hands did he reveal the quivering need that hammered through him, the heat, the hunger.

At first Abigail struggled fiercely, but after a moment she went still, her body taut beneath his. He could feel the tremors rippling through her. For a brief moment he let himself believe the reaction stemmed from desire, but he knew that it was more likely disgust. Maybe even fear.

The thought overrode his base instincts, giving him the strength to pull away, though his body clamored for more.

He raised his head and looked down at her. Somehow he managed to keep his expression impassive, almost bored. "You see. We both feel nothing. Right?"

He watched her throat work as she swallowed. Her lips were puffy and wet from his kiss, the area around them red where his whiskers had abraded her skin. She stared at him, her pale eyes round and unblinking, and gave a hesitant nod.

"Good. Now that you know the chemistry just isn't there, you can quit worrying about it and we can both get some rest. Okay?"

"O-okay," Abigail whispered.

Releasing her, David flopped over onto his back. "Now, how about making that damned dog shut up. That mutt makes more racket than a horde of crazed teenagers at a rock concert."

As David switched out the light, Abigail issued a firm one-word command. At once Chelsea's barking ceased. The darkened cabin pulsed with thick silence.

Several inches separated them, but David could feel Abigail lying rigid beside him. He rolled onto his side, facing away from her. The bed rocked. He punched his pillow. "Go to sleep. You need to get some rest. Tomorrow's gonna be one helluva day."

The silence stretched out. After a while Abigail murmured a subdued good-night and turned over, too, taking care not to touch him. She scrunched up against the bulkhead, putting as much space between them as she could.

David pretended to snore. Finally, after what seemed like hours, he felt her relax and heard her breathing grow slow and deep.

He stared into the darkness and gritted his teeth.

Oh, yeah. You're in trouble all right, Blaine. Deep, deep trouble.

Chapter Five

As they did every morning, Abigail's eyes popped open at precisely five minutes before five.

Arms overhead, she arched her back and stretched, but her fledgling smile collapsed into a frown when she focused on the unfamiliar ceiling.

This wasn't her bedroom!

The thought had barely registered when memory returned—the trip, the two thugs, David Blaine's grudging assistance...

David!

Abigail's head snapped around. Sure enough, there he was, sprawled out beside her, sound asleep.

Catching her lower lip between her teeth, she raised on one elbow to study him. She couldn't believe she had slept with him. Well...beside him. She hadn't expected to get so much as a moment's rest, but she had slept like a log all night.

Though, considering the day she'd had, that wasn't so surprising. The excitement of the trip, then the fright and tension, to say nothing of her clashes with David, had left her exhausted. And, yes, she grudgingly admitted while examining his rugged face, there was something about this tough, overbearing man that made her feel secure. Despite his gruffness and his grousing, somehow she knew that David would do everything in his power to keep her safe.

She studied him as though he were an alien species that she'd never seen up close before. In a sense, he was; in her thirty years, Abigail had never encountered a man quite like David before. He was a battle-scarred warrior—granite hard, world-weary, cynical—a man who had dealt with life's seamier side, seen things Abigail knew she couldn't even imagine, and walked away, a trifle battered, perhaps, but whole.

Beneath the whisker stubble, the bruise on his jaw had turned a livid purple. So had the larger one on his shoulder. He hadn't complained of either, but Abigail knew they must be painful, and she had to resist a disturbing urge to run a comforting hand over his battered flesh. Her eyes flickered to the small cut above his left eye. She wondered if it would leave a scar, one more mark of experience on his lived-in face.

Her smile returned, tinged with whimsy. No, he didn't exactly fit the image of a knight in shining armor, but there was no denying that he'd come to her rescue. And he was appealing—in his own roughshod way.

In that unguarded moment he didn't look quite so dangerous or formidable. His harsh face was softened in sleep, his lips parted and slack, making him appear vulnerable. Well...almost. He looked rumpled and utterly relaxed with stubble shadowing his jaw and his dark hair mussed and hanging across his forehead. But even in sleep he exuded a strange earthy appeal.

She sighed. If only he weren't so impossible.

Not that it would make any difference. He'd made his feelings crystal clear. Skinny librarian types didn't turn him on. Which suited her just fine, because he wasn't her type, either.

Of course, in all honesty, Abigail wasn't sure she even had a type, since her experience with men was so limited. But if she did, it wouldn't be the likes of David Blaine, she assured herself. Of that she was positive.

Abigail's gaze turned to his mouth, and her heart began to thump. His kiss had come as a shock—or at least, her reaction to it had. It wasn't fair that he could so easily turn her into a quivering lump, especially since he'd only kissed her to prove a point.

Oh, she had agreed with David when he said that the kiss had sparked no feelings between them. After all, she had her pride. It was distressing, and painful—downright humiliating—to admit, even to herself, that she had experienced such mindless pleasure when he had so obviously felt nothing.

It also annoyed her no end. David Blaine was the last man she wanted to respond to that way. The whole idea was ludicrous. They were like oil and water, for goodness' sake!

The only reason it had happened was that she had been frightened and exhausted and her defenses had been down, she told herself. That and this bizarre situation in which they'd found themselves. Under normal, everyday conditions she would have felt nothing. Except perhaps revulsion.

All at once it occurred to Abigail that David might wake up any second. Unnerved by the thought, she turned back the cover, scooted to the foot of the bed and eased out, keeping a watchful eye on him all the while. This situation was awkward and embarrassing enough without them waking up in bed together.

The instant she opened the folding door and stepped into the main cabin, Chelsea jumped down from the banquette seat and wriggled joyously around her feet, whining and licking her ankles. Chelsea always slept at the foot of Abigail's bed, and the little dog was almost frantic over being separated from her overnight.

"What's the matter, girl? Did you miss me?" Abigail crooned, scooping the animal up in her arms and cuddling her close.

But even after the greeting was over and Chelsea had been fed the half dozen or so dry pellets of dog food she had each morning, she still was not satisfied. While Abigail dressed in her clean undies and rumpled shorts and shirt, the little Yorkie restlessly roamed the boat—going up on deck, coming back down, trotting urgently around the cabin and giving her mistress desperate looks.

"I know, girl," Abigail sympathized. "It's been a long night, hasn't it?" She measured coffee into the basket and slid it into the maker. As water began to gurgle into the glass pot, she glanced toward the forward cabin. "Well, don't worry, he'll be up soon and we'll take care of it."

The delicious smell of coffee brewing filled the cabin. When that failed to rouse David, Abigail set about making breakfast, casting expectant looks at the folding door as she banged pots and pans and hummed a cheerful tune.

David woke with a start and shot up in the bed as though he were spring-loaded. What the *hell* was that?

His gaze darted around, but all was peaceful. Then a crash sounded in the galley, and he flinched.

He sighed, and his spine bowed as he slumped and dragged his hand down over his face. Hell, he should've known. Every disagreeable thing that had happened to him during the past twelve hours had involved Abigail Stewart. And waking up in the morning was high on his list of disagreeable things.

Another clattering bang sounded, and David held his head and groaned. The woman was making more noise than a demolition crew.

Bleary-eyed, he glanced around the cabin. A pale lavender light seeped through the window above the bed; Jeez. The sun wasn't even all the way up yet.

David threw the cover back, swung his feet to the floor and staggered to the door. Grinding his teeth, he shoved aside the folding partition. God, she was humming, too. The woman had to be a sadist.

"Dammit, what is all that racket?"

Abigail looked up from dumping oatmeal into a pot. David filled the doorway, his hands gripping the frame on either side at shoulder level. He hadn't bothered to dress or even put on a robe. He just stood there like a big, grumpy bear, glaring at her, wearing nothing but those outlandish purple bikini shorts.

Avoiding the splash of color, Abigail's gaze flickered over his brawny chest, those powerful arms and legs, tanned and corded with muscle and dusted with hair. Her mouth went dry, and her eyes flickered away again. Lord, didn't he have an ounce of modesty?

"Oh, good. You're awake!" she chirped with false brightness.

"I am now. What the hell were you trying to do in here, wake the dead?"

"No, just you." She sent him a cheery smile. "You said you wanted to get an early start on the engine. Remember?"

"Not this early. Hell, even roosters aren't up yet."

"Oh, but this is the best part of the day," she protested. "It's so quiet and peaceful, and everything is fresh and new. It's a shame to waste this time sleeping."

"Aw, jeez. Don't tell me. Let me guess. You're one of those people who jumps out of bed at the crack of dawn all bright-eyed and bushy tailed and disgustingly perky. Right?"

"Well...I...I am at my best in the morning."

He rolled his eyes heavenward. "Why me? Huh? What did I do to deserve this?"

"Oh, don't be such a grump," Abigail chastised, but her voice held a hint of laughter. She gave the oatmeal a quick stir. "Haven't you heard? It's invigorating to get up early. And it's good for you."

"If you're a bird, maybe. But I don't happen to like worms. So if that's what you're cooking for breakfast, count me out."

Scratching his chest and yawning, his eyelids drooping at half mast, he lumbered into the galley and headed for the coffeepot. Chelsea lifted her lip at him as he walked by. David lifted his back.

He poured himself a mug of coffee, propped a hip against the counter and took a big swig. It had no sooner gone down than he made a horrible face and jerked upright, coughing and sputtering. "What the hell is that?"

Abigail bristled. Her benevolent morning mood vanished like the steam rising from the mug he was eyeing so suspiciously. "It's coffee," she snapped. "I'll admit it may be a little strong—I'm not used to that kind of coffee maker—but there's nothing wrong with it, so you needn't act as though I'm trying to poison you."

Abigail was sensitive about her coffee-making skills. She was a better-than-average cook but somehow she'd just never gotten the hang of making coffee. She used to brew it for her customers at the bookstore, but her efforts were so bad she ended up throwing away more than was consumed. Now she just provided a pot of hot water and a jar of instant and let them make their own.

"A *little* strong? This stuff would float an iron wedge. Why, I've seen battery acid that didn't have this much bite."

Abigail lifted her chin and gave the oatmeal another brisk stir. "Since you find my coffee so objectionable, I suggest that you throw it out and make some more yourself."

David's eyes narrowed on her haughty expression. "You know, I'm getting real tired of that nose-in-the-air attitude of yours, Legs. Say the least little thing and you get as prickly as a hedgehog. Loosen up a little, why don't you?"

Least little thing, indeed. The man was a mannerless oaf. Abigail sniffed, and her chin went up another notch.

"Fine. Have it your way." He slammed the mug down and turned on his heel.

She ignored him until Chelsea pawed at her ankle and whined, reminding Abigail of the reason she had awakened him in the first place. She dropped the spoon and took a quick step after him. "Where are you going?"

"Where do you think? To the john."

Abigail felt her face grow pink. She suspected he was deliberately trying to embarrass her but she met his challenging gaze head-on and refused to acknowledge her discomfort. "As soon as you're done, I'm afraid you'll have to row Chelsea and me to shore."

"To shore? You mean before breakfast? What the devil for?"

"Chelsea needs to relieve herself, too, you know. For that she needs a bit of soil, preferably a grassy area. She's an exceptionally well-behaved dog, but there are limits to her... well, to her... uh... capacity. So you see, you must take us ashore. Just for a few minutes. Unless, of course, you don't mind a puddle or two on your decking."

For his expression you would have thought she was suggesting they tap-dance over the teakwood decks in cleats. He stared at her, appalled. Then his face hardened.

"C'mon." Ignoring her growl, he scooped Chelsea up in one hand and went up on deck. Abigail turned off the burner under the oatmeal and followed on his heels, feeling victorious, though a bit surprised that he'd agreed so readily.

But instead of inflating the raft, as she expected, he stalked to the railing and held the dog out at arm's length over the side.

"Since she's got to go so bad, she can go here," he said, and let the little Yorkie drop.

Abigail gasped and rushed forward in time to see Chelsea hit the water. She rounded on David. "You... you... beast! How *could* you?" she screeched, kicking off her sandals.

"Aw, what's the big deal? Dogs can swim. It's not as though— Hey! Hold on! What are you doing? Get down from there ri—"

His protest was cut off by a tremendous splash when Abigail jumped, feetfirst, from the railing.

She sank beneath the crystal-blue waters like a rock. A few seconds later she bobbed back up coughing and sputtering. Ignoring David's shouted orders and outstretched hand, Abigail sucked in a deep breath and started after her dog.

On deck, David gaped in astonishment. Never in his life had he seen such a pathetic attempt at swimming. Abigail flailed through the water with all the style and grace of a threshing machine.

Hell, the damned dog was doing a hundred times better than she was.

The glass-calm waters of the cove presented no problem for the terrier, who paddled furiously for shore, steadily lengthening the distance between herself and her mistress. Yards behind, Abigail flogged the water, whipping up such a froth he doubted she could see at all.

Keeping his eye on her, David dashed over to the fiberglass case that housed the inflatable life raft.

"Damn fool woman." He flipped open the latches and fumbled for the cord. All right, so maybe he shouldn't have tossed the mutt into the drink, but, dammit, the woman had a way of lighting his fire. Whenever she got that prune-faced expression and her mouth drew up like the pucker on a tight drawstring, it made him so mad he couldn't see straight, much less think straight.

And it wasn't as if he'd been trying to drown the little fuzz ball. Anyway, what kind of idiot jumps in after a dog when she can't swim any better than that?

Locating the cord to inflate the raft, he gave it a hard yank. Nothing happened.

"What the—" He pawed through the folds of rubber. "Well, that cuts it!" David cursed and poked his forefinger through the bullet hole in the raft. Bending over, he located the corresponding one in the fiberglass case and cursed again.

Throwing the useless pile of rubber down in disgust, he raced back to the side.

With the instinctive fear of a poor swimmer, Abigail was fighting to keep her head above the surface and failing miserably. Coughing and choking, she sucked in a mouthful of water with every desperate gasp.

David knew she was using up her energy. As he watched, the furious splashing diminished and she began to sink.

Snatching up a life buoy with a rope attached, he slung it out into the water. It landed a few feet from Abigail. "Grab hold! Grab the ring! C'mon, you can do it!" he shouted through his cupped palms.

But Abigail was in the grip of panic and neither saw the buoy nor heard David's instructions. She thrashed at the water, fighting a losing battle.

"Aw, hell."

The curse had barely left his lips before he was over the side and slicing through the water with long, powerful strokes. Abigail's wretched swimming had not taken her far, and he reached her before she went down for the final time.

When she realized that he had come to her rescue, she grabbed him in a stranglehold. "Oh, David. Th-thank... God," she choked.

"Dammit, will you let go! Just relax and I'll—"

Water closed over their heads, and the remainder of the stern command came out in an indecipherable "glub, glub."

A powerful kick from David sent them shooting back up. They broke the surface coughing and sputtering, David struggling to free himself from her clinging arms and Abigail struggling just as hard to hold on.

"Let go, dammit! You're gonna drown us both!" At last he managed to peel her off and push her away, but Abigail made another grab for him. "Now cut that out!" he roared, but she was beyond reason. Thrashing and clawing, she lunged again. "All right, dammit. You asked for it."

Left with no choice, he drew back his fist and clipped her one on the jaw.

Abigail's eyes glazed over and crossed, and her body went limp. He hadn't hit her hard—just enough to addle her for a moment. Before her head could clear, he cupped her chin and towed her to the life buoy.

Though still dazed, Abigail instinctively hung on to the buoyant ring with a death grip as David towed it and her back to the boat.

Once on board, she collapsed in a sodden heap in the middle of the deck. She sat, gasping for breath, bedraggled and forlorn. Her clothes plastered her body, and limp strands of hair that had worked loose from the braid clung to her face. Water streamed around her in an ever-widening puddle.

"You *hit* me," she accused, gingerly fingering her jaw.

David stood over her, his legs braced wide, his chest heaving. Wet, the purple bikini underwear was even more indecent. "Yeah, well you didn't leave me any choice. If I hadn't, we both would've gone down like a rock. And just what the hell were you thinking of anyway, jumping in the water that way when you can't swim worth a plug nickel?"

"I was *thinking* of my dog," she snapped back. Her eyes widened. "Oh, my Lord, Chelsea!"

Abigail scrambled to her feet and rushed to the side. Gripping the rail with one hand, she shaded her eyes with the other.

With her long fur plastered to her body and coated with sand, the little dog resembled a clump of seaweed, and at first Abigail didn't see her standing on the small, crescent-shaped beach. Then Chelsea shook herself, sending up a shower of drops. Abigail sagged with relief. "Thank God."

She recovered the next instant and whirled on David. "You have to go get her."

His brows shot upward. "You gotta be kidding."

"It's your fault she's over there. That was a horrid thing you did."

"All right, all right. I'm sorry. I shouldn't have tossed your dog into the water. But hell, Legs, it didn't hurt her. You baby that mutt too much, you know. She swam ashore just fine, and when she's ready, she'll swim back. No big deal."

David could feel his anger slipping away. He tried to hold on to it, but he was distracted by the way the soaked shirt molded Abigail's breasts and abdomen.

"Chelsea has never been in the water before. She's not used to swimming. If you're really sorry, you'll go get her."

His breath grew shallow, and a hot heaviness settled in his loins as he stared at the baggy shorts clinging so provocatively to her fantastic long legs. It took a second for her statement to penetrate.

"What? Oh. Well, forget it. No way."

"Very well. If you won't go after her, I will."

The huffy pronouncement barely registered with him and was quickly dismissed as bluff.

She brushed past him and bent over to retrieve the life buoy. His mesmerized gaze homed in on her tight little derriere. Beneath heavy lids his brown eyes smoldered as they traced the round shape and the enticing panty line so clearly revealed by the clinging wet cotton. She had one leg over the rail and was about to launch herself back into the water before he realized her intent.

With a muttered oath, David leaped across the deck and hooked an arm around her waist. "Are you nuts?" he raged, dragging her back. "You almost drowned five minutes ago trying to swim across that cove!"

Abigail turned her head and looked at him over her shoulder. Her aquamarine eyes glittered with a sheen of moisture, and David felt a sharp tightening in his gut when she whispered through quivering lips, "Please. You don't understand. Chelsea is all I have."

Within seconds he found himself slicing through the crystal waters with the life buoy in tow. With every stroke he called himself a chump, but he knew that even if she'd asked him to swim the Atlantic, he couldn't have refused the heartfelt plea in those gorgeous eyes. What the hell, he told himself. A swim would cool his blood. It was that or a cold shower.

Chelsea refused to cooperate, and David chased her around the sandy beach three times before he caught her. The ungrateful little beast rewarded him with several sharp nips for his trouble.

Grinding out a string of colorful epithets that would have done a longshoreman proud, he tossed the snarling terrier onto the life buoy, uncaring whether she managed to hang on or not, and stroked furiously back to the boat. By the time he reached it, temper and the expenditure of energy had purged him of every trace of lustful feelings.

Unfortunately, one look at Abigail in the clinging cotton garments, and they all came rushing back.

As a result, so did his temper.

"Here. I hope you're happy now," he snarled, thrusting the drenched Yorkie into Abigail's outstretched arms. "And I'm warning you, that had better hold her for a while, because I'm not making that swim again anytime soon."

Abigail cuddled her pet close as Chelsea greeted her ecstatically. Water dripped from the little Yorkie's long coat, soaking Abigail even more, but she didn't seem to notice.

Arms crossed over his chest, David leaned back against the side and watched a drop trickle down her neck and collarbone and disappear into the shadowy cleavage at the top of her shirt. Desire surged through him in a hot wave. He clenched his teeth and lowered his gaze, only to encounter those luscious, endless legs.

Damn. There ought to be a law against prim librarians having legs like that.

Stroking Chelsea's head, Abigail looked at David curiously. "Why swim? Why didn't you just row ashore?"

"Because those two goons shot a hole in the life raft, that's why," he said with an unmistakable note of accusation in his voice. Scowling, he looked around. "Would you look at that!" he squawked, jerking away from the side when he spotted another hole in the bulkhead. "And here's another one."

The discoveries led to more, and before long David was darting from one side of the boat to the other, inspecting holes and splintered gouges in the wood and dents and scratches in the brass fittings.

It was the first opportunity he'd had to take stock of the damage in daylight, and with the discovery of each new blemish on his precious craft his face became darker.

"They shot up my boat!" he bellowed. "Those dirty rotten bastards shot up my boat! I'll kill 'em! I'll strangle the scum with my bare hands!"

Chelsea leaned out over Abigail's arm and curled her lip at him in a snarl. Abigail backed up a step. "I . . . uh . . . I'm sure it's not as bad as it looks," she ventured. "Wh-why don't you come below and let me fix you a nice hot breakfast?"

"Breakfast be damned! I'm going to try to repair the engine. As soon as I do, we're heading back to San Cristobal. No one is gonna shoot up my boat and get away with it!"

He disappeared below deck, and the sounds of doors slamming and drawers banging shut echoed through the companionway. Moments later he was back, dressed in the disreputable cutoffs of the day before, a half-smoked cigarette dangling from his mouth. Stomping past her with a determined look on his face, he flicked the butt over the side and jerked open the engine well.

All morning, while David worked on the engine, Abigail did the prudent thing and stayed away from him. After eating a solitary breakfast, she bathed Chelsea, then showered, scrubbed the salt water from her clothes, and washed her hair. When done, she purloined one of David's cotton sports shirts to wear while her outfit dried.

To stay busy, she decided to clean and put things in order below deck. Abigail had noticed that topside all was shipshape and spotless, but the same could not be said for the living quarters.

While not exactly a pigsty, the cabin was a far cry from Abigail's idea of tidy. Overflowing ashtrays were everywhere. Rolled charts and maps had been tossed haphazardly onto the ledge above the banquette, along with pencils, a straight edge, a sextant, an elaborate reel and a spool of heavy line. A billed cap swung from the handle of an overhead storage compartment, and a shirt was hooked over the knob on the wardrobe door. An assortment of hooks, lures, sinkers and bobbers cluttered the bedside table in the forward cabin, and a gaff and landing net stood propped beside the folding door. Mystery novels with lurid covers were crammed into almost every nook and cranny. And to Abigail's outrage, she discovered a girlie magazine wedged beneath the cushions on the banquette seat.

And all that, she knew, was just the tip of the iceberg; she hadn't forgotten the jumbled mess David had made of the drawers the night before.

Rolling up her sleeves, Abigail dived right in. She started by gathering up all the paperback books. She reached for the skin magazine to add it to the pile, but at the last instant her hand stilled.

Curiosity tugged at her. The magazine lay in the center of the table where she'd tossed it, its outrageous name, *Babes,* emblazoned in bold block letters across the top of the slick cover. She stared at it and felt a forbidden stirring.

Tapping her fingers on the tabletop, she pursed her lips and covertly glanced up through the door that led topside. Her forefinger riffled the pages at one corner over and over, ran up and down the edge of the pages, then casually slipped inside and flipped the magazine open.

Abigail gasped. Her jaw dropped. She stared, disbelieving, at the naked bleached blonde.

The picture was shamelessly explicit, a brazen appeal to a man's most prurient instincts. The bimbo knelt beside a pool, cupping her enormous breasts like an offering while she smiled at the camera with a scorching, come-hither look that had probably melted the lens. Her eyes gleamed beneath the sultry droop of her eyelids, and her lips were parted, the tip of her tongue peeking out from between her teeth. Long wet hair lay sleeked back from her face, and her oiled skin, beaded with drops of water, glistened in the sunlight. At the apex of her thighs, more moisture glistened in the dark feminine triangle.

Abigail slammed the magazine shut. Her body pulsed with embarrassed heat from her toes all the way to the roots of her hair. *David Blaine, you ought to be ashamed of yourself!*

Making an aggravated sound, Abigail thrust the offending periodical into the overhead storage above the bed and threw herself into the housekeeping chores with a vengeance.

For the next several hours she went through the boat's living quarters like a tornado, burning up her ire and embarrassment in an excess of activity. When she had finally calmed, she chided herself for overreacting. After all, she should have expected such from a chauvinistic ruffian like

David Blaine. When—or *if*—she got home, she was going to have to write to her congressman about the caliber of men the government hired.

She had just finished below deck and was admiring her handiwork, when David loped down the steps.

He brought with him the smell of sweat and engine grease and maleness. His nearness, his size, his state of undress, all unnerved Abigail, making her skin prickle. She stepped aside as far from him as she could and averted her eyes from his body.

Without so much as a word to her, he reached into a cabinet above the sink and extracted two cigarettes from an open pack, his movements a study in unselfconscious masculine grace.

The action tightened his buttocks and caused muscles in his broad back to ripple. Abigail gritted her teeth. The man oozed a raw, animal magnetism and a supreme self-confidence that made her insides flutter and aroused in Abigail, a woman who prided herself on her self-control and even temperament, the totally uncharacteristic desire to give him a good swift kick.

David lit one of the cigarettes and stuck the other behind his ear. His eyes flickered over her, taking on a strange glitter as he noticed her attire. Then he looked around.

He frowned. "What the devil have you done to this place?"

"I cleaned it and straightened everything up. Doesn't it look better?"

"Oh, great! Now I'll never find anything. What the devil have you done with all my stuff?"

"Your fishing gear is in the locker up on deck, your clothing is in the wardrobe and drawers, and your books are in the overhead storage."

At the last, David shot her a startled look, and Abigail returned it coolly.

"Along with your...ah...*other* reading material, of course." Her arch tone and expression left no doubt as to what she meant or her opinion of it.

For an instant David appeared uncomfortable, but he quickly recovered, and his heavy brows lowered in a glower. "You can get that snooty look off your face. Just because a guy buys a skin magazine doesn't mean he's a sicko."

Abigail widened her eyes. "Did *I* say anything?"

"It so happens I didn't buy the damned thing for the pictures. That magazine contains excellent articles and book reviews—"

Her snort cut him off, and David skewered her with a killing glare. He fumed in silence for a full thirty seconds before throwing up his hands. "I don't know why I should even try to justify myself to you. What gives you the right to sit in judgment, anyway? If you don't like my choice of reading material, keep your priggish little nose out of it."

He spun away and stalked up the steps, muttering under his breath, leaving Abigail feeling properly chastised.

On one level, her brain and her conscience told her that he was right. But another part of her—the emotional part—still simmered with outrage...and a totally irrational, inappropriate feeling that was very close to jealousy, though she would have bitten off her tongue rather than admit it.

Abigail gave an indignant sniff and stiffened her spine. So what if the man got some sort of voyeuristic thrill out of ogling naked tootsies in trashy magazines? It was no concern of hers.

Her gaze fell on the partial pack of cigarettes he'd left on the counter, and her eyes narrowed. In fact, she told herself with just a hint of smug satisfaction, instead of criticizing the man, she ought to do something to thank him. After all, he had saved her life. Twice. Of course, the second time it had been his fault that she'd almost drowned, but he *had* saved her.

She picked up the cigarettes, fingering the cellophane. A tiny, dangerous smile tipped up the corners of her mouth. What better way to show her appreciation than to help him quit smoking?

A half hour later there was nothing left to do but braid her hair. It, however, was still damp, despite the hours that had passed since she'd shampooed it. When loose the thick mane hung to below her waist and was the very devil to dry, even with a hair dryer—and Abigail's was back in her hotel room in San Cristobal.

She wasn't anxious to get anywhere near David, but she needed to be outside so that the wind and sun could dry her hair. Besides, Abigail reasoned, it might be wise to be someplace where there was a bit more maneuvering room.

Resolutely she took her hairbrush from her purse, picked up Chelsea and went topside. The bridge was far enough away, she decided, settling herself on the companion bench. From there she couldn't possibly bother him.

She was driving him nuts. Stark, staring mad.

Straining, David grunted as he bore down on the wrench, but the stuck bolt wouldn't budge. He cursed and swiped the sweat from his forehead with the back of his arm.

Involving him in her troubles. Waking him up at the crack of dawn. Looking one minute like she'd spook if he said boo and giving him orders in that prim, schoolmarm voice the next. *"As soon as you're done, I'm afraid you'll have to row Chelsea and me to shore,"* he mimicked silently.

Between her and the fuzz ball, he'd soon be bouncing off the walls of a rubber room somewhere.

That is...if he managed to get them out of this mess she'd dragged him into.

He banged on the stubborn bolt with the side of the wrench. Thanks to her, his boat was shot to hell and gone, the engine was crippled and the KGB was after his ass. And to top it all off, little Miss Mouse In Starchy Drawers was down there cleaning and organizing his boat. Soon it'd look like that damned purse of hers, with everything all neatly labeled and in its proper place.

Well, he didn't need or want a housekeeper. He wasn't exactly a slob. He kept his boat clean and orderly. Sort of. Anyway, a little clutter was comforting. Made a place seem lived in.

He wiped his sweaty palms on the seat of his cutoffs and gave the wrench another try, putting all his weight behind it.

And then there were those beautiful eyes and that fantastic little body with those knockout legs. He'd lain awake half the night, thinking about how they'd feel wrapped around him, those silky thighs clamping his hips as he—

The sound that came from David was very close to a snarl, and he gave the stubborn bolt another vicious whack. This time when he applied pressure, it gave with such suddenness, his sweaty palms slipped off the wrench and he scraped three knuckles.

He was in the midst of grinding out a string of colorful curses, when he heard Abigail come up on deck. Breaking off in midspate, he peered over the top of the engine well in time to see her climb the ladder to the bridge.

He ducked back down, banged on the engine a few times, then stood up and pretended to arch the kinks from his back while he slanted another furtive glance her way.

The instant he saw her, he went utterly still. He felt as though someone had dealt him a blow to the solar plexus.

With Chelsea curled at her feet, Abigail sat on the end of the bench, her eyes closed, running a brush through her hair from scalp to tip with slow, smooth strokes.

Lord, how could he have thought, for even a moment, that she was just attractive? With her hair loose around her face instead of scraped back in that hideous tight braid— why...she was lovely. Not drop-dead gorgeous, maybe, but striking—in a quiet, understated way that grabbed his gut.

He had assumed her hair was plain light brown, but the thick cascade glittered in the sun with golden highlights, a long, straight curtain of shimmering silk that hung past her hips.

His hands clenched. He wanted to run his fingers through that luxurious mane, gather it up in his hands and bury his face in it, inhale its clean scent. Feel it slide against his skin. Tangle with the hair on his chest . . .

A shudder of desire rippled through him, constricting his breath and sending blood surging through his body, straight to his loins.

Hellfire, he was in trouble. Big, big trouble.

Shakily, never taking his gaze from her, David hoisted himself out of the engine well onto the deck. The throbbing heat pounding through him robbed him of strength, and with a deceptive nonchalance, he stood and rested his hips against the rail and crossed his long legs at the ankles. He reached for the spare cigarette behind his ear but it was gone, and he remembered that he'd already smoked it.

Damnation. He couldn't have another for at least an hour. Already he was over the limit he had set for himself that day.

He stuffed his shaking hands into the pockets of his cut-offs and stared at Abigail's legs. She was wearing one of his shirts. Below, earlier, he'd tried not to notice how sexy she looked in the masculine garment, but now all he could do was stare. It swallowed her slight frame and the tails hung down to her midthigh. He wondered if she wore anything under it.

Tipping her head to one side, Abigail noticed him watching her. Instead of turning away or feigning indifference, her gaze found his and held.

The sun beat down hotly. A salt-scented breeze toyed with the ends of her hair. Water lapped at the hull of the boat, and from ashore came the distant raucous call of a bird. All else was still. Quiet. In the somnolent afternoon, they looked at each other. The air between them pulsed and sizzled with something wild and electric, something irresistible.

Abigail licked her lips, and David's chest grew tighter. The slow, heavy beat of his heart reverberated through his body. She gazed at him steadily, her aquamarine eyes glazed, unblinking, helplessly fascinated. As though of its own volition, the hand holding the brush continued its slow, mesmerizing strokes.

"Aw, the hell with it," David growled, and shoved away from the side. "I need a cigarette. Now."

The spell broken, Abigail watched him disappear below deck, her heart pounding like a wild thing in her chest. She was inexperienced where men were concerned, it was true, but she wasn't so naive that she didn't know what had occurred between her and David just now. It was called chemistry, sexual attraction, the age-old pull between male and female. And it had been primal. Hot. Dangerous.

Her cheeks flamed at the memory, and she covered them with her hands. She understood what had transpired, all right, but what confused her was how such a thing could have happened between her and David!

She was left with no time to ponder the matter, however, because at that instant David shot up out of the cabin like a scalded cat.

"Dammit, Abbey!" he roared. "Where the hell are my cigarettes?"

Chapter Six

Abigail sucked in her breath. Whoops. In the past few minutes she had forgotten all about the cigarettes.

Which was hardly surprising. That sizzling interlude had practically rendered her a mindless lump of quivering flesh. Even now, faced with David's fury, her breasts still tingled, and a pulsing heat persisted at the core of her femininity, making it difficult for her to concentrate.

David glowered up at her from the deck below. With his fists planted on his hipbones and his stance wide and aggressive, he radiated anger.

Abigail cleared her throat and shifted on the bench. "I...uh...I thought you were trying to quit."

"I am. Where are my cigarettes?"

"Ha-have you ever given any thought to just, uh... stopping? You know...cold turkey?"

David's eyes narrowed. "What have you done with my cigarettes, Legs?"

A shiver rippled through her at the soft demand, but she hid her trepidation behind false bravery. "Well, I didn't throw them overboard," she snapped. "Though for your sake I should have."

"Don't do me any favors, okay? Now where the hell are my cigarettes?"

Abigail drew a deep breath and screwed up her courage. "I hid them."

"You *what?*" His eyes bulged, and his jaw dropped. Then, like a thundercloud, his face darkened. His lips tightened into a white line, and a muscle twitched in his cheek.

"You hid my cigarettes?" he asked slowly, softly. And then, exploding, he shouted, "You *hid my cigarettes?* Dammit, woman, do you have a death wish?"

Roused from her sleep, Chelsea looked down over the edge of the bridge and growled.

"No. But apparently you do. Good grief. If you had any sense you'd know that at the very least you should cut down." Abigail gripped the hairbrush with both hands, unaware of the bristles stabbing into her palm.

"Woman, I'm going to ask you one more time. *Where are my cigarettes?*"

Abigail tipped her chin up. "I won't tell you. If you must have the noxious weeds, you'll just have to find them yourself."

Fury, astonishment, disbelief, frustration, then back to fury—David's expression ran the gamut. If ever a man looked ready to fly apart, he did. Everything about him, his rigid stance, the glitter in his eyes, the fists opening and closing at his sides, screamed of rage barely held in check.

Abigail knew that he wanted to throttle her. Still, she managed to ignore her quaking insides and meet his glare without flinching.

Normally she would not have dared to tweak a grizzly's nose, but there was something about David that stirred in her a strange recklessness that overrode her normal caution.

The tense, silent confrontation went on for a full minute with neither budging. She was beginning to wonder how much longer she could keep up the defiant front when David muttered something under his breath, which she had no doubt was obscene, and stormed below deck.

The horrible banging and slamming that ensued reached such proportions that Abigail could not stand it. Scooping up Chelsea, she scrambled down from the bridge and hurried below. She arrived just as David pulled one of the stashed bundles from behind the small TV in the forward cabin.

"What's this," he demanded, dangling the plastic bag between his thumb and forefinger.

"As you can see, it's your disgusting cigarettes."

Abigail's mouth compressed as she took in the mess he'd made of the cabin. All her work, ruined.

"There are only four in here."

"Well, my stars. You don't think I'm stupid enough to hide them all in the same place, do you?"

"You mean you've stashed bags like this all over the place?"

Her reply was a smug look that brought a growl from David. Chelsea answered it with one of her own.

"Aw, shut up you miserable little dust mop, or I'll throw you overboard again."

Abigail gasped and clutched her pet closer, but David was too busy tipping up the mattress and pillows and searching through the wardrobe to notice.

After five minutes, when his efforts failed to turn up another cache, he was so desperate for a smoke, he gave up and lit one of the precious four he had. After a long, blissful drag he exhaled slowly, shot Abigail a murderous glare and stomped past her. "Damned interfering, pain-in-the-butt women. Nothing but trouble, the lot of them. Always sticking their noses in . . ."

He disappeared up the steps, and Abigail didn't catch the end of the muttered tirade, nor did she care. Fuming, she was already straightening the bed and snatching up the books and other articles he'd tossed aside in his search.

For the next hour they stayed away from each other. David worked on the engine, banging and cursing with what

Abigail felt was unnecessary force and frequency. She occupied herself retidying below deck.

No sooner had she finished, than he reappeared and told her to get ready to swim ashore. "I can't fix the engine without a new part. Which means we're going to have to walk back to San Cristobal."

"Walk back? But that's miles."

"You got a better idea how we can get there?"

"Well . . . no. But why do I have to go? Can't I just wait here for you?"

"Sure," he said with a disinterested shrug. "If you don't mind taking the chance on those two KGB guys coming back for a closer look and finding you, why should I care?"

David waded ashore and tossed the plastic garbage bag containing their dry clothes on the sand. He looked around just as Abigail found her footing and stood up. Groaning, he cursed under his breath.

He had tried to get her to strip down to her panties and bra for the swim to shore, but she had been shocked, and adamantly refused. He felt like telling her that her modesty would have been better served if she'd taken his suggestion. The soaked shirt plastered to her body was a helluva lot more provocative than any bikini he'd ever seen, and his body reacted to the sight in the normal, if annoyingly zealous, manner.

Gritting his teeth, David turned away as she dragged the flotation ring with that ridiculous purse and even more ridiculous dog perched on top up onto the beach. He'd tried to get her to leave that satchel and the mutt behind, but at the mere suggestion she'd clutched the purse to her chest and looked at him as though he'd suggested something unspeakably heinous.

"Where I go, Chelsea goes," she'd informed him. "And I always carry my purse with me. I . . . I might need something from it."

No amount of arguing or reason had budged her. With the purse riding on a life buoy and Chelsea perched on top of it, she had hung on to the flotation ring and propelled herself and the mutt to shore by kicking her feet.

Damned stubborn female, he thought as Abigail came walking toward him with the clinging shirt molding every line and curve and sending water sheeting down over those gorgeous legs.

David snatched up the plastic bag and tore it open. "Here, put these on," he ordered, tossing dry clothes at her. "And make it snappy."

His rude manner caught her by surprise, and Abigail blinked at him. For some reason the hurt look in her eyes, which she quickly tried to hide, darkened David's mood.

"Well, get a move on if you're going with me," he snapped. Unhampered by modesty, he had stripped down to his skivvies for the swim ashore. Ignoring her, he hooked his thumbs under the waistband on his maroon briefs and pushed them downward.

Abigail made a choked sound and scurried for the bushes, her face flaming.

As soon as he was dressed, he set off through the forest without a word to her.

"Wait! Wait for me!"

He glanced back and saw Abigail scrambling after him, hopping and skipping as she struggled to roll up the legs on her jeans while on the run.

Three hours later, shoving aside a clump of brush, David looked back over his shoulder, sighed, and stopped once again to wait for Abigail to catch up.

She struggled along the narrow animal trail, swatting at bushes, trailing vines and insects, huffing and puffing like a steam engine, lugging that absurd purse and that pitiful excuse for a dog.

At least she was dry now, thank God, David thought, watching her gird herself to leap over a small stream. It seemed to him that she'd spent most of the time since they'd met drenched to the skin. And driving him crazy.

He had to give her credit though; she was a game little thing. She'd complained some, mostly when he'd gotten too far ahead of her, but not as much as he had expected, even though the going had been rough in spots. He'd lost count of the number of times she'd stumbled and fallen. Once she'd even lost her footing and slid down the muddy bank of a ravine on her backside.

Her attire didn't make it easier. Her shorts had been unsuitable for hiking through the woods, but it had to be awkward, tromping along in a pair of his jeans with over a foot of the legs rolled up and the bunched waist secured with a piece of rope. The shirt she wore, which fit him perfectly, flopped around her knees and caught on every twig and bramble. Neither of them had on hiking boots, but at least he was wearing sneakers, which were a helluva lot better for walking over rough terrain than those flimsy leather sandals of hers.

"David, can't we please rest for a little while?" Abigail moaned as she came trudging up the path behind him. He opened his mouth, but before he could reply, an enormous snake dropped out of a tree onto the path between them.

Abigail cut loose with an ear-piercing scream that could be heard clear to the next island, and covered the ten feet or so that separated them in one superhuman leap. Before David could react, she was astraddle him, purse, yapping dog and all, her legs clamped around his waist and her arms wrapped around his neck in a choke hold. She was shaking so hard, her bones were rattling like castanets.

"Snake! Snake! Oh, help, help! Do something!" she blubbered.

"Abbey... for God's... sake, let go!" He coughed and choked, clawing at her locked arms.

Between her own babbling, Chelsea's incessant barking and the mindless terror that had her in its grip, she didn't hear a word he said. The more he tried to pry her loose, the more she tightened her hold.

Tiny dots were beginning to appear before David's eyes. Just when he was beginning to think she was going to choke him to death, Chelsea jumped to the ground, snarling and barking, and attacked the snake.

The next instant David was free. Bending over, he braced his hands on his thighs and sucked deep draughts of blessed air into his lungs while Abigail hopped around shrieking like a banshee. "Chelsea, stop that! Oh, David, *do* something!"

"Wh-what?" he choked.

"Kill it! Kill it!"

"You want me to kill that snake? Jeez! Woman, are you nuts? That thing is eight feet long!"

"Well, do *something!*"

The reptile, which had been slithering away into the underbrush, changed directions and curled back toward its attacker.

Abigail let loose with another ear-piercing scream.

Cursing, David grabbed her hand, snatched up the snarling dog and ran.

By the time they stopped, they had put a good half mile between themselves and the snake.

"Pl...please. I ha...ha...ave to re...re...rest," Abigail gasped.

"All...right," David agreed, struggling to control his own labored breathing. "But only for...a few minutes."

Dropping to the ground, he leaned back against a tree and draped his wrist across his upraised knee. He watched in silent amusement as Abigail checked around the base of a small boulder, before gingerly settling onto it.

His gaze turned sour as it settled on Chelsea, who was still snarling in leftover fury.

Nutsy dog. Acted like she thought she was a German shepherd or something. That snake could've swallowed her whole.

Abigail pulled a package of cheese and crackers and a bag of raisins from her purse.

David shook his head. "God, you've got everything but the kitchen sink in that thing. It's a wonder you don't have a permanent list to one side from carrying it around."

"They're all useful items. It never hurts to be prepared, you know." She glanced up from peeling open the cellophane wrapper on the crackers and caught him eyeing the snack. "Would you like some?"

"No, thanks. I'm not hungry."

The lie was hardly out of his mouth when his stomach growled. Without a word, Abigail dug another bag of raisins from her purse and handed it to him, along with half her crackers. Then she spoiled the gesture by adding, "Of course, if you had let me make sandwiches to bring along, as I had wanted to, we wouldn't have to make do with crackers and raisins. Neither of us had any lunch, after all."

"I'm in a hurry. I don't relish the thought of trying to find my way to San Cristobal in the dark. As it is, we have only an hour or so of daylight left to make it."

It was a bold-faced lie. He had an excellent sense of direction and the skills to find his way out of a maze in pitch-blackness. When he had hustled her off the *Freewind,* he'd had one thought in mind: clearing up this situation as fast as possible so he could get one Miss Abigail Stewart out of his life. Hopefully, before he did something foolish.

Chomping a cracker, David glanced at her out of the corner of his eye, and a reluctant grin tugged at his mouth. She did look a sight. He hadn't given her time to braid her hair, so she had twisted it up and pinned it on top of her head to keep it dry during the swim. In the past couple of hours the thick coil had loosened and now it sat askew over one ear. Low branches and brambles had snagged long tendrils free, and they straggled around her face and shoulders. In those clothes, with leaves and debris clinging to her wild hair and her face streaked with mud, she was a comic sight.

So why, he wondered, did he still have this itch?

Blast the woman, she appealed to him! Though damned if he knew why. He tipped up the bag of raisins and chewed as though he were pulverizing rocks with his teeth.

Well... actually, she wasn't so bad. A bit repressed and starchy, maybe, but from what he'd gathered about that aunt of hers, that was understandable. And he had to admit, when she wasn't making him so mad he wanted to strangle her, he thought it was kind of cute the way she stood up to him, all huffy and indignant. Especially when he could see in her eyes that she was scared spitless.

And he had to admire the way she'd kept her head and eluded those two goons. She was soft and vulnerable, but there was an intelligent, gutsy lady beneath that prim and proper exterior.

His mouth twitched again as he recalled how flustered she'd gotten when she'd seen his purple underwear. Erin, his irrepressible, thoroughly maddening sister, had given him a whole box of racy skivvies for his birthday as a joke, X-rated briefs in every color and style, including flesh-colored mesh, a leopard-print jersey and a passion red, French silk G-string. Shoot, if she thought the purple knits were shocking, she'd faint dead away if she got a look at the ones he had on now.

"What are we going to do when we reach San Cristobal?" Abigail asked, breaking in on his amused thoughts.

"We'll head for Pepe's. From there I can call my cousin, Travis McCall. *He's* still *with* the FBI," he said, giving her a pointed look. "I'll get him to check out this Patrice Johnson woman you sat next to on the plane. One of Pepe's boys can get the part I need while you and I pay a visit to your hotel."

He thought she blanched a little at that, but he couldn't tell in the shadowy light.

"Do, uh—" She stopped and cleared her throat. "Do you think we'll find whatever it is those men were looking for?"

"Not really. They've had plenty of time to search your things. If it was there, they've found it by now." He shrugged. "But it's a place to start. Anyway, there's always the chance they overlooked something."

"And if we don't find anything? What then?"

"We'll pick up the part I need at Pepe's and borrow his skiff to get back to the cove. When I get my boat fixed, we'll go to my twin sisters' summer place over on Rincon Island while we're waiting on Travis to find out what he can."

"*You* have *sisters?*"

The question was asked with such artless astonishment that David took immediate offence.

"Yes, I have sisters," he returned in an affronted tone. "A mother and a father, too. What did you think? That I crawled out from under a rock somewhere?"

"No, of course not. It's just that...well...you seem like such a loner that I just never thought of you as having a family. That's all."

David wasn't mollified. He rolled to his feet in one smooth motion, his face set. "C'mon. We've wasted enough time."

"Wait a minute." Abigail dug two small sealed packets from the bowels of her purse and handed one to him. Frowning, he turned it over in his palm as she unwrapped hers.

"What's this?"

"A moist towelette to wipe your hands with," she said, suiting actions to words.

"Aw, for... We're in the middle of the woods, Legs. Not at a church social." He stalked off down the narrow trail, disgust evident in every line of his body. "Heaven spare me from neurotic women!"

"I am *not* neurotic!" Abigail scrambled to her feet, scooped up Chelsea and hurried after him. "And for goodness' sake, will you please stop calling me by that ridiculous name!"

"Quit your bellyaching. I can think of worse things to call you."

"And *I* you," she returned in her snippiest voice. "Like mannerless oaf. Or how about boorish brute? Ruffian? Hooligan?" Issuing deliberate insults was as foreign to her nature and upbringing as perfume was to a pig. Aunt Harriet would be appalled. But it felt good, Abigail discovered.

"Listen, Legs, if you..."

Like a couple of children, they squabbled every step of the way to San Cristobal. By the time they reached Pepe's Cantina, Abigail had decided that she detested David Blaine. Just when they were finally having a halfway civil conversation, he had to go and spoil it. The clod.

They arrived under the cover of full darkness and slipped inside the cantina as inconspicuously as possible, considering that Abigail looked as though she'd been jerked through a knothole backward.

Standing in the shadows beside the door, she slanted a resentful look at David as he checked out the room. They had just trekked miles through a mountainous forest. Her hair was tangled and sticking out every which way, she had blisters on both feet, and mud and no telling what else between her toes. The clothes she was wearing, which at the best of times made her look like a clown-school reject, were stained and dirty, the shirt ripped. Her back ached, her legs ached, her feet ached—even her shoulders ached from toting her purse and Chelsea. And yet he looked no worse for wear than if he'd been out for a refreshing stroll. It wasn't fair.

"It looks safe. I don't see anyone but the regulars," the object of her ire murmured. "C'mon."

"Señor Blaine! Señorita Stewart!" Pepe's face registered profound shock and relief at the sight of them. Hearing him, Constanza came bustling out of the kitchen chattering away in excited Spanish as he rounded the bar and greeted David with a hearty clap on the back. "*Dios mio, mi amigo,* it is good to see you! Both of you! We heard about what happened. My cousin, Raphael, he was bringing his fishing boat in to the pier when the men, they grabbed the *señorita.* He saw the whole thing."

"*Sí, sí. Ai yi, mi pobrecita,*" Constanza wailed, enveloping Abigail in a squashing hug that nearly suffocated her. "Can you ever forgive me, little one, for not taking your problem more seriously? I should have let Pepe go with you. I should have—"

"It's all right, Constanza. Really," she assured the tearful woman, patting her fleshy arm. An hysterical giggle bubbled up in Abigail's throat at the thought of Pepe acting as her protector, but she stifled it. It was clear that Constanza thought her scrawny little husband was *muy macho.*

"But, *señorita,* you could have been killed!" She gasped, and her hand flew to her mouth. "*Madre de Dios!* What

have I been thinking of. Are you all right, little one? Were
you hurt?"

"No. No, I'm fine."

"Ah, *muy bien.*"

Pepe's thin chest puffed out. "You see, *señorita,* I told
you that Señor Blaine would protect you."

"As to that," David inserted, "I think that you and I
need to have a little talk, *mi amigo.* Now." Clamping his
broad hand around the back of Pepe's neck, he steered him,
none too gently, toward a secluded table in the corner.

Assured that Abigail was unharmed, Constanza recovered her composure and ushered her into the family's
living quarters at the rear of the cantina. "Come. You will
feel better once you have a bath and proper clothes. These
things," she said, wrinkling her nose at the oversize jeans
and shirt. "They are filthy. And fit only for an hombre. My
daughter, Louisa, she is about your size. She will have
something for you to wear. Something *muy bonito.*"

Abigail didn't stand a chance against Constanza's mater-
nal bullying. Her protests were halfhearted at best, anyway. The thought of a warm bath and something clean to
wear, something that she didn't have to keep hitching up
every few minutes, was simply too tempting to resist.

When Abigail returned to the cantina a half hour later,
most of her soreness had been soaked away. At Constanza
and her daughter's insistence, she had donned a full gathered print skirt and a gauzy, long-sleeved, aqua peasant
blouse that did marvelous things for her eyes and skin and
made her feel deliciously feminine. Clean and relaxed,
smelling of Louisa's best perfume, her hair in a loose French
braid, Abigail felt like a new woman—an attractive, intri-
guing, sensual woman.

The looks she received from the male patrons reinforced
her budding sense of feminine allure as well as bolstered her
confidence. As a result, she was much more kindly dis-
posed toward David and greeted him with a smile when he
turned from hanging up the pay telephone located in the
back corner of the cantina.

He had used the time to clean up as well. His hair was still damp from the shower and, though he wore the same trail-stained jeans, he had purloined a fresh shirt from some-where, a rusty brown chambray that complemented his eyes and brought out the red highlights in his dark hair. The rough material stretched taut across his broad shoulders and massive chest, and the sleeves were rolled up to his elbows, exposing brawny forearms sprinkled with dark hair. He looked rugged and heart-stoppingly male.

Abigail's throat went dry, and she swallowed hard. "Di-did you get through to your cousin?"

David treated her to a quick, frankly masculine ap-praisal, a strange glitter in his brown eyes as his gaze lin-gered on her creamy shoulders and the swell of her breasts beneath the soft batiste. Abigail felt the look all the way to her toes, but when he answered, his voice was flat, almost curt.

"Yeah. He's on his way to headquarters to check out Pa-trice Johnson on the computer." David had also asked Travis to run a check on Abigail. He was confident that she was clean, as she claimed, but it didn't hurt to play it safe. Pulling a cigarette from a fresh pack in his shirt pocket, he lit up and inhaled. "I'll call him again when we get back from your hotel to see what he found out, if anything."

Dammit, a prim librarian had no business looking like that. All soft and curvy and sexy as hell. Made a man want to cart her off someplace where it was quiet and iso-lated . . . someplace like his boat.

The errant thought jolted him. He must be nuts! Him and Miss Starchy Drawers? Uh-uh. No way. She was nothing but trouble. Besides . . . she wasn't even his type.

"And just where did you get that?" Abigail demanded, her eyes on the glowing cigarette. "I know it's not part of the stash you found in the flour canister before we left the boat. You smoked those on the way here. So where did it come from?"

"From Pepe's vending machine."

"David, you know—"

"Don't start with me, Legs," he warned, giving her a quelling look.

He was in no mood to lock horns with her again over his smoking habit. Especially not after the frustrating session he'd just had with Pepe.

Fat lot of good it had done to read his imaginative friend the riot act for getting him involved in Abigail's problems. Trying to get it through the man's head that he was no longer an agent was an exercise in futility. He might as well try to convince him that the Pope wasn't Catholic.

No matter what he'd said, or how angry he'd gotten, or what dire threats he'd used, Pepe responded with a conspiratorial look and an earnest: "*Sí, sí.* I understand, *mi amigo.* You are head of security for Telecom International. You are just here for the fishing. Do not worry. That is all anyone will get from me. Pepe knows how to keep his mouth shut."

What was worse, the difference between FBI and CIA was, at best, blurry in Pepe's mind. He seemed to think David was some kind of international spy. Dammit, he hated being mistaken for a spook!

Abigail opened her mouth, but Pepe rushed up before she could say more.

"Juanito has just returned from the hotel, *mi amigo.* It is all set. Rico will let us in through the back entrance. But come. We must hurry."

"Who is Rico?" Abigail asked, as David took her arm and fell in behind Pepe.

"Pepe's cousin. Between him and Constanza, they're kin to half the people on this island. I figured they'd have a relative working at the hotel, and I was right." He started out the door, but Abigail hung back.

"Wait. I have to get Chelsea."

"Leave her. Pepe's kids are playing with her in the back. She'll be fine until we return."

"Oh, but—"

"Dammit, Legs, the object is to sneak in without being spotted. We're not taking that yapping dog, and that's final."

Abigail didn't like it, but he had a point.

Pepe led the way, his scrawny chest puffed out with self-importance and his eyes dancing at the prospect of taking part in what was shaping up to be a real, honest to God, dangerous intelligence mission.

They covered the three blocks to the hotel quickly, hugging the shadows beside the buildings and cutting through alleyways whenever they could. On the streets of San Cristobal Abigail felt exposed, her nerves raw and jangled. Once, when a yowling cat streaked past them, she almost jumped out of her skin and barely managed to stifle a scream.

"Here we are," Pepe whispered when they reached the back of the hotel. He gave the door three quick raps, paused, then knocked twice more. From the other side came a burst of four raps, followed by two more.

David rolled his eyes.

Pepe lifted his hand to knock again.

"Oh, for cryin' out loud!" Rudely, David shoved him aside and put his mouth close to the door. "Rico, this is David Blaine. Unlock the damned door. Now."

At once the door swung open.

Pepe looked crestfallen, but David ignored him and hustled them inside. The door had no sooner closed behind them than Rico took off. From his nervous manner it was obvious that he did not share his cousin's enthusiasm for playing spy.

David eased open the lobby door a crack. "Damn," he snarled.

"What? What is is?"

Hearing the urgency in Abigail's voice, Pepe edged closer. "Trouble, *señor?*"

"One of those apes who tried to grab Abbey is keeping watch in the lobby. There are others out there, too, so he may have company. It's hard to tell. One of them looks familiar, though." Frowning, David studied the man through the crack. "Dammit, I've seen that guy somewhere before. But where?"

He tried to recall but could not place the man, and after a while he released the door and took Abigail's arm. "Pepe, you stay here and keep an eye on the lobby. If anyone—and I mean anyone—goes near that elevator, you hightail it upstairs pronto and warn us."

"*Sí, mi amigo.* You can count on Pepe," he replied, swelling up importantly at the assignment.

They climbed the three flights carefully, making as little noise as possible. Abigail felt a chill, recalling the mad dash she'd made down the same stairwell the day before, her sandals clanging against the metal treads and Chelsea barking. Had it been only a little over twenty-four hours ago? It seemed as though an eternity had passed since then.

The fourth floor hallway was deserted. They hurried down the carpeted corridor and let themselves into the room with Abbey's key. Once inside she collapsed back against the wall beside the door, her heart pounding in her chest.

David flipped on a light and started searching with a quick efficiency that spoke of experience.

"Why...they're empty!" Abigail exclaimed, staring at the drawers he had opened. She jerked open the closet doors and gaped at the bare hangers. "My things! They're gone!"

"Looks that way," David replied without pausing in his search.

"But why would they take my clothes and things? They weren't worth much."

"Could be so they can go through everything at their leisure. Or it could be that they figure they'll have to eliminate you, so they're trying to make it look like you never arrived on Alhaja Verde. I'd be willing to guess that the hotel no longer has any record of you ever being registered here. And if the airline lists you as a passenger at all, they probably show that you deplaned in Mexico City." He glanced her way, gauging her reaction. "If family or friends make inquiries, it's easier to hide what happened if they're following a false trail."

"Oh, my stars," she whispered, looking at him, aghast. "Th-they really mean to kill me!"

"Not if I can help it."

Under the circumstances, Abigail was not reassured. She knew that David would do his best to protect her, but he was just one unarmed man pitted against the vast resources of the KGB.

Feeling suddenly sick, she staggered into the bathroom. She stood braced against the sink until the wave of nausea passed, then splashed cool water over her face and neck.

"Don't move."

Abigail froze, her eyes widening above the towel she was using to dry her face. That wasn't David's voice!

She turned slowly, but there was no one in the doorway.

"We have been waiting for you, Mr. Blaine," came the voice again.

Abigail crept to the door and peeked around the edge of the frame. The man stood just a couple of feet away with his back to her, but from his size she knew it was Shovel-face. He was holding a malevolent looking pistol pointed straight at David's heart. David stood motionless on the other side of the bed, his expression watchful.

"Why don't you save yourself a lot of pain and tell us where it is? Huh?" the man said in accented English.

"Where what is?" David returned with commendable calm.

Shovel-face uttered what sounded like a curse. Abigail bit her lip. Oh, Lord, she had to do something. David was powerless.

"Don't get smart. I can make things very unpleasant for you, Mr. Blaine. In fact . . . after what happened on the pier yesterday, I would enjoy it. Now where is it?"

She needed a weapon. Quickly Abigail searched her purse. All she had that might do was a small pocket knife, but it wasn't big enough to inflict serious damage. Besides, she knew she could never bring herself to stab someone. Abigail cast a panicked look around, but the only thing in the bathroom other than towels and soap was a vase of fresh flowers.

She picked up the vase, flowers and all. Taking a deep breath, she raised it high and eased out into the room with as much stealth as she could manage.

To David's credit, he didn't so much as bat an eye, though she knew that he saw her. As she crept up behind the man Abigail was terrified that he would hear her heart thundering.

"I told you, scum bucket, I don't know what you're talking about."

Abigail's eyes widened. She couldn't believe it! David's tone was deliberately goading, his cocky grin a taunt in itself.

The man tensed, and Abigail's heart leaped. Without giving herself time to think about it, she brought the vase crashing down on his head.

He folded like a poleaxed ox, his knees buckling under him, pieces of shattered ceramic, water and flowers raining down over his head.

"Atta girl! Way to go, sweetheart!" David leaped over the bed and was at her side in an instant.

Her stunned gaze went from the collapsed man to David, and at the look of beaming approval on his face, fear and horror faded and a strange lightheartedness began to take hold. "I—I did it."

"Yeah, you sure did, sweetheart. You did great."

Elation and triumph bubbled up inside her. She grinned at him. "I really did, didn't I?"

He chuckled and took her arm. "You're learning, I'll give you that. Now, c'mon, honey. It's time to get the hell outta Dodge."

"Where did he come from?" Abigail gasped as they raced back down the stairs. "Pepe was supposed to warn— Oh, my stars! Do you think something has happened to him?"

"Naw. Shovel-face was probably keeping a lookout from the room across the hall. Don't worry about it, just run. That goon has a head like concrete. He won't be out long."

Abigail didn't need any more prodding. They loped down the stairs without regard for caution or silence. On the ground floor they were relieved to find Pepe still keeping watch on the lobby. Without stopping to explain, or even slowing down, David grabbed his arm and jerked him along with them. "C'mon, let's get the hell outta here! Run, man! Run!"

Chapter Seven

They tore out the back and down the dark alley as though the demons of hell were after them.

David's long stride ate up the ground. With a hand clamped around Abigail's wrist, he hauled her along with him. Gasping, her cumbersome purse slapping her hip with every step, she strained to keep pace, her feet just skimming the ground. For a big man, David ran with amazing speed and agility.

A few feet to the rear, Pepe pounded after them, his skinny legs and arms pumping like pistons.

They had almost reached the alley entrance when the back door of the hotel crashed opened. Unable to resist, Abigail peeked over her shoulder and let out a squeak. A man stood silhouetted against the light from the open door, one arm extended.

"Oh, my stars! They're going to shoot!" she yelped, even as a bullet whacked the building on their left and sent a chip of adobe plaster flying.

"*Dios!*" Pepe gasped.

David gave Abigail's arm a jerk and turned on more steam. "Run, dammit! Haul that cute little butt before you get it shot off!"

Shouts and pounding footsteps followed them. They reached the entrance, skidded around the corner and took off down the side street. They sprinted down the sidewalk for all they were worth, but they were still a few yards shy of the next corner when four men erupted from the alley behind them.

"C'mon, you two. Haul it!"

David ran a twisting course. For what to Abigail seemed an eternity, the chase wound through the back streets and alleys of San Cristobal, deserted at that hour but for a few derelicts and late-night revelers. David jerked her along in his wake, exhorting both her and Pepe to run faster, but no matter how much they strained, they could not outdistance the four men.

Finally Pepe gasped, "This way, *señor*. I know a place we can hide. Follow me."

He darted into a narrow alley, and David had no choice but to follow. After a hundred yards or so, another alley bisected the one they were in. Pepe turned down it and screeched to a halt at the first doorway.

"Dammit, Pepe, what the hell are you doing?" David spat as the little man felt along the frame. "Jesus! We're dead meat if those goons catch us."

"This shop... it belongs to m-my... cousin Juan," Pepe panted. "He hides a... ke-key along... he-here somewhere."

Abigail leaned against the wall. Her lungs were on fire, her heart was in overdrive, and her legs had turned to putty. Both she and Pepe were huffing like steam-driven locomotives. She didn't think she could run another step—not even if Freddy Krueger himself materialized in front of her. David was breathing hard, his massive chest heaving, but he seemed otherwise unaffected. If anything, Abigail noticed with disgust, he seemed to crackle with energy and leashed power.

Flattening his back against the wall, David peaked around the corner the way they had come. "Well, hurry up and find it, will you? They'll be here any second."

"It is under... Ah, hcre it is!" Pepe removed a palm-sized slab of plaster from the adobe. Quickly he picked out a key from a small hole and set the plaster back into place.

"Good. Now quick! Get that door open! Hurry, man! Hurry!"

Pepe fumbled with the lock. David peeked around the corner again, and his voice lowered with new urgency. "Hurry, dammit. Here they come."

Abigail felt her racing heart lurch. She wrung her hands and switched from one foot to the other, her frantic gaze fixed on Pepe's hands. She was on the verge of pushing him aside and dealing with the balky lock herself when the door flew open so suddenly that Pepe fell inside.

Abigail didn't need any urging to follow. David darted in behind her, so close she felt his chest against her back. In one smooth, continuous motion he shut the door, turned the key and shoved her to the floor.

"Stay down. And don't move," he commanded.

Less than a heartbeat later, running footsteps crunched to a halt in the intersection of the two alleys. A quick, short exchange was rapped out in guttural voices.

Crunching steps separated from the others. The three crouched against the door exchanged a tense look. The fine hairs on Abigail's arms stood on end.

The four men had split up, and one was coming their way stealthily, as though he knew they were there.

Gravel crunched right outside the door. Abigail's frightened eyes sought David. He laid a finger across his lips in silent warning, but even so, when the doorknob rattled, both she and Pepe started.

They tensed and waited. In the ominous quiet, all Abigail could hear was their labored breathing and her own thundering heartbeat, booming in her ears like a kettledrum. She was terrified the man outside could hear it through the door.

The quiet stretched out. Then, at last, the footsteps moved on.

Abigail started to sag with relief, but David gave her a warning look and again signaled for quiet. Minutes later the man returned, just as the other three entered the alley from the opposite direction.

They stopped to confer, and Abigail looked at David again, her eyes growing huge. They were standing right outside the door! Not more than three feet away!

They could hear every word. Unfortunately, the low-voiced discussion was in Russian. At least, that was what it sounded like to Abigail. They also sounded angry, their voices sharp. After a minute or two they moved on, and the voices faded as they turned the corner and walked away.

No one in the storeroom moved for several minutes—not until David heaved a sigh.

Abigail sagged in a heap on the floor. She released her own pent-up breath and closed her eyes. When she opened them, David was grinning at her, a cocky, triumphant grin. She couldn't help it. A giddy happiness filled her, and she grinned back. "We made it."

"Damn right, we did," he said with hard satisfaction, and before she realized his intent, he cupped his hand around the back of her neck, jerked her close and planted a firm kiss on her mouth.

The kiss was brief but powerful. Abigail felt its punch all the way to her toes. When David released her, he bounded to his feet, leaving her sitting dazed and disoriented, her heart doing a wild dance in her chest.

"C'mon, Legs. Let's get out of here," David said impatiently, and she realized that he was standing over her, his hand extended to help her up.

Once on her feet, she brushed off the back of her skirt and strove to appear unaffected. "What...uh...what do we do now?"

"Now? Now we're going to do some stalking of our own."

His voice carried a gritty edge. All thought of the kiss left Abigail as she caught the glitter in David's eyes. He looked granite tough. Savage.

"I'm damned tired of being hunted," he continued in the same dangerous tone. "From now on we're going to do the hunting."

Abigail shifted on the cracked vinyl seat, but still the broken spring poked her bottom. She sighed. Pepe's dilapidated pickup was not the ideal vehicle for a stakeout.

She glanced at the two men on either side of her and was struck by the contrast between them. Pepe leaned forward in the seat, chewing on his lower lip, making his thin mustache twitch. His dark eyes glittered, and his wiry body pulsed with eager excitement.

David sat motionless, one elbow hooked over the edge of the open window, his other arm straight out in front of him, his wrist draped over the top of the steering wheel. Between the first two fingers of his dangling hand hung a glowing cigarette. He stared straight ahead, his eyes fixed on the hotel entrance in the next block. He looked harsh, determined. Dangerous.

"How long are we going to wait," Abigail asked in a hushed voice.

"As long as it takes."

"But what if they don't leave?"

"They'll leave. Shovel-face and his pals aren't the brains behind this operation. They're just muscle. Sooner or later they're going to have to report that business at the hotel to whoever is in charge. They probably have a set rendezvous time."

Abigail fell silent, her thoughts again drifting back to that wild chase. She had been so terrified, and yet there was no denying that mingled with the fear, and later with the relief, had been a bubbly feeling of... exhilaration. Of excitement. Happiness almost. It was strange....

Abigail's train of thought was lost when Pepe jerked to attention beside her. *"Señor—"*

"I see them," David said in a low rumble. Following the direction of his gaze, Abigail spotted the three men who had just emerged from the hotel. They conferred a moment, then one walked off into the night and the other two climbed into a long black car at the curb.

"Abbey and I will take the two in the car. Pepe, you follow the one on foot. And for God's sake, don't try to play James Bond. Just stay out of sight, find out where he's going, then meet us back at the cantina."

Pepe, his eyes glittering with excitement, nodded and slid from the cab of the truck.

Driving without lights and staying well behind, David followed the black car to the harbor. He coasted to a stop on the quayside road a block behind where the sedan parked, his gaze locking on the pair that climbed out.

Both men paused and looked around. When they were satisfied, they headed down Pier One.

"C'mon. We have to get closer," David commanded, and reached for the door handle.

Abigail swallowed hard, but she eased her door open and slid out, too.

Pier One ran along the curving arm of land that formed one side of the harbor. On the landward side it was lined with warehouses, bait and tackle shops and small storefront places that rented everything from boats and windsurfers to scuba gear. Staying a hundred yards or so behind and hugging the shadows cast by the buildings, David and Abigail trailed the two men.

Near the end of the pier, the men stopped and took another look around. David jerked Abigail into a recessed doorway. Pressed back against the wall, they stood motionless for several seconds, then David peered around the edge of the embrasure.

"They're going aboard that big yacht down near the end," he whispered. He squinted his eyes. "It looks like her name is... *The Wanderer II*. Yeah, that's it. Ah-ha, who's this?"

Abigail edged closer and peeked over his shoulder. The two they had followed were on the deck of the yacht, engaged in a serious discussion with a third man. From where they were standing, it was impossible to make out his face, only that he was tall and slender and had an air of command about him. He appeared to have dark hair, though what color was difficult to tell. The only thing certain was that the hair at his temples was completely gray. Even from a distance it gleamed like silver wings in the dim light on deck.

"I'd be willing to bet we've just found Ms. Johnson's contact," David murmured.

They were so intent on the three aboard the yacht they did not hear the man approaching from behind until he was almost on them. When the footsteps registered, David's head whipped around.

"Holy shi—"

He bit off the whispered expletive, and before Abigail knew what was happening, he had her backed up into the doorway, locked in a passionate embrace, his broad back shielding her from view.

"David, wha—"

"Someone's coming. Just shut up and kiss me."

His mouth closed over hers with commanding force, scaling off any further attempt at protest.

The use of brute strength, however, was unnecessary. Abigail was too stunned to utter a word. It was all she could do to stand.

She felt the heat of the kiss in every cell of her body. Her toes curled in the skimpy sandals. Her stomach tightened. Her fingers clutched handfuls of his shirt and held on, while her heart thrummed and her head spun and her knees turned to mush.

After a moment David raised his head a few inches. Glittering hotly, his brown eyes probed her face. Surprise and wary fascination marked his expression. Stunned, Abigail could only stare back, her eyes wide and bewildered.

David's gaze dropped to her parted lips, still wet from his kiss, and after a moment he lowered his head again.

All the harshness was gone. This time he kissed her with greedy hunger, his mouth devouring hers. Abigail's lips quivered and parted. His tongue stabbed into her mouth. She thought she would die from the exquisite sensation that speared through her. Tremors began to dance along her nerve endings. She touched his tongue with hers, caressed it, felt the shudder that ran through him.

Emboldened, she went up on tiptoe and twined her arms around his neck. His arms tightened, pulling her closer still. Her breasts flattened against his massive chest. One hand cupped her bottom. He pulled her up against him, and she felt the hardness of him pressing against that part of her that ached with need. Her knees went weak. She made a mewling sound into his mouth and melted against him like overheated caramel. Nothing in her life had ever felt so good.

His hips rocked against her, and Abigail moaned. David swallowed the sound and kissed her like a man dying of hunger.

She wasn't aware of the man passing by, or of his crude snicker when he saw them, or even of where they were. All that existed for her was David, the feel of his arms around her, the magic of his lips.

Even conditioned as he was by years of training, it took a moment or two for the sounds to register with David, and another moment of delayed reaction before he placed them. At last he broke off the kiss, pausing just long enough to give Abigail another penetrating look before peering around the edge of the door again.

"He's on board. C'mon." Grabbing Abigail's arm, David stepped out onto the pier and hauled her toward the quayside road. "Let's get the hell out of here while we can."

The putt-putt of the outboard engine on Pepe's skiff floated across the dark water. The only other sounds were the occasional slap of a wave against the side of the boat and the distant crash of breakers against the cliffs to their right.

The boat had a spotlight attached to the side, but David didn't want to risk being seen, so he guided the small craft through the darkness unaided, hugging the shoreline just beyond the breaking surf. Gripping the steering arm, he stared straight ahead, his face set.

Abigail sat on the bow seat, facing him. She held on to the side with one hand and stroked Chelsea with the other. Gnawing the inside of her lower lip, she watched him covertly.

She knew he was disturbed that he'd been unable to reach his cousin. When they'd returned to the cantina he had placed a call to Travis, but all he'd gotten was the answering machine. They'd hung around for more than an hour and he'd tried several more times but the result was always the same, even though by then it had been almost dawn in Washington, D.C. Still, Abigail knew that the awkward silence between them was due to more than concern over his cousin or his need to concentrate.

He hadn't said a dozen words to her since they had stepped out of that doorway at the harbor. On the drive back to the cantina his expression had been so remote she hadn't dared utter a sound.

Abigail sighed and looked over her shoulder when David altered course and began to steer the skiff toward the narrow inlet.

She sneaked another quick peek his way to find that he was staring at her. The instant their gazes collided, both looked away. The dark intensity she had glimpsed in David's eyes vanished, and he focused straight ahead, his face expressionless.

Abigail strove to appear unaffected as well, but her heart began to pound, and she could feel heat spreading over her face and neck and across her chest above the low-cut blouse. She gave silent thanks for the concealing darkness.

Was it possible that David had been as moved by that kiss as she had? The question had been hovering at the back of Abigail's consciousness for the past hour, but the minute her mind voiced it she panicked.

No. Of course not. Don't be foolish, Abigail. You're acting like the love-starved old maid he accused you of being. Though perhaps a bit rough around the edges, David was a man of the world. He had probably kissed hundreds of women. Thousands. Probably many in the line of duty.

Anyway, he's made it clear more than once that you aren't his type.

That kiss had just been an expedient action. A sham. It had meant nothing. No doubt if he knew what havoc it had wreaked on her system he'd bust a gut laughing, the clod. She pressed her lips together and looked out across the ocean and reminded herself that she detested David Blaine.

A whine from Chelsea caught her attention, and with a guilty start Abigail realized that she had been scratching the dog's tiny head so hard she'd created a tender spot.

She lifted her pet in her arms and crooned an apology. David gave a disgusted snort, earning himself a withering look as he guided their little craft through the narrow passageway into the cove.

Once on board the *Freewind,* they moved around each other in stiff silence, each taking great pains to keep a distance between them and not to look at the other.

While David secured the skiff and unloaded the engine parts, Abigail went below. Feeling hurt and irritable, she marched into the forward stateroom, deposited her purse and Chelsea on the bed and shook out the sack of clothing that Constanza had provided.

To Pepe's profound disappointment, the man he had followed had merely walked around the corner to an all-night pharmacy for a bottle of aspirin and returned to the hotel. Pepe had been back at the cantina for almost an hour when she and David arrived, and by then Constanza had gotten the whole story out of her husband. On learning that all of Abigail's things had been taken, she had sent one of her daughters out to acquire a few essential replacements.

"*Ai yi,* do not fret, *señorita,*" she'd said when Abigail expressed amazement that she had managed the purchases at that late hour. "It was no trouble. Tía Lupe, my aunt, she owns a dress shop. She lives above it. When Louisa woke her and told her of your problems, she was happy to open the shop."

It had been a thoughtful gesture, and Abigail was touched and grateful. The only problem, she thought, gazing at the pile of ultra feminine clothes, was that seventeen-year-old Louisa had stars in her eyes.

The girl, and all the other females in the Morales family, thought that David was one *muy macho* hombre, and that the two of them being thrust together was exciting and romantic. Earlier, when Louisa had gathered up the mud-splattered clothes Abigail had worn on the hike through the woods, she had been vocal in her disapproval of Abigail's plain undies. Evidently she had used the shopping spree to remedy that deficiency.

Dismayed, Abigail looked at the shorty nightgown and matching panties on top of the pile of clothes. The garment was low cut and frothy and just skimmed the tops of her thighs. The pink cotton was opaque, at least, but that was the only good thing she could say about the gown.

Abigail sighed and snatched up the skimpy garment, along with her toothbrush, and started for what David called the head. "Silly name for a bathroom," she mumbled to herself, stepping into the molded compartment that was not only a shower stall but housed the toilet and washbasin as well.

David came below a few minutes later, just as she emerged from the tiny cubicle with the clothes she'd borrowed from Louisa draped over her arm. She halted at the sight of him and tugged at the hem of the short nightgown, but he barely spared her a glance before sliding past her.

After eyeing the two humans, Chelsea curled up on the banquette bench with her toy puppy and stayed out of their way.

Abigail was relieved when David disappeared into the head. When he returned a few moments later, she was hanging a sundress in the closet. If he noticed her anger at all, it didn't show. His face was as remote and unreadable as stone. Except for giving her a hard, "I dare you to say a word" look as he lit a cigarette, he didn't so much as glance her way.

He sidestepped around her to the built-in bureau and pulled open a drawer. Her eyes narrowed on his back. With a sniff, she lifted her chin and made a show of giving him a wide berth, moving past him to sit down on the end of the bed. While she folded the frilly panties and bras Louisa had purchased, David pawed through the open drawer like a badger digging a hole. One of the very drawers that she had straightened and organized just that morning, Abigail thought, grinding her teeth.

He withdrew a scrap of cloth and tossed it onto the bed. He toed off his sneakers, bent and peeled off his socks and tossed them aside. Nonchalantly, as though she weren't even there, he jerked his shirt free of his jeans and began working the buttons open. Abigail didn't notice. She stared, transfixed, at the pair of scanty leopard-print silk briefs that lay on the bed. My stars! Didn't the man own anything but X-rated underwear?

At the rasp of a zipper her head whipped around. Her jaw dropped as David hooked his thumbs under the waistband of his jeans and shoved them down. At eye level, not three feet from her face, her gaze encountered a narrow strip of red-and-white polka-dot knit stretched across lean hips. Helplessly she stared at the impressive bulge at the front of the minuscule briefs, and the straining placket that covered it. Her mouth went dry.

"Wh-what do you think you're doing?" she sputtered.

He paused with his jeans around his knees and shot her a puzzled glare. "What the hell does it look like? I'm getting ready to hit the sack. But first I'm going to change my underwear. The ones I have on got wet when waves splashed over the stern of the skiff."

"You could at least have the decency to change in the bathroom."

"Forget it. I can't strip down in there. I bang my knees and elbows against the walls just trying to shower."

"Well, you could have warned me so I could turn my back or go up on deck. Which I'm going to do right now." She shot him a scornful glare as she stomped past. "Pervert."

"Oh, yeah!" He turned to follow, but the jeans around his ankles acted as hobbles and he almost fell flat on his face. Cursing a blue streak, he hopped after her on one foot while tugging and yanking at the denim pant leg covering the other. "Well, I'd rather be a pervert than an uptight old maid!"

"*That* is an antiquated expression. And for your information I am single by choice," she retorted over her shoulder.

"Ha! You know what your problem is? You're a prude. I'll bet you've never had a boyfriend in your life. No man in his right mind would want to get lashed up with a hoity-toity, introverted, prissy, little puritan."

That hit a nerve. Abigail sucked in her breath and spun around. She was sensitive about her meager experience with the opposite sex. Not that she was plain or ugly. She was attractive, in a quiet way. Even Aunt Harriet had grudgingly conceded that. She just didn't have the knack for attracting men. Or for holding their interest. Her one excursion into romantic waters had been a disaster.

"You're so hung up on playing it safe and 'always being prepared,'" he mimicked in a nasty singsong, "that you don't even know what life is all about."

"That's not true!"

"Oh, yeah? You ever made love? Or even gotten hot and bothered? From the way you kiss I sure as hell don't think so."

Abigail gasped at the jeer. While she sputtered, he continued in a sneering voice, "Hell, there's not enough passion or daring in you to light a fire in any man. It's no wonder you're an old maid."

She hit him then. She, who until now had never struck another human being, who rarely raised her voice, who didn't believe in violence, hauled off with a roundhouse swing and slapped him right on his bruised cheek. So hard her hand stung. So hard his head snapped around. So hard he yelled.

And then she promptly burst into tears.

Chapter Eight

Before David could react, she spun around and fled topside.

He stood there in his garish underwear with his jeans bunched around one ankle and his face blank. Gingerly he rubbed his cheek and grimaced at the sound of her racking sobs. He glanced at Chelsea, and she lifted her lip at him.

"Yeah, well. For once I agree with you, fuzz ball," he muttered.

His shoulders slumped. What the hell was the matter with him? He'd never said anything like that to a woman in his life. Hell, he'd decked other men for less.

But dammit! There was just something about this particular female that got under his skin, made him say and do things he ordinarily wouldn't dream of doing. Just being around her made him antsy, for some reason.

He raked a hand through his hair. Who was he kidding? He knew why he'd done it. Because he *was* attracted to her. And it scared the hell out of him.

Abigail Stewart was no Maxine; she was no bimbo out for a good time. Back in Crockett, Texas, where he came from, she was what was known as a good woman. A lady. The kind you took home to meet Mama and the family.

Panic fluttered through him at the thought. Hell, he wasn't ready for that. He enjoyed his freedom and liked his life just the way it was.

That kiss at the docks had shaken him, though. The feelings it aroused had been so strong they'd made him forget for a moment all the reasons why he didn't want to get involved with a respectable woman.

So you lashed out at Abigail. Great going, you jerk.

He sighed. Hell, he deserved a good kick in the butt. It was too bad his sister Erin wasn't there. She'd be more than happy to give it to him.

Abigail's piteous weeping floated down into the cabin, long gulping sobs that sounded as though they were torn from her soul.

David winced. Hell, he couldn't take much more of this. Feeling like the lowest form of life, he started for the steps—and promptly tripped on the jeans still tangled around one ankle. Cursing, he yanked off the denim pants, gave them a vicious kick across the cabin and took the steps in two leaps.

She was standing by the stern with her back to him, her head bent. With each racking cry her hunched shoulders shook. The sounds were raw and raspy and painful to hear.

"Abbey..."

She flinched when he touched her shoulder. "Go a-away! Just le-le-leave me alone!"

"I can't. Aw, honey, don't cry."

The sounds became even more anguished, and she tried to scuttle away from him. He followed, but this time when he touched her, she whirled on him and fought like a wildcat, slapping at him with both hands.

"Dammit, Abbey...!"

She was so upset it was impossible to fend her off without hurting her. With an impatient growl, David locked his arms around her and jerked her close, trapping her hands between them.

"C'mon, honey, calm down."

Frustration added to her woes, and after a moment she gave in and collapsed against him, her raw cries coming out in torrents.

David rocked her from side to side. "Aw, honey, don't. I'm sorry, babe. I didn't mean it. Not any of it. Honest. You've probably noticed I'm not the most tactful guy at the best of times, and when I lose my temper I pop off and say things I don't mean. Hell, if you want the truth, I, uh . . . I acted like a horse's rear . . . well, because I *am* attracted to you. And I don't want to be," he added with a touch of belligerence.

His words hadn't the slightest effect. Feeling powerless and awkward, David stroked her back above the low neckline of the nightie and blurted out the first thing that came into his mind. "Now I'm not saying that you're not a prissy pain in the butt, 'cause you are. You make me madder, quicker, than any female I've ever known. And with my sisters, that's saying something, believe me. You've been nothing but trouble from the word go, stuck your nose in where it didn't belong and aggravated the living hell out of me. Why I should be attracted to you, I don't know, but, God help me, I am."

"N-no you're not," she gulped. "N-no man ev-ever . . . is."

"The hell you say! I guess I kn—" A renewed spasm of crying overtook her, cutting off his blustery rejoinder. His arms tightened, and his voice went low with concern. "Hey, now. Honey, c'mon now, don't cry like that. You're gonna make yourself sick."

He might as well have told the wind to stop blowing. She sobbed against his bare chest as though her heart would break. Frowning, he leaned his cheek against the top of her head and rocked her, real alarm growing in him.

There was more behind this jag than mere hurt feelings, he realized. His taunts had been nasty and uncalled for, but they should have sparked anger, not this soul-wrenching despair. In the short time that he and Abbey had been together, he'd learned enough about her character to know that she didn't dissolve over a few crass remarks. This sprang from something much more serious.

Some bastard must've hurt her badly, he thought. He looked out across the calm waters of the cove, his eyes narrowing. Unconsciously his jaws clenched.

Over the years, David had had enough experience dealing with his twin sisters to know that when a woman was that distraught, the only choice was to let her cry it out. Gritting his teeth against her tears and drawing a tight rein on his own impatient nature, he held her close and murmured nonsensical words against the top of her head while his big hands roamed her back and hips in long, soothing strokes.

She worked her arms free, and they came around him. Clutching him, she burrowed closer, burying her face in the thick mat of hair on his chest. She clung with all her might, as though he, and he alone, offered the solace her battered heart so desperately needed.

David's nose stung. His throat tightened. Something shifted and expanded in his chest.

He stood with his legs braced on either side of hers. From their ankles to the top of her head their bodies were pressed together, bare skin to bare skin except for his minuscule briefs and the wisp of a nightie.

Though he told himself he was a heel for noticing at a time like this, he was aware of every sweet inch of her—her breasts flattened against his chest, the softly rounded belly and that feminine mound snuggled against his burgeoning manhood, the enticing flare of womanly hips that just begged for a man's hands. And—oh, God—those long luscious legs, so smooth against his, so strong and perfectly formed.

It struck him as almost funny that here he was, alone with a desirable woman in a tropical paradise, the two of them almost naked and embracing beneath a lovers' moon...and there was no way in hell it was going to get him anything but a long night of frustration.

He sighed and massaged the back of her neck beneath the thick braid. She felt so small and fragile in his arms. And she was so damned vulnerable.

After a while her sobs decreased to sniffles and hiccuping little sighs. With calm came awareness and embarrassment. He felt her tense an instant before she took a step back and eased out of his arms. Sniffing, she swiped at her drenched cheeks with the backs of her hands and looked down at the deck.

"I . . . I'm sorry. I shouldn't have—"

"Hey. I'm the one who should apologize, not you."

He tipped her head up with a forefinger beneath her chin. "Abbey," he whispered. "Look at me, honey."

Her lips quivered, but slowly her gaze lifted. David looked into those tear-drenched aquamarine eyes, and his heart squeezed.

Light from below spilled out on deck, illuminating her pale face. The emotional storm had given her a blurry, out-of-focus look and left her fair skin blotched. Her mouth was puffy. So was the flesh around her red-rimmed eyes. Tears spiked her lashes and glistened on her cheeks. She looked fragile and infinitely sad, her eyes swirling with hurt and despair.

"You want to tell me about it?"

The uncharacteristic gentleness in his voice caused fresh tears to well up. Abigail's chin wobbled. "There . . . there's nothing to tell. I, uh . . . I just overreacted. That's all."

"C'mon, Legs. There's more to it than that, and we both know it."

She sniffed and looked out over the water. For a moment he thought she wasn't going to answer. "I . . . I almost married once," she said in a wistful little voice.

"So what happened?" David prodded after a moment when she didn't elaborate.

"He . . . he left me standing at the altar."

"*What?*"

Abigail jumped. "Well, not literally *at* the altar, of course. I never got that far. I, uh . . . I was waiting in an anteroom off the church vestibule."

David muttered a curse under his breath, but she didn't seem to notice, so lost was she in the painful memory.

"When Ted didn't show up at the appointed time, Aunt Harriet kept saying that he wasn't coming, but I didn't believe her. She had never liked him and hadn't wanted me to marry him." Abigail's mouth twitched. "Actually... Aunt Harriet didn't like men, period. She was furious when I started dating Ted during my sophomore year in college. She predicted that I was just going to end up getting hurt, but for once I wouldn't listen to her.

"I waited for over an hour, but finally I had to accept that he wasn't coming." A bitter smile tilted Abigail's mouth, and she looked at David with wounded eyes. "I had given myself to him—heart, body and soul—and he didn't even bother to send a note. He just didn't show up. Later, I learned that he had eloped that morning with his former girlfriend. It seems he had met me on the rebound."

This time David spat out a string of profanity that she could not fail to hear. The thought of her pain and humiliation filled him with rage and an aching sympathy. *Damn that slimy bastard to hell! He ought to be horsewhipped!*

Reacting instinctively, he reached out and hauled her back into his arms. "God, I'm sorry, Abbey." He cradled her close and rubbed his cheek against her crown. "That must have been awful for you."

She made an embarrassed sound but snuggled against him. "At least I got to hide in the anteroom. Poor Aunt Harriet was the one who had to go out there and tell all those people that the wedding was off."

Humph. Poor Aunt Harriet, my ass, he thought. He'd be willing to bet the old battle-ax enjoyed the hell out of it.

He understood a lot of things better now—the reason for her prickly front, the insecurity behind it, her overcautiousness. He shuddered to think of what Abigail's life must have been like, being raised by that straitlaced old harridan. The one time she had defied her strict upbringing and her Aunt's dire warnings, it had ended in disaster. Hell, she'd probably been toeing the line ever since.

"Jeez, when I think about the lousy things I said to you I'm amazed you didn't clobber me."

"I did." To his surprise, Abigail giggled. It was a weak sound but it made his heart soar.

He tipped his head to one side and looked down at her. "Wanna do it again? C'mon. I'll let you take your best shot."

"Don't be silly," she protested with another watery giggle.

"Why not? I deserve it."

"No doubt. But I'm not going to do it. I can't just *hit* someone."

"Oh, I don't know. You bashed that guy back at the hotel pretty good," he teased.

Abigail groaned and buried her face against his chest. "Don't remind me. I don't know what's happening to me. I've never done anything so barbaric before."

David chuckled. "Don't fight it, Legs. You need to loosen up a little and let fly now and then—learn to take things as they come."

He could feel her breath stirring his chest hairs, feel its moist warmth against his skin. She gave a shuddering sigh, the last tattered remnant of spent emotion, and sagged against him.

"C'mon. Let's put you to bed. It's been a helluva day, and you're so exhausted you can barely stand."

She did not demur, but leaned against him as he led her below. Once tucked in, however, she clung to his hand. "Aren't you coming to bed, too?"

He hesitated, and her grip tightened. "Please, David." She caught her lower lip between her teeth and looked up at him, her expression at once embarrassed and beseeching. "I . . . I need to be held," she said in a quavering whisper. "Just for a little while."

It was not a smart move. He knew that. He had intended to fiddle around until she was asleep before coming to bed. He looked at those liquid eyes, and sighed. What the hell.

"Just let me douse the lights. It won't take long."

He was back in less than a minute. No sooner had he slid in beside her and settled his head on the pillow than she moved into his arms and snuggled her cheek against his shoulder.

"Thank you, David," she whispered. She tipped her head up and gazed at him earnestly, her face a pale oval in the moonlight filtering through the window.

A sweet ache invaded David's chest. She looked so damned fragile and sweet. His gaze lowered to her mouth. It was slightly parted, still a bit puffy, and so soft and tempting that he could not resist.

He caught the slight widening of her eyes, felt her go utterly still, but she did not try to pull away. Slowly, delicately, as though she might shatter at the slightest pressure, his lips touched hers.

A whisper, a brush of flesh upon flesh, a moist mingling of breaths—that was all it was, yet the impact was staggering. David felt as though he'd been zapped by a bolt of electricity. The fire sizzled all along his nerve endings.

He pulled back a few inches and saw the confusion and heat in Abigail's expression, and he knew that she had felt it, too.

His heart boomed, and he could barely draw breath. His blood surged through his veins and pooled, hot and heavy, in his loins. Every cell in his body tingled.

David gazed at her, knowing he should stop. He had meant to keep it light and innocent, a kiss of comfort, a soft good-night. But that brief taste had started a conflagration that was already out of control, and with a groan, he lowered his head again.

This time he kissed her with gentle savagery, his open mouth rocking across hers, rubbing, nipping. She lay utterly still, her fingers clutching his chest hair. With a slow, mesmerizing rhythm, his hand glided back and forth over the curve of her hip and thigh. One finger riffled the lace edging on the leg of the pajama panties and trailed a feather-light line of fire along her thigh. He felt her tremble.

Holding the kiss, David stilled, waiting, his hot breath dewing her skin. After a moment her lips quivered under his. Then, hesitantly, they parted.

Desire raced through David with the force of a locomotive. With a low growl, he plunged his tongue into the sweet warmth of her mouth and rolled her onto her back. In slow, sinuous strokes, his tongue rubbed hers. The taste of minty toothpaste lingered there, the refreshing sweetness mingling with the salty tears that had gathered at the corners of her mouth.

His broad shoulders and massive chest covered her upper body, pressing her into the mattress, flattening her breasts. The kiss deepened, grew hotter, more demanding. His tongue swirled through her mouth like a hungry marauder, exploring every sweet recess, gliding over her teeth, tracing the curving roof. His bent knee slid between her legs and pressed intimately against her. Abigail sucked in her breath. He pressed harder and rubbed, the slow movement matching the indolent rhythm of his thrusting tongue.

Abigail clutched his bare back and moaned.

The tiny sound stoked the fires burning inside David. He ached for her, wanted desperately to strip the flimsy nightgown from her body and bury himself in her sweet warmth.

But even through the morass of need and want, his conscience prodded him.

"Damn!"

The whispered curse was wrenched from him, raspy and harsh in the silent darkness. Abruptly releasing Abigail, he flopped back against his pillow and draped his forearm over his eyes. His other hand clenched in a fist at his side. For a moment the only sound in the cabin was his stertorous breathing.

"David? Is ... is something wrong?"

The timorous question made his jaw clench. "No. Nothing's wrong," he managed, grating the words out through his teeth. "Things ... just got out of hand. That's all. I shouldn't have kissed you. I'm sorry. Now go to sleep."

Silence followed—thick and strained. It lasted perhaps ten heartbeats.

"I see," Abigail said in a wobbly voice. "It's because you don't find me attractive enough, isn't it?" David jerked his forearm away from his eyes and rolled his head on the pillow. He stared at her through the gloom as though she'd lost her mind, but she rushed on before he could reply. "Well, fine. I'm certainly not interested in being anyone's charity case."

She tried to flounce over onto her side and scoot away from him, but David grabbed her shoulder and rolled her back. "What in the name of hell are you talking about?"

"You kissed me out of pity and you know it," she shot back, though it was obvious she was battling tears. "You think I'm just a pathetic, prickly old maid and you felt sorry for me. Well, don't do me any favors!"

She tried to roll away again, but this time he grabbed both her shoulders and pinned them to the mattress. He loomed over her, his face like a thundercloud.

"Woman, you're not only a royal pain in the butt, you're also nuts! Not *want* you? Hell, I want you so bad, for the first time in my life I'm tempted to ignore my own code about women like you. I want you so bad I can't think of anything else but what it would feel like to be inside you. Dammit! I want you so bad I hurt," he snarled in a dark, rough voice that made her eyes widen and sent a shiver rippling through her. "Believe me, I would like nothing more than to strip you naked and make long, slow love to you until neither of us could move." He grabbed her hand and held it against his lower body. "Does that feel like I don't want you?"

Abigail sucked in her breath. Against her palm his arousal was hot and hard, throbbing. "Then...why did you stop?"

"Because, you're upset and it wouldn't be fair. Or right."

"But I wa—"

"Dammit, Abbey, you're vulnerable right now. You've managed to get yourself into one hell of a dangerous situation, you're holed up with a man you barely know, to whom you've just spilled your guts after coming down off a world-class crying jag. I may not be an expert on women, but I know vulnerable when I see it. So you can just quit looking at me with those big eyes. I don't take advantage of women.''

Hurt and anger fled, and Abigail gave him a melting look. ''Oh, David. That's so sweet.'' She snuggled against him and tried to wind her arms around his neck, but he grabbed her wrists and pulled them down.

''Now, cut that out. We are not going to make love, and that's that. I may be a hooligan and a barbarian and all those other things you called me, but I'm not that big a bastard.''

Smiling tenderly, she stroked his cheek, her fingertips threading through the five-day growth of beard. ''No. You're not,'' she agreed in a whisper-soft voice. She raised her head and gave him a quick kiss. ''You're not a bastard at all. What you are, David Blaine, is a very nice man. Even though you do work hard at trying to hide it.''

David's gaze bore into her. ''Don't kid yourself, Legs. I'm the meanest hard case you'll ever meet. When I have to, I fight low down and dirty. Whatever it takes to win. I've seen and done things that were anything but 'nice,' so don't make the mistake of romanticizing me into some kind of hero. I'm not.''

A smug smile curved her mouth, and her eyes sparkled at him. ''Whatever you say.''

''Dammit, I mean it, Legs.''

''Mmm-hmm.'' Giving him a placating smile and a pat on the cheek, Abigail snuggled her head against his shoulder.

David gritted his teeth. God save him from starry-eyed females.

Abigail sighed and settled against his side like an exhausted puppy. Within minutes her breathing was slow and even.

David held her close. He was acutely aware of her soft breasts pressing against his side, the small hand that lay curled on his chest, her warmth burning into him. His hand, resting on her hip, rubbed hypnotically. He stared through the darkness and listened to her even breathing. He'd been called a lot of things by a lot of people, but never, *never,* a nice man. He didn't know whether to be pleased or insulted.

One corner of his mouth twitched. Oh, baby. If you only knew. Hell, he was holding on to his lofty principles by his fingernails.

He needed a cigarette. Bad. For a long time he lay without moving. When he was sure she was asleep, he reached out with his free hand and groped across the bedside table. Cellophane crinkled as his fingers closed around the pack.

"Only a fool would smoke in bed, you know," came Abigail's sleepy murmur.

Damn!

The next morning Abigail awoke at her usual time. She dressed, fed Chelsea and took her ashore in the skiff, and was back in the galley preparing breakfast by the time David stirred.

He was grumpier than he'd been the morning before. Rumpled and bleary-eyed, wearing his threadbare cutoffs, he stomped around like a bear with a sore head. When he tasted her coffee, he spewed it out, along with a string of curses that would have made a longshoreman blush, and shot her a look that accused her of trying to poison him. Muttering under his breath, he stormed up on deck with the pot and flung the contents over the side. He snarled at Chelsea, glowered at Abigail, and complained about everything from the noise she made cooking to the way she scrambled his eggs.

They had no sooner sat down to eat than he gave her a narrow-eyed look and snapped, "What the hell happened to your face?"

"My face?"

"It's all red."

"Oh...that." Abigail touched her upper lip and felt heat rise up her neck. "It's nothing. Just, uh . . . whisker burn," she mumbled.

David stared at her abraded skin. To her surprise, and amusement, a dull red spread over his cheeks. Ducking his head, he dug into his meal without another word.

They ate in silence. Afterward, while she did the dishes he disappeared into the head. When he emerged, he was clean shaven, and there was a tiny scrap of toilet tissue stuck to a cut on his chin and another along the left side of his jaw.

Abigail was amazed. Clean shaven, that battered face looked almost handsome.

Glowering at her, he lit a cigarette and blew smoke at the overhead. The look in his eyes dared her to say a word. Abigail was tempted but she wisely refrained, and he stomped past her and went up on deck. Within moments the sounds of banging and grunted curses came from the engine compartment.

All day he was gruff and distant. Every chance he got, he growled at Chelsea and was abrupt with Abigail if she so much as opened her mouth.

A few days before she might have been hurt by his treatment, or even frightened. But not now. She wasn't fooled. She knew that he was striving to put their relationship back on its former footing.

It was too late, of course; she had glimpsed the man beneath David's rough exterior. Not that she had any illusions. She knew he was as tough as nails, a warrior who could and would fight dirty if he had to. But deep down, where it counted, he was a decent, good man, a man who would never hurt her. Not deliberately.

On principle, she responded to his barbs and growls with cool primness, but she was well aware that things between them had shifted subtly, and that they would never again be the same. She suspected that David knew it as well.

David finished the repairs to the *Freewind* late that afternoon, but they waited for the cover of darkness to head back to San Cristobal. Because he was concerned that the boat would be recognized, they left it in the cove and took Pepe's skiff.

The first thing he did when they reached the cantina was place a call to Travis. He bit out a curse when his cousin's answering machine clicked on, but the next instant his expression cleared. His eyes sharpened and he stilled, suddenly alert.

"Oh, no. Don't tell me he still doesn't answer?" Abigail moaned, when he replaced the receiver and dug into his pants for more change.

"No. But that's okay. The message on his machine has been altered. Just a bit. If you didn't know what to listen for you'd never notice the difference. It's a signal between Travis and me. It means the line may be bugged, and to call him at another number—one known to just the two of us."

David wasted no time putting the call through. At the first ring the receiver at the other end was snatched up.

"Dammit, Cuz, what the hell kind of mess are you into now?"

Travis was a laid-back, daring devil who sauntered through life with a cocky grin and rarely turned a hair over anything, not even in the diciest situations. The agitated edge to his voice put David on alert at once.

"Why? What's happened?"

"Well, for starters, the file on Patrice Johnson is red flagged as top secret, and access is on a need-to-know basis, so I couldn't do anything there. About all I managed to find out about Abigail Stewart is she's a former librarian turned bookstore proprietor."

David started at the mention of Abigail's name. He'd almost forgotten he'd asked Travis to check her out. Subconsciously, he'd already accepted that Abigail was who and what she claimed. Not very professional, but sometimes a man had to go on instinct. "That jibes with my information. What else you got?"

"Well . . . she's thirty, never been married and has no criminal record. She was orphaned at a young age and raised by an old maid aunt." Travis's dry chuckle came through the earpiece. "Sounds like a real tough customer. I'd watch myself if I were you, Cuz."

"Funny. You're a regular barrel of laughs, McCall. Now tell me the rest."

"Not much left to tell. There was a little more in the file, but before I could finish reading it someone pulled the plug.

"I knew it had hit the fan when the computer screen went blank," Travis drawled. "But before I could shag my tail outta there a whole swarm of our upper echelon guys and three CIA spooks were on me like ugly on an ape. Thanks to you, Cuz, I spent a damned uncomfortable night trying to explain why I was so interested in Miss Stewart. And why I'd tried to access the Johnson woman's file. To tell the truth, I've been wondering the same thing. I don't suppose you'd like to fill me in?"

"You're right. I wouldn't."

Travis sighed. "That's what I thought."

"So what did you tell them?"

"Well, I tried to tell them that I was just checking out two of my lady friends, but they didn't buy it. I finally had to fess up and admit I was doing you a favor."

There was a pause, and Travis added, "I gotta tell you, Cuz, they weren't pleased. It took me the rest of the night to convince them that was all I knew and that I had no idea where you were. They're going after this hot and heavy. It seems they're real anxious to know Miss Stewart's whereabouts. Yours, too, now. And believe me, Cuz, they're not looking to pin any medals on you."

David's mind was working ninety to nothing, but he replied with a noncommittal grunt and a terse, "What else?"

"That's about it. By the time they let me go, I figured they'd had plenty of time to bug my telephone, so I changed the message and came here."

"Thanks, Travis. I owe you one, buddy."

"Hey, man. That's what kinfolks are for. But look, now that I've got my butt in a sling for you, the least you could do is tell me what's going on."

"Forget it. Believe me, the less you know, the better off you are."

"Okay, Cuz, have it your way. But watch your ass, will you? I don't know what the hell's shaking, but take it from me, you've stumbled into it deep. The big boys are in on this one."

David hung up the telephone and turned to find both Abigail and Pepe hovering over him.

"Well?" Abigail demanded. "Did he find out anything?"

David gave her a sour look. "Hell, Legs, when you get into trouble, you do it up brown, don't you? Not only are the KGB on your tail, now you've got the FBI and the CIA after you, too. After both of us."

"Dios mio," Pepe murmured, his face alive with anticipation.

"Our agents are looking for me? But that's wonderful!" Her excitement fizzled when she noticed David's dark look. She caught her bottom lip between her teeth. "Isn't it?"

"That depends on why. If Patrice Johnson is working for the other side—and it looks that way—and they think you're in cahoots with her, then you could be in as much danger from our people as from the bad guys."

Chapter Nine

Heads swiveled, and the eyes of every patron zeroed in on them when they entered the bar. David faced the sullen silence with a flinty stare and a to-hell-with-you expression that Abigail could only admire. Not matter how hard she tried, she could not suppress the prickle of fear that rippled over her skin. The sensation made the hair on the back of her neck stand on end.

Perched, as usual, in the side pocket of Abigail's purse, Chelsea poked her head over the side and bared her teeth at the room in general. Abigail put a restraining hand on the dog's head and edged closer to David.

The waterfront dive in no way resembled Pepe's Cantina. Stale air reeked of sweat, cheap tequila, and cheaper tobacco. Dirt gritted underfoot on wooden floors that hadn't seen a coat of wax or even a mop in years. Flies buzzed around spills on the pocked and water-ringed bar and tables. All were littered with overflowing ashtrays, bottles and cloudy glasses.

The rhythmic creak of an ancient ceiling fan marked the tense passage of time, but the blades' lazy rotation did little to stir the haze of blue smoke hovering along the low ceiling. Here and there a few hard-looking women lounged on bar stools or at the tables, but most of the patrons were men—toughs and back-alley crawlers who looked as though they would cut out your heart for the price of a bottle. Most sat hunched over their drinks, watching Abigail and David.

"There's Bates. C'mon," David said, and started for the table in the far corner.

Abigail scurried after him, her nerves jangling. As they cut a zigzagging path between the tables, she noticed a cockroach the size of man's thumb scuttling along the back of a chair and another feeding at a spill on a nearby table, antennae waving. Abigail shuddered and averted her eyes.

Halfway across the room her gaze happened to meet that of a man at the bar. He looked her over in cold calculation, and Abigail's heart lurched. She scooted closer to David and grabbed the back of his shirt with both hands.

He frowned at her over his shoulder and muttered out of the side of his mouth, "Lighten up, Legs. It's not smart to let these guys see that you're uneasy."

He turned his attention back on his quarry, and Abigail's glare bounced off the back of his head.

Uneasy? *Uneasy?* She wasn't uneasy. She was scared spitless! Terrified! Her heart was about to club her to death, for heaven's sake!

It wasn't every day she found herself the target of the intelligence agencies of two world powers. At the moment, however, even that paled in comparison to the immediate situation. She shivered again and gripped David's shirt tighter. Lord, help them. It would be a miracle if they got out of this dive without getting their throats cut.

She didn't care if she was acting like a ninny. She hung on to David for dear life and kept her gaze fixed on a spot between his shoulder blades. In a world gone mad, he was her only security.

So far he'd kept her safe. She had to believe that he would continue to do so. There had been a shaky moment or two when he told her what he'd learned from Travis, but when she had blanched and stammered, "Wh...what do we do now?" he had not even hesitated.

"We'll make contact with our guys and set up a meeting—on our own terms—and try to find out what the hell is going down."

"How do we do that?"

"Don't worry. I know—or know of—most of the deep cover operatives in the western hemisphere. It may take a while, but a few phone calls, the right word in the right ears, a triggering phrase—and the message will be received loud and clear. I guarantee it."

Sure enough, two hours after he'd begun sending out feelers, a teenage boy had arrived at Pepe's with a note for David. It said simply:

Meet me at El Gallo Enfadado at one.
Leo

David came to a halt, and Abigail slammed into his back. "Oh, for Pete's sake."

Heaving a sigh, he reached behind him and pried her fingers loose from his shirt. With a hand clamped around her wrist, he hauled her around in front of him and stuffed her into the corner booth opposite an unsavory-looking character.

"Hi ya, Blaine." The man's oily grin didn't reach his eyes. "It's been awhile, ol' buddy."

"Cut the crap, Leo. I want to know what the hell's going on."

"Hey, man!" Leo affected a wounded look. "Ain'tcha even gonna introduce me to your lady friend?"

He leered at Abigail and smiled around the filterless cigarette dangling from the corner of his mouth. She shrank back on the seat and tried not to grimace.

Sly yellowish eyes, sharp features and pointed, nicotine-stained teeth combined to give the man a foxlike look that made Abigail's skin crawl. Brown hair hung across his forehead in greasy strings. His sallow skin was pockmarked, and a scar puckered his lower lip on one side. Dark stains formed half circles beneath the arms of his grimy shirt, and an unpleasant odor emanated from him.

He was neither as big nor as muscular as David, but there was something feral and menacing about him that Abigail found chilling. Of all the sleazy characters in the place, she knew, instinctively, that Leo Bates was the most dangerous. That he worked for the U.S. government amazed and appalled her.

"Just answer my question, Leo. What's this operation about?"

Leo took a drag on the cigarette and blew out a stream of smoke. As it drifted upward to join the cloud hugging the ceiling, he flicked an inch of ash onto the floor. His scarred mouth quirked in a taunting smile. "What operation?"

"Don't give me that. I want to know what you Langley spooks want with a small-town bookstore owner?"

"Hey, man. If someone's interested in Miss Stewart, I don't know anything about it."

"Is that right? Then how is it you know her name?"

Leo took another pull on his cigarette and considered David with his foxy eyes. "You're quick, Blaine. But then, you always were. Never could figure out why you left the Bureau. Seems like a waste of talent, if you ask me."

"Like I said, Leo, cut the crap, and just tell me what you know."

"I'm telling you, I don't know nothing. Except that everyone in the sector is suppose to be on the lookout for the two of you and report your whereabouts if they spot you."

"Why?"

"How the hell would I know? I'm just a lowly field man. You think they tell me anything? Look, I need another drink." He stubbed out his cigarette and slid from the booth. Pausing, he swept them with a sardonic look. "How about you two?"

Abigail almost gagged at the thought of consuming anything the place might serve. David waved Leo off. As he ambled toward the bar, Abigail shivered. "He's, uh...an unusual man."

"He's pond scum." David fished a cigarette out of his pocket and lit it, squinting his eyes against the curl of smoke. Ignoring Abigail's pointed look, he flipped the match into the ashtray and inhaled. "But useful pond scum," he added. "A sleaze like Bates can infiltrate at levels that most agents can't. He has hundreds of contacts in Mexico and Central America who feed him all sorts of useful information."

"How did you know he was on Alhaja Verde?"

"I didn't. For all I know, he may not have been. I placed a call to a number on the Mexican mainland."

Leo returned with a mug of dark Mexican beer. After taking a deep draught, he expressed his appreciation with a gusty exhale, swiped his mouth with the back of his hand and let loose a booming belch.

Abigail clamped her lips and looked at her hands clasped together in her lap. Leo grinned again. His yellow eyes glittered with malicious glee.

David watched him, his face impassive. "I want you to set up a meeting for us with your superiors."

"I got a better idea. Why don't you just dump the broad and let her fend for herself?"

Abigail sucked in her breath. She darted a look at David, but his hard profile gave nothing away.

"Hell, man, you don't want to get involved in this," Leo went on. "You're a civilian now. Why don't you just leave it and walk away. Our guys won't hassle you. I guarantee it."

"And Miss Stewart?"

Leo shrugged and spread his hands.

"David . . . ?"

Under the table his hand closed around Abigail's twisting ones. "Don't worry, honey. I'm not going anywhere."

David's gaze stabbed into Leo, but the other man was too busy studying Abigail to notice.

His scarred mouth lifted in a sneer. "Well, well. Like that, is it? Funny. I didn't think you went for the prissy librarian type, ol' buddy. Must be a lot hotter than she looks."

It happened so fast, Abigail barely had time to blink. One instant Leo Bates sat slouched against the opposite seat, smirking. The next, David jerked him halfway across the table by his shirtfront.

"Hey—!"

"Just shut up, Bates. I don't want to hear another word about Abigail come out of that filthy mouth of yours. Got that? She is what she is, and if you're too blind or too dumbass stupid to see how appealing that is, then that's your problem. Abbey's a decent woman. A lady. Something a creep like you wouldn't know anything about, so just keep your comments to yourself."

Abigail stared at David, her mouth sagging open. The last thing she expected was to hear him defend her. That he'd done so, and with such emphatic fury, warmed her heart.

Emotion swelled in her chest, and as she gazed at him, her surprised expression changed to melting tenderness.

With his elbow braced like an arm wrestler's, David held Leo sprawled off balance over the table. His bicep bulged, and the tendons and veins stood out along his arm. The two men stared at each other nose to nose, one face wary, resentful—the other rigid, muscles twitching with restrained menace.

Jaw clenched, David held Leo suspended for several seconds longer. Finally he shoved him back onto the bench seat. "Now pay attention, Bates. I want a meeting with your superior. Or whoever is running this show. And I want it fast. So set it up."

"All right, all right. I'll see what I can do."

"Don't see—just do it." David took Abigail's hand and slid out of the booth. "I'll expect to hear from you by tomorrow night."

Leo nodded, and without another word, David turned away.

Abigail's every instinct urged her to run for the nearest exit, but he kept a firm grip on her hand. With bold unconcern, he strolled with her through the room of hostile faces and out into the balmy night.

The instant they stepped through the door, the air of brazen challenge vanished, and his entire body tensed like someone had flipped a switch. "C'mon, Legs, move it," he urged, and hustled her away into the shadows at something just under a run.

"What do we do now?" Abigail gasped as they hurried through the dark streets. Every so often she had to break into a trot to keep up with his long stride.

David checked back over his shoulder again, an action he repeated every few seconds. "We hotfoot it back to the *Freewind* and get the hell off this island. After tonight our Rooskie friends will know we're still here and you can bet they'll search every inch of it. If they should find the cove I want to be long gone."

The sudden reduction in engine speed brought Abigail awake with a start. She jerked upright on the companion bench and looked around the bridge, lit by the soft glow of light from the console. David stood at the wheel with his legs braced wide, his gaze trained straight ahead.

Abigail rotated the stiffness from her shoulder and rubbed the back of her neck. She hadn't meant to fall asleep. Guiltily she glanced up. Stars still glittered overhead, so at least she hadn't dozed long.

David cut speed even more until they were moving at a slow idle. The engines chugged in the quiet night, the sound blending with the swish and slap of the water.

Her mind drifting, Abigail gazed out over the side. When the boat bumped something solid, she jumped and gave a startled yelp. Concerned, she hurried over to stand beside David, and her eyes widened. They had come to an idling stop against a wooden pier.

"Hold the wheel steady," David said, and lifted her hand onto it before she could protest. At once she felt the drag of water and overcompensated, and the boat bumped the pier again, harder. "Dammit, I said steady," David barked as he skimmed down the ladder.

He jumped to the pier and disappeared into the darkness. Abigail felt a dart of panic. Where was he going? She wanted to run after him, but she had her hands full trying to control the bobbing boat.

A few seconds later, a light came on inside the boat house just ahead. Steel rollers rumbled, and a rectangle of yellow spilled out over the water as the door slid upward, revealing two slips. A small speedboat occupied one. The other stall was empty.

By the time David returned, Abigail had bumped the boat against the pier three more times.

"Jeez, Legs, what the hell are you trying to do, beat a hole in the side?" He stepped up behind her and reached for the wheel. Abigail relinquished it gladly.

"Where are we? Whose boat house is that?" She had expected they would spend the night at sea or anchored off an uninhabited island.

"We're on Rincon Island. It's about twenty miles, as the crow flies, from Alhaja Verde. This place belongs to my sisters and their husbands."

Abigail squinted. On a slight rise beyond the beach, she could just make out the shape of a sprawling one-story house. "But...do you think we should just barge in this way?"

"No problem. They're coming down next week for a few days of R and R. I'm supposed to join them. But until then no one will be here. Besides, I have the use of the place anytime I want."

He guided the cruiser into the slip and cut the engines. "We should be safe here, but just in case anyone comes looking, the boat will be out of sight."

While David secured the boat, Abigail went below and gathered up her meager belongings and Chelsea, who lay curled up on the banquette with her toy puppy.

The wood and glass house had been designed with casual comfort and roominess in mind. Elevated on stilts and built in the shape of a wide-spread V, with a generous deck stretching along the seaward side, it enjoyed an uninterrupted view of the white sand beaches and the blue waters of the Gulf of Mexico.

"There are bedrooms on either side," David said, leading her into the large, high-ceilinged room at the center of the structure, where the slanted wings converged.

Feeling like a trespasser, Abigail stood just inside the door and looked around at gleaming wood floors dotted with rattan furniture with linen-covered cushions in a splashy yellow-and-white tropical print. At the back of the room, separated from the living area by a bar lined with stools, was an immaculate modern kitchen. Overhead, patches of stars twinkled through numerous skylights in the vaulted ceiling. During the day, Abigail realized tiredly, those same skylights would flood the room with sunshine.

"Erin and Max use the left-hand wing, and Elise and Sam the right one," David said. "Each has a master suite and two guest rooms, so you have your pick. So long as we're on the same side of the house, I don't care where I flop."

Abigail gave him a sharp look, and he sighed and rubbed the back of his neck. "Look, I know I said we'd be safe here, and we probably will be, but I'm not taking any chances. If there's trouble, I want you within reach. Okay?"

Giving him a wan smile, Abigail nodded. "Okay."

"Good. Now c'mon. I don't know about you, but I'm bushed."

He showed her to a pleasant room at the end of the right wing. "The bathroom is through there," he said as he moved from window to window, checking locks. "It connects with the bedroom I'll be using. I want you to keep the hall door locked at all times and both bathroom doors open when it's not being used. And don't lock them even then. Got it?"

"Ye-yes. I understand."

Abigail set her purse and the sack containing her clothes on the chaise lounge beside the windows. Chelsea climbed out of the side pocket and stretched sleepily. Scratching at the chintz cushions, she turned in a circle three times, before dropping her toy and curling around it with a sigh.

David and Abigail looked at each other, then away. Quiet settled, as thick as pudding. They'd been alone together for over two days, most of the time on a cramped boat, but this was different. More intimate. This was a real house. A real bedroom. A real bed.

Awkwardly, each waited for the other to speak. Abigail fiddled with the trim on the pocket of her sundress. David shifted from one foot to the other and looked at everything but her, his mouth grim. The silence stretched out, uncomfortable, endless. Then David broke it so abruptly she jumped.

"Oh, for Pete's sake, Abbey, go to bed," he snapped, and stalked from the room.

Abigail watched him disappear through the connecting bath, feeling shaky and hurt, and strangely abandoned.

Lying in the queen-size bed with his hands clasped beneath his head, David listened to the gush of the shower. He'd hurried through his own in the master bath across the hall, uneasy with being separated from Abbey for even the few minutes it had taken.

He was probably being overcautious. They hadn't been followed; he was sure of that. The boat was hidden. And apart from Pepe and Constanza, no one on Alhaja Verde knew that he was related to the Delanys and the Lawfords, the two couples who jointly owned a summerhouse on Rincon. For some reason—probably ingrained caution held over from his days with the Bureau—he'd chosen to keep that bit of information quiet.

Of course, if anyone cared to dig they could find out, and sooner or later they would. But he figured they had a few days grace before that happened.

If he was wrong and they were found, at least no one could sneak up on them. Their bedrooms were at the back where the windows were too high to reach, unless you happened to be a cat burglar. Across the deckside of the house, four sets of French doors opened from the master suites and the living room, but he'd rigged each with a cook pot suspended by a string, the end of which was caught between the top of the door frame and the jamb. If a door were opened, even slightly, a pot would hit the wooden floor with a clatter that would wake the dead. Crude perhaps, but effective. By the time they kicked in a bedroom door he'd be ready for them.

A hard smile curved David's mouth as he slipped a hand beneath the pillow and closed it around the grip on the .45 automatic. *Sam Lawford, you big wary bastard, I love ya, man.*

It was not a sentiment David had ever expected to experience, but at that moment if that damned taciturn brother-in-law of his had been there, David would have been hard-pressed not to kiss him.

It would never have occurred to Max to keep a gun squirreled away for protection, but the isolation of the beach house had been a concern for Sam. His brother-in-law had mellowed out a lot since marrying Elise, but he still didn't trust his fellow man a whole helluva lot. Thank God. On David's last visit Sam had shown him where the weapon was stashed. Just in case.

David fumbled a hand over the top of the bedside table and located the plastic sandwich bag—the one he'd found taped to the bottom of a drawer in the *Freewind's* galley. He extracted a cigarette and lit it. Only two left. Hell. He'd have to search the boat again. Why the devil hadn't he thought to buy more before they left Pepe's?

The sound of running water halted. David's gaze shifted to the bathroom door. Through it he heard the rattle of the shower curtain rings, and he gritted his teeth.

He'd been doing his damnedest not to think of Abbey standing naked beneath the spray, all sleek and soapy, the mounds of lather sliding down her body, caressing her the way his hands itched to. But now, in his mind's eye he could see her, stepping from the tub, reaching for a towel, her wet hair streaming down her back to her hips, her skin rosy and beaded with water. If he were in there with her, he would sip every droplet from every inch of her. David's body tightened, and he groaned. God! He could almost taste it.

Dammit, Blaine, will you knock it off! Think about something else, for God's sake!

But it was no use. He wanted her. He wanted her more than he could ever remember wanting any woman in his life. Why that was so, he didn't even want to think about.

The whole thing was insane. This wasn't the time to get mixed up with a woman. Any woman. If he was going to get them out of this mess, he needed to stay sharp, keep his edge. Anyway, Abbey wasn't even his type, for goodness' sake!

Oh, hell, who was he kidding? He sighed and stubbed out the half-smoked cigarette with a hard jab that broke it in two. It was crazy, but he liked everything about the woman, from her sharp little tongue, to those wide aquamarine eyes to her ladylike manner to her sexy little body. He liked her soft voice, her openness, her fierce love and protectiveness for that silly animal, the cute way she said "Oh, my stars" whenever she was upset. He liked her sharp mind and her stout heart and her courage and grace under pressure. She'd been caught in a dangerous situation and frightened out of her wits, but even under fire she hadn't crumbled.

Shoot, he even liked the way she stood up to him. David's mouth twitched. He didn't know any other woman who was gutsy enough to hide his cigarettes. Not even Erin had that kind of nerve.

Yeah, he liked her all right. The truth was, he *more* than liked her. And that made him uneasy.

Marriage wasn't part of his game plan. At least, not anytime soon. Hell, he'd just managed to get himself into a position to enjoy life. He had a good thing going with his new job, his boat, his bachelor life-style. He'd figured on enjoying it all for a few years before settling down.

Dammit. He wasn't ready to fall in love.

The bathroom door opened. A cloud of moist air roiled into the room, warm and evocative, redolent with the scents of soap, shampoo, talc and woman. David groaned as the heady combination filled his senses and sent fire streaking to his loins.

The light went off, leaving only a soft glow spilling through from the other bedroom. Abbey's voice floated out to him, whisper-soft and shy. "Good night, David."

His jaws clenched. "Night, Legs."

Silence. Then after a moment the light clicked off, and from the other room came the faint squeak of the bedsprings.

Aw, hell.

Abigail flounced onto her side and winced when the bed squeaked again. It was no use. For twenty minutes she'd lain there willing sleep to come, but she was as wide-awake as an owl.

She slipped her legs over the side and eased out of bed. She crossed to the windows, but all she could see were sand dunes and salt grass, tinted an eerie blue by the moon, and beyond that the line of trees where the forest took over and began its climb toward the mountains.

She pivoted away and paced back and forth across the room, her bare feet soundless on the wood floors. Chelsea lay with her snout on her paws, button eyes tracking the restless movements.

Abigail halted beside the windows again and stared out at nothing. She folded her arms across her midriff and massaged her elbows, her fingers moving in agitated little circles.

There was no point in lying to herself any longer. David was the reason she couldn't sleep. She wanted him—wanted to feel his arms around her, wanted him to kiss her, wanted him to make love to her . . . to love her.

It was crazy. Common sense told her she couldn't be in love with him. They'd known each other barely three days, for heaven's sake! What's more, they didn't even get along. They couldn't go more than a few hours without clashing like two gladiators.

My stars, Abigail, the man is rude, bossy, bad-tempered and as hard as nails. The two of you have nothing in common.

She sighed again, her shoulders slumping. But despite all that, despite the tension and fright of the past few days, despite the danger they still faced, she had to admit, she had never felt so alive, so...so...energized. And yes...so happy. And it was all because she was with David.

Abigail glanced toward the open bathroom door. Her heart warmed as she recalled the way he'd championed her to Leo Bates. His gruff tenderness the night before when she'd been upset. The way he'd held her, kissed her. How he'd refused to take advantage of her in that vulnerable state.

And he *had* come to her rescue. Oh, he'd grumbled a lot and stomped around like a bad-tempered bear, but she was beginning to realize that all that growling and snarling was for show. At least, it was where she was concerned. He'd groused and cursed and threatened, but he'd still done everything in his power to keep her safe and help her get out of this crazy mess.

For all his rough edges, beneath that irascible exterior, David Blaine was a kind and caring man. A modern-day chivalrous knight, almost. The corners of Abigail's mouth turned upward. She could just imagine how he'd react to *that* description.

She sobered, longing and a touch of panic in her eyes as her gaze again turned toward David's room. Who knew what tomorrow would bring? Or even if they would live to see another tomorrow? David had been careful not to worry her any more than he had to, but she knew the odds were against them. Even if they survived the predicament they were in, they probably wouldn't have a future together. She knew that, too.

But suddenly it didn't matter. None of it. With the exception of that debacle with Ted, all of her life she had been cautious. Every step she had ever made had been carefully considered. She had played it safe, prepared for every eventuality, protected herself at every turn and behaved in a circumspect manner—and all it had gotten her was a life as dull as dishwater.

Well, no more. Squaring her shoulders, Abigail drew a deep breath and started toward the connecting bathroom. From that moment forward she was going to forget caution and live for the moment. For too long she had watched from a safe distance while life passed her by. Foolhardy or not, she had fallen in love with David, and for however long they had, whether it was years or days or even hours, she was going to grab what happiness she could.

That he might rebuff her, she refused to even consider. Not that she deluded herself into thinking that he loved her. But he wanted her; he'd demonstrated that quite convincingly. Though she might yearn for more, she would accept whatever she could get.

Her heart hammered in her chest as she crossed the cool tile floor of the bathroom. At the door to David's room she paused.

He lay on his back with one hand beneath his head, the other resting on his chest, his legs spread. The top sheet lay bunched around his feet, and in the darkness his fuchsia bikini briefs glowed. So did the tip of his cigarette.

The soft words of seduction Abigail had been about to utter flitted right out of her mind.

She cleared her throat and opened her mouth to berate him for smoking in bed again, but she didn't get a chance to utter a word.

She had never seen anyone move so fast. At the first sound David bit out a curse and dived from the bed. In one fluid motion, he hit the floor and rolled to his feet braced in a crouch, holding a wicked-looking gun in his right hand.

"Freeze!"

Chapter Ten

"Oh, my stars!"

"Abbey?"

"That's a gun! You've got a gun!" she babbled, and sagged against the door frame, her hand over her heart. Goggle-eyed, she stared at the weapon gleaming malevolently in the moonlight, her gaze fixed on the ugly black hole in the end of the barrel.

"Dammit, Abbey!" David's aggressive stance collapsed. He snapped on the beside lamp and glared. "What the hell are you doing, sneaking around in the middle of the night?"

"Wh-where did you get that gun?"

"Don't you realize I could have killed you?"

"Is . . . is it lo-loaded?"

"Dammit! Will you forget about the gun and answer me!" He threw the weapon down on the bed and planted his balled fists on his hips. "What the hell were you doing creeping around in the dark?"

His tone cut through her shock and raised her hackles. She lifted her chin and gave him a look guaranteed to freeze lava. "I was *not* creeping."

"Oh, yeah? Well, I don't know what else you'd call it. What the hell were you doing, tippy-toeing in here like that?"

"If you must know, I came in here to seduce you!" she snapped.

"Well, that was a damned stupid thing to do!" he roared back almost before the words were out of her mouth.

"If I'd known you had a gun I wouldn't have done it!"

"That's beside the—" He stopped, his face going blank. His voice changed from a shout to a croak. "Wait a minute. Did you say...? You mean...? You came in here to...*seduce* me?"

Abigail sniffed and lifted her chin a notch higher. "Yes. But I've changed my mind."

In rapid succession a series of expressions flitted across David's face—from shocked to intrigued to downright lustful. Then his eyes flashed annoyance and his mouth flattened. "Well, great! Because I wouldn't let you anyway! I told you last night—" He broke off and sniffed, his scowl deepening. "What the hell is that smell?"

"Oh, my stars! Your cigarette!" Abigail cried. "It set the sheet on fire!"

"Dammit all to hell!"

The fire, which had been no more than a smoldering ring around a charred hole, burst into flames at that precise moment. Tiny tongues of orange and red leaped up and danced across the flowered sheets and smoke spiraled upward.

Instantly a high-pitched, pulsating alarm went off overhead.

Abigail screamed and covered her ears. Cursing, David grabbed a pillow from the bed and began to pound at the blaze.

Pandemonium reigned. David scrambled across the bed on his knees, whacking the mattress and spewing obscenities. Abigail squawked and dithered like a demented chicken. The ear-splitting alarm nattered on endlessly.

Chelsea tore in through the bathroom to enter the fray, barking hysterically and twirling in circles like a tiny dervish, as she was prone to do when excited. Between David's shouted profanity, Abigail's squeaks, the electronic blare of the smoke alarm and the terrier's yapping, the decibel level in the room was torturous.

For several seconds Abigail hopped around, alternately flapping her hands and holding her ears. Finally gaining a modicum of control, she dashed into the bathroom and snatched a towel from the rack. She wet it under the bathtub faucet and raced back into the bedroom with it, dripping water everywhere.

At the foot of the bed she hauled off and slung the sodden towel at the smoking remains of the fire—and missed the mark by a mile.

The towel smacked David across the nape with a *splat* and wrapped his head like a fishing line whipping around a tree branch. In a blink the saturated cloth encased him from the shoulders up like a freshly wound mummy.

Abigail sucked in her breath and gaped. "Oh...my... stars!"

David, who almost toppled under the impact, let loose a roar that not even the folds of wet terry cloth could completely muffle. He dropped the pillow as though it had suddenly caught fire and grabbed with both hands at the clammy binding that threatened to suffocate him.

"Oh, David! Oh! Oh! Oh, I'm so sorry!" Abigail clambered across the mattress to him on her knees. She tried to grab the end of the towel but David was twisting and flailing around so much that she couldn't. "Here, let me— David, if you'll just be still— Oh! Oh!"

Finding the end, he unwound the soppy cloth with impatient jerks and slung it across the room. The towel hit the wall with a splat, stuck for an instant, then plopped to the floor.

Bending forward, David braced his hands on his thighs and gulped in several deep breaths. Then he turned on Abigail with a vengeance, his brown eyes shooting fire.

He opened his mouth to say something, but instead snapped it shut again and leaped to his feet. He did a bouncy stomp across the bed, yanked the cover off the smoke alarm and jerked out the battery.

"Now for God's sake, shut that damned dog up!" he shouted at the top of his lungs.

At a word from her mistress, Chelsea's barking dropped to a throaty growl. For several seconds she maintained her aggressive stance and lifted her lip at David, leaving no doubt about whom she blamed for the disturbance.

"Hush, Chels," Abigail ordered when David shot the animal a black look. Chelsea obeyed, and after one last "ruff" of protest, she trudged back into the other room.

Abigail sighed and closed her eyes. The cessation of noise was heaven, but the respite did not last long.

"Would you mind telling me why in holy hell you whacked me with that damned wet towel?"

David dropped to his knees before her, his face like thunder. His dark hair was soaked and plastered to his head. Water beaded his face and streamed down his body. Drops created dark splotches on the strip of fuchsia knit around his hips.

Abigail's face set. "I was simply trying to smother the flames."

"The bed was on fire, not me! Anyway, by then I'd already put the fire out."

"I was rattled, okay? I..." She looked at the yard-wide hole burned in the sheet and the charred mattress pad it exposed, and her haughty demeanor melted away. When her gaze returned to David, her eyes were tender and teary. "Oh, David. I was so scared you would be hurt," came her shaky whisper.

He stared, helpless, into her shimmering aquamarine eyes, his expression that of a man who'd just had the props knocked out from under him. With those few simple words anger fled and the atmosphere in the room became charged with a much different emotion. Lusher. Deeper. More intense.

Face-to-face, only a foot or so apart, they knelt on the singed bed while smoke drifted around them in a lazy cloud and the acrid smell of burned cotton hung in the air. It stung their noses and made their eyes water, but they didn't notice. Silence stretched out, thick and pulsing with tumultuous emotions. Hearts pounded, chests tightened and eyes searched.

Slowly each leaned forward, drawn by a yearning too strong to resist. Abigail's head lifted. David's dipped. Eyelids drifted downward. Warm breaths mingled, and a sweet ache of anticipation squeezed Abigail's chest.

Their lips met, the touch soft, tentative, testing. With mouths open and slanted together, they sampled the delight that beckoned them to take their fill. Even so, the pleasure was piercing. It stabbed through Abigail with a sharp sweetness. Need spiraled and desire swelled under the self-imposed restraint, making her quiver and ache.

When Abigail could stand it no longer, she moaned and lifted her hands to clasp the sides of David's waist, leaning in closer, blindly seeking to intensify the kiss. For an instant David responded in a like manner, but then he grasped her shoulders and pushed her away.

"Abbey...no. We've got to stop this." Desire swirled in his eyes and his voice came out raspy and uneven, but the set of his jaw told her he meant it.

Abigail felt a touch of panic, and her eyes pleaded. "But...why? Why must we stop, David?" She edged closer and placed her hand flat on his bare chest. His muscles jerked at the contact. Against her palm she felt the crisp springiness of his chest hair, the warm hardness of male flesh, the thud of his heart that told her he wasn't immune to her.

Abigail drew a deep breath and gathered her courage. "I want you, David," she said, and struggled to ignore the blush that climbed her neck and flooded her cheeks. "And I know you want me." Turning her hand over, she let the back of her knuckles trail downward over his midriff and stomach.

"Abbey..." The warning came out choked.

Holding on to her nerve by a thread, Abigail slid her knuckles down farther, until they rested on the inch-wide elastic banding the top of his minuscule briefs. She felt him suck in his breath, saw his face tighten. Her eyes limpid, she looked straight into his and whispered, "It's not something you can hide."

"That's not—" David stopped to clear his throat. "Whether or not I want you isn't the point." He scowled, and tried to catch her meandering hand. She moved it to his thigh and raked her nails through the dusting of hair there.

"Then what is?" she asked with husky innocence.

"I told you last night, I'm not going to take advantage of y— Oh, God, Legs," he groaned when she leaned forward and nuzzled her nose in his chest hair.

"I know," she murmured against his skin as she strung a line of kisses across his chest. "I'm going to take advantage of you."

"Abbey— Ahhh..." David sucked in his breath when her tongue found a tiny nipple. She lathed it with meticulous care, then nipped. His body jerked, and he arched his head back and bared his teeth. His hands tightened on her shoulders, flexing now with pleasure. "Ah, Abbey... Abbey. Sweetheart this... this isn't right. You're reacting to the... stress of the situation," he gasped as her finger delved into his navel. "I've seen it ha... happen lots of... ti... times. Oh, God, Legs!"

Abigail's mouth found the other nipple. At the same time she ran her fingertip down the leg edge of his bikini briefs from his hipbone to that part of him that throbbed and yearned. Oh, so slowly, her finger glided against his skin, her touch feather light, tormenting. A hard shudder shook David.

"Don't worry," she murmured, nipping his shoulder. "I know what I'm doing." Taking advantage of his momentary debility, she gave him a push that sent him sprawling onto his back.

"Wha—"

He started to rise on his elbows, but Abigail straddled his body on her knees and pushed him back down with a hand on each shoulder. She bent over him, her eyes heavy lidded and sultry, her lips parted. Her breasts, exposed by the gaping neckline of the nightie, pointed toward his chest, saucy and as lush as ripe fruit on a tree, their shape molded by gravity. "Just lie back and relax, darling," she purred, smiling.

It had taken every ounce of nerve and daring Abigail could muster to initiate the seduction, but emboldened by David's response, she was beginning to enjoy herself. Especially now that she was getting the hang of it.

"Abbey, honey..." David gave a discomfited chuckle, his expression a mix of chagrin, concern and longing. "If we become lovers you're probably going to regret it later," he argued, but his voice held so little intensity, Abigail suspected he merely felt obligated to try to talk her out of proceeding.

She lowered herself until she sat astraddle his hips and smiled as she watched his pupils expand. Leaning forward, she braced her forearms on his chest, her face just a few inches from his. "I'll never regret it," she whispered with such passion that he almost looked convinced.

Abigail framed his face with her palms. "Listen to me, David. I've made up my mind. I'm through playing it safe. With you I feel...I don't know...really alive for the first time in my life, I guess. And I like it. If we get through this—" He frowned and started to protest. She put her hand over his mouth, stopping him. "*If* we get through this I don't want to go home to Waco regretting what might have been. And if we don't...well, then, I will have at least had this night."

David's hands settled on her back and massaged gently. His dark eyes searched her face. "Abbey...I want you. And if you're sure this is what you want, I'm not going to deny us. Maybe I should. Hell, I know I should. Even if you weren't overwrought and vulnerable, you're not the kind for a casual fling. But—" his mouth twisted "—despite my old man's teachings, I guess I'm just not that much of a gentleman. Sweetheart, before we go any farther, first I gotta tell you—I can't make you any promises, Abbey. I don't know where this is leading us, or how long it will last. Or even if it will last. Marriage, commitment—I just don't know. Hell, I'm not sure I'm even the marrying kind.''

"It doesn't matter."

"You sure?"

Abigail nodded, and after a moment David's arms tightened around her. His eyes darkened, and desire hardened his face. "In that case, come here, woman," he said in a raspy whisper.

As their lips met, he rolled with her until she lay with her back against the scorched mattress and he lay half over her, his muscular leg hooked over both of hers. They kissed hungrily, endlessly, the want that had been building for days springing free.

Abigail twined her arms around his neck and tunneled her fingers through his hair. The light rake of her fingernails against his scalp sent shivers of delight coursing through David. Oh, God, it felt so good. She felt so good.

Her mouth opened to him like a flower, innocent and eager, and he drank greedily of her. Tongues swirled and rubbed in a mating dance that sent heat streaking through them and made their pulses pound.

Like the one that first night on the boat, and the one the night before on the pier, the kiss stunned David. It punched him in the gut with its sweet sensuality and stole his breath away. He had told himself—had half convinced himself—that the pleasure he had experienced before had been the result of an adrenaline high, that it would have been the same no matter what woman had been with him. It had just happened to have been Abbey, that was all. Now he knew better.

"Abbey, Abbey, Abbey." He whispered her name in a feverish litany, dewing her skin with his moist breath as his mouth slid across her cheek. He found her ear, and the tip of his tongue traced each delicate swirl. He felt her shudder, heard her weak "Oh, David," and a fresh wave of pleasure washed through him. He nipped her earlobe with gentle savagery, then lathed the tiny pain with his tongue.

She moaned, and her hands clutched his shoulders, her fingers digging deep into his flesh.

Bracing on one elbow, David grasped the hem of the shorty nightgown. He tugged it upward, lifted her, and with a deft movement whisked the garment over her head and tossed it aside. Just as quickly, he hooked his fingers into the bikini panties and stripped them down her legs. The scrap of pink cotton fluttered to the floor and settled beside the nightgown and the soggy towel as he eased Abigail back down onto the bed.

David stilled, his gaze fixed on her bare breasts.

Abigail blushed crimson and made an instinctive move to cover herself.

"No, don't. Let me look at you."

He took her hand and returned it to his shoulder. For several seconds he stared, rapt. Her breasts were perfect, just full enough, the nipples pink and pouty, the creamy skin around them showing a tracery of blue veins. "Oh, God, Abbey. You're so beautiful," he whispered in a ragged voice.

He cupped one lush mound, and Abbey's breath caught.

"Do you like that sweetheart?" he asked in a seductive whisper.

"Ye-yes. Oh . . . yes."

He watched her face as he kneaded the soft globe, lifted, stroked, molded, squeezed. With delicate brushing strokes his thumb brought the nipple to an erect peak. Abigail writhed and moaned, and David smiled.

Bending over, he buried his face in the silky valley between her breasts and traced an erotic pattern on her skin with his tongue. "And this? Do you like this?" he asked in a strained voice as his mouth trailed up over the pearly mount to its crest.

Abigail cried out as his mouth closed around her aroused nipple, her back arching off the mattress. "Yes. *Yes!* Oh, David!"

In restless passion, her hands ran over his shoulders, his neck, down his chest. Her fingers threaded through the springy hair, tugged, kneaded.

As he lavished the same attention on her other breast, his broad palm slid downward. Abigail whimpered when his hand stroked her belly. The whimper turned to a moan when seeking fingers found the moist core of her desire.

David lifted his head from her breast and looked down at her, his face taut and flushed with passion. "Oh, Abbey! I can't wait any longer!"

With jerky movements, he stripped the fuchsia briefs from his body and sent them sailing.

When he turned to Abigail, she smiled. Her arms enfolded him, and as their lips met, David slid his hands beneath her hips and lifted her into his possession.

Abigail gasped, her body taut and trembling as she absorbed the shock, his heat, his hardness.

David stilled. "Did I hurt you?"

"No. No!" Her hands clutched his bare shoulders. "I...oh, David."

Bracing up on his forearms, he looked at her, and his frown faded. Seeing in her flushed face and dazed eyes the helpless passion she could not hide, he smiled, a slow, wicked smile that did wonderful things to his battered face. "I know, sweetheart. I know."

He rotated his hips against her, and the smile deepened at her little groan. He repeated the action.

"Oh...please." It was both a cry for mercy and a plea for more.

Lowering his head, he nibbled the sensitive skin beneath her jaw. With a slow undulation, he moved within her. The warm, moist heat of his breath filled her ear as he whispered, "Ah, Abbey, love. You're so tight. So perfect." His tongue dipped into the fragile shell, wetting it, stroking it, the tiny thrusts matching the rhythm of his rocking hips.

Abigail made a desperate little sound and arched her neck. She kneaded his back, her fingernails digging into the hard muscles.

David grunted. Abruptly he abandoned his teasing torment. His breathing grew harsher, his movements stronger, more deliberate. Abigail wrapped her legs around him and matched his urgent movements, her hips rising to meet each powerful thrust. "Oh, Lord, Abbey! Yes! *Yes!*"

"*Da . . . vid!*"

The delicious tension became more than they could bear, and as their hoarse cries blended, the world shattered in an explosion of pleasure.

They collapsed together, spent and sated, their legs tangled, their bodies boneless and as limp as melting caramel.

Abigail heard David's labored breathing in her ear, felt the press of his expanding chest against her breasts, his weight pushing her deep into the mattress. He was so heavy, she could barely breathe, but she was too tired and too satisfied to care. A heavenly lethargy seeped into every cell of her body. Her eyelids drooped as though weighted with lead. Making no effort to fight the pull of sleep, she drifted off, content.

Sometime later, she emerged from the depths of slumber just enough to be aware of David lifting her in his arms and carrying her.

"Mmm, what . . . ?"

"Ssh. I'm just moving us to the other bedroom. This one stinks like burned feathers. Just go back to sleep, love."

Abigail needed no urging. She was barely aware of being carried through the connecting bathroom. When David laid her down on the bed, she sank into oblivion the instant her head touched the pillow.

Waking in the morning was not something David relished, or did with good grace...or speed. Resentfully aware of the trill of birds beyond the window and the light that tried to penetrate his closed eyelids, he made a sleepy sound and rotated his head on the pillow.

Damn. He had to quit smoking. He felt as though he had a five-pound weight on his chest. A warm, furry weight.

He yawned, then paused, scowling. Furry?

With painful slowness, his eyelids lifted partway, and he found himself staring into Chelsea's button eyes just inches from his face.

He blinked and started.

The dog lifted her lip and growled.

Ah, hell! The little fur ball was perched on his chest, snarling as though she meant to savage him.

The Yorkie's manicured toenails dug through his chest hair and into his skin. David was certain her doggy breath would peel paint at ten paces.

His first instinct was to shove the mutt aside. He lifted his hand, intending to do so, when it occurred to him that Abbey wouldn't be thrilled if he manhandled her precious pet. After what happened between them the night before, the last thing he wanted was to upset her. The sight of those bared little needle teeth, just inches away from his face gave him pause, as well.

"Abbey?" he said with a warning edge in his voice. "Abbey, do something about this animal, sweetheart. She seems to think she's some sort of vicious attack dog. And to be honest, I don't like the way she's looking at my nose."

Chelsea's growl grew more threatening, but from the other side of the bed came only silence. David reached out to shake Abigail.

"Abbey. Abbey, honey, wake up. I—" His hand patted bare mattress, and his heart lurched. He forgot about the dog. "Abbey?" His head snapped to the side, but all he saw was a dented pillow and rumpled sheets. David's eyes grew wild. Holy hell! She was gone!

He grabbed the gun from under his pillow and bolted out of bed in one great lunge, tumbling the tiny dog to the mattress without a thought. Stark naked, he flew across the room and jerked open the unlocked door, nearly tearing it off its hinges. The wooden panel crashed against the wall as he pelted down the hallway. Chelsea came streaking after him, barking and snapping at his heels.

David ran for all he was worth, arms and knees pumping, muscles straining. His heart pounded somewhere in the region of his throat. Oh, God, Abbey. Abbey, baby! Dammit, if they hurt her somebody would pay!

He rounded the corner at the end of the hall and burst into the living room at full speed. Momentum carried him to the center of the room before he caught sight of Abigail in the kitchen and skidded to a halt.

Dressed in Elise's white terry-cloth robe, she stood stock-still, gaping at him over the counter, her expression startled. In one hand she held a slice of toast, in the other a knife with a glob of butter on the end. "David! What in the world—?"

"Dammit to hell, Abbey!" he exploded. "What are you doing in here?"

"Ma-making breakfast. I found bread in the freezer but I had to raid the *Freewind's* refrigerator for the butter. I hope you—"

David spit out a vicious curse that made her jump. He stormed the rest of the way across the room to the counter and glared at her over its surface. "You mean you went out to the boat!" he raged. "In broad daylight? Alone?"

"Well . . . yes. But just for a min—"

"Dammit, woman! I told you to stay in that bedroom with the doors locked!"

"But that was last night. This morning when I woke up you were still sleeping, so I thought I'd cook breakfast, and—"

"Breakfast, be damned!" He stomped around the end of the counter and towered over her with his hands on his hips and his bare feet spread wide. "Woman, you don't have the sense God gave a goose! What the hell were you thinking of, sashaying outside in broad daylight after all you've been through?"

He was not in the least self-conscious about his nakedness. If anything, he appeared unaware that he was storming around, ranting and raving like a madman, without a stitch on. Abigail, on the other hand, was acutely aware of every glorious inch of him.

The sight of that hard, battle-scarred body, the memory of how it felt to run her hands over him, to bury her face against his hairy chest, to make love with him, caused every nerve ending in her body to jump and hum. Standing so close, she could feel his heat, smell his musky scent. She swallowed hard, remembering the slight salty taste of his skin.

She had awakened feeling unsure of herself, and a little shocked at her own wanton behavior. And now her disturbing reaction to his brazen lack of modesty rattled her even more. It was that, as much as his domineering tone, that put her back up.

Her mouth primed, and her chin lifted. "I'll thank you not to talk to me in that manner," she said in her haughtiest librarian voice.

"I'll thank you not to talk to me in that manner," he mimicked back in a nasty singsong. Bending, he stuck his face so close to hers their noses almost touched. "You can just knock off the prissy old-maid talk, sweetheart, because it doesn't work with me. Not after last night."

Abigail gasped and stepped back. "Oh! You...you... Oh!" She spun on her heel and stalked away. "I should have expected something like that from a...a ruffian."

"Like what? Something like what? Hey! Where are you going? Come back here! I'm not through talking to you, Legs!"

"Well, I'm through talking to you. And don't call me Legs! And, for heaven's sake, put some clothes on!" Ignoring his low curse, Abigail marched through the living room and down the hall. David stomped along right behind her, his bare heels thudding against the wooden floor like blows from a rubber hammer.

"What the devil are you angry about? I'm the one who almost had a heart attack when I woke up and found you gone."

"What am I angry about? What *am I* angry about?" At the door to the bedroom they had shared she whirled to face him, and he almost cannoned into her. "I don't appreciate that crack about...about last night. *That's* what I'm angry about, as if you didn't know."

David looked puzzled. "Crack? What crack?"

"Oh!" Incensed, Abigail slammed the door in his face.

She had taken two steps when the door was thrown open again so violently it crashed against the wall. Abigail jumped and whirled around in time to see David stomp into the room in all his naked fury.

The righteous indignation, embarrassment and insecurity that had fueled her defensive ire fizzled under that blistering look. She backed up a couple of steps, but two long strides brought him to within inches of her. He loomed over her, glowering down from his great height. A muscle along his jaw twitched and his nostrils flared and whitened. "Woman, don't you *ever* slam a door in my face again," he ground out through his clenched teeth. "You got that?"

"Don't . . . don't you dare tell me what to do, David Blaine," she sputtered with her last gasp of false bravery.

"Oh, I'll tell you all right. But we'll argue that point later. Right now I want to know what has you so bent out of shape."

"Oh, please. You needn't pretend you don't know." She gave him a cool look and her mouth drew up as though it were on a pucker string. "Male chauvinist that you are, I suppose I should have expected you to evoke the old double standard and accuse me of being a . . . a . . . loose slut!"

"What! Are you crazy? I didn't do that!"

"Oh, really? It wasn't you I heard say that my 'old maid' talk didn't work with you . . . after last night?"

"And you thought I meant . . . ?" In a blink, David's irate scowl melted into an expression so tender Abigail grew flustered and could not meet his eyes. She looked away and firmed her mouth to keep her chin from quivering like a hurt child's.

"Ah, Abbey, honey. All I meant was that I know all that prickliness is just a cover-up. That the woman I held in my arms last night is no snooty ice queen. I don't think you're loose." He angled his head to one side and tried to make her look at him, but she blinked and stared at the opposite wall as though it were the most fascinating thing she'd ever seen. "I happen to think you're pretty wonderful," David added in a husky murmur.

Abigail sniffed and cut her eyes around at him. "Really?"

"Really." A blunt finger beneath her chin brought her face around to his. "But I meant it about doing as I tell you. From now on, when I say stay put, you stay put. Got it?"

Abigail nodded, and he bent and pressed a soft kiss to her lips. Her toes curled, and she felt a tiny zing of electricity race through her body.

"Okay. Now that we've got that settled, why don't we go back to the kitchen and eat that breakfast you made."

He slipped an arm around her waist to propel her toward the door, but she hung back. "David . . . wait. Uh . . . don't you think you should . . . well . . . put some clothes on first?"

"Why, Abbey. You're blushing." Chuckling, David wrapped his arms around her and hauled her close in a rough, tender embrace. "Aw, sweetheart, you're a wonder. One night you seduce me and the next morning you're embarrassed to see me naked."

"I didn't seduce you," she mumbled against his chest.

"You didn't? It sure felt like you did."

"Well, I didn't. I was going to, but then you took charge and I never got the chance."

"Did I? Oh. Well, in that case . . ."

"David!" she squawked when he gave the cloth belt on her robe a quick jerk and the borrowed garment spread wide. Underneath she was as naked as he was. Grinning, he grabbed the lapel edges and pushed the robe off her shoulders before she could stop him.

"David, for heaven's sake, what are you—"

He stopped her dithering protest with a hard kiss. Tightening his embrace, he lifted her up, walked to the bed with her hanging in his arms. Twisting, he fell backward onto the mattress with Abigail sprawled naked on top of him.

He kissed her long and hard, and when their lips parted, he spread his arms wide in exaggerated surrender and grinned. "I'm all yours, sweetheart. Now's your chance to have your way with me."

His look was so wickedly sensual, Abigail felt fire lick through her belly. Lying atop him, feeling his body's response, seeing the suggestive challenge on that sexy, lived-in face, she experienced a giddy sense of power that was new to her. It was exhilarating, and Abigail found she wanted to indulge herself to the fullest.

Her slow smile was pure provocation. He answered it in kind, his hot gaze daring her, luring her. Accepting the challenge, Abigail's eyes grew heavy-lidded as they locked with his and she began to move, her body shifting and arching, undulating against him in a slow, sinuous stretch.

Every muscle in David's body tightened. His eyes darkened and narrowed. His nostrils flared as his breathing grew harsh.

Abigail experienced a rush of excitement. Her sense of power burgeoned and her teasing grew bolder. She blew an intricate pattern through his chest hair, trailed her fingertips along his shoulders and neck, traced the outline of his lips, shifted from side to side so that her breasts swayed against his chest, watching all the while for his reaction.

Through it all, David lay motionless with his arms still outstretched in docile acquiescence. Only the tenseness of his body and the hot glitter of his eyes betrayed him.

Finally Abigail held his face between her palms and slowly—oh, so slowly—lowered her mouth to his. She kissed him with unabashed hunger, her open mouth rocking over his as though she would devour him. Her lips nipped and rubbed, her tongue swirled in his mouth, darting in, retreating, darting in again.

David remained passive and supine, luxuriating in the kiss and the lavish attention with all the greedy self-indulgence of an eastern potentate.

Letting herself go, Abigail bit his shoulders, his earlobe, the side of his neck. Her fingertips explored his biceps, the tender skin at the bend of his elbows. The soles of her feet rubbed sensuously up and down his hairy calves.

Her pointed tongue delved through the springy curls on his chest and drew a wet pattern on his skin. David groaned and twisted beneath her. "Oh, yes, sweetheart. That's it. That's it."

Abigail raised her head and looked at his flushed face, and smiled, experiencing another rush of power. "You like that, hmm?'' she murmured, mimicking the sweet torment he'd dealt her the night before.

"Yes. Lord, yes!"

"And this?"

"Yes. Yes."

She lifted up on her hands and knees. Her aquamarine eyes burned down at him with sultry heat, and as she slowly lowered her hips, David groaned.

"Ahhh, Abbey. Sweetheart!"

Chapter Eleven

The day that followed was the most wonderful Abigail had ever known. For twelve hours, beyond keeping a lookout for unwanted visitors, they gave little thought to their situation—not to the danger they faced, nor to the men on Al-haja Verde who pursued them, nor to the reasons why. For that brief space of time Abigail and David pushed aside everything else and concentrated on each other.

Wearing borrowed terry-cloth robes belonging to David's sister and brother-in-law, they ate breakfast, smiling all the while into each other's eyes, trading bites and sips of coffee, and stopping often to kiss and touch.

Afterward, while doing the dishes together, a playful nudge in the ribs escalated into an all-out tickling match, and they ended up making love on the kitchen floor.

When they floated back to earth and the hardness of the tile floor registered, Abigail made no protest when David scooped her up and carried her back to the bedroom wing.

There, for the first time, Abigail experienced the sensual pleasure of sharing a shower with the man she loved. She washed him and he washed her, drawing the chore out, both luxuriating in the freedom to touch and explore, to learn every line, every texture, every hard muscle and sinew, every soft curve and dip of their lover's body.

Inevitably the activity lead to another round of lovemaking. The warm water sprayed down and steam roiled around them, but neither noticed. With David's palms braced flat against the wall on either side of her hips, Abigail stood with her back pressed against the cool tiles, one leg hooked over his arm, lost in an erotic haze of pleasure as their soap-slick bodies rubbed together in the sinuous rhythm of love.

In the way of new lovers since time began, when passion was spent they talked for hours, learning secrets, making discoveries, sharing hopes and dreams.

David told Abigail about growing up in the small east Texas town of Crockett, about hot summer days spent at the local swimming hole, about the rambling old house his family had lived in—that his parents still lived in—where the doors were never locked and which seemed to always be overflowing with relatives and friends.

Abigail told him what little she could remember about her early years with her parents, and about Aunt Harriet's immaculate, pre-World War II house filled with a profusion of bric-a-brac, which had to be dusted at least twice a week, and the stiff, uncomfortable furniture, which her aunt had sworn promoted good posture and encouraged one to sit in a decorous manner.

He told her about his old-fashioned mother who still knitted her own sweaters, canned fruits and vegetables from her garden, and taught Sunday school every week. He told her about his father who was an attorney, in partnership with Travis's dad, and was the "salt of the earth" type with strong notions about things like honor and ethics and doing what was right, notions he'd done his best to instill into his children.

"Once when I was eight, some of my buddies and I, out of boredom more than anything else, stole some watermelons out of old man Buxton's patch," David reminisced. "He must have been about eighty at the time, and every summer, to supplement his retirement income, he sold watermelons from a little stand out in front of his house.

"Well, we ate a few of the melons we took, but most of them we just used for target practice. We all had BB guns and slingshots, and for about an hour we had a high old time busting those melons to smithereens...until my old man caught us. Dad turned my friends over to their parents, and they either got their hides tanned or a lecture and had to pay Mr. Buxton for a share of the melons we'd taken. But not me. Every spring and summer after that I had to hoe old man Buxton's garden once a week," David recalled with a wry chuckle.

"And of course, you resented it." Abigail smiled. She could imagine David as a barefoot, sweaty, freckle-face boy in overalls and a straw hat, chopping weeds in a garden.

"In the beginning. But by the end of that first summer I had gained a healthy appreciation for just how hard that frail old man had to work for his few pennies. After that I never took anything that didn't belong to me. And to this day it makes me see red when anyone takes advantage of someone too old or too young, or some who's just not equipped to stand up for themselves."

"You mean like a lone, defenseless woman?" Abigail teased, earning herself a long, hard kiss.

She told him about Aunt Harriet, who had a platitude for every occasion, and whose opinions and attitudes were as stiff and unbending as the boned corsets she had insisted upon wearing.

"She sounds like a witch," David commented when Abigail recited some of her aunt's strict rules.

"She just had her own way of doing things," Abigail defended. "She was much older than my father, and set in her ways by the time I came to live with her. It couldn't have been easy on a woman who had no tolerance for messy, noisy children to be suddenly saddled with her brother's child at her age."

David told Abigail about his sisters, who were identical twins; daring, irrepressible Erin with her insatiable curiosity and wanderlust; soft, gentle Elise who possessed a quiet strength that had surprised them all.

He filled her in on Max Delany, the globe-trotting entrepreneur whom Erin had married, and Sam Lawford, Max's best friend and partner, a reserved man who had spent four years as a prisoner of war and had returned a cold emotionless shell of a man, until Elise had thawed the ice around his heart.

He regaled her with stories of his sister's high jinks over the years, the worry and trouble they'd caused him, and how he was glad they both had husbands now to watch out for them. But beneath his gruffness and grousing, Abigail heard the pride and love.

Fascinated, she listened to it all with the intense interest and envy of one who had grown up alone in a sterile home, longing for brothers and sisters, the warmth of a family.

That whole day they did not leave the house. Lunch and dinner were consumed, though neither could have said an hour later what they had eaten. They talked for hours and spent quiet, reflective times wrapped in each other's arms, both aware of the minutes ticking by, but loath to bring the matter up.

And they made love repeatedly.

All too soon, however, the idyll ended. As the setting sun splashed ocean and sky with red and orange, the *Freewind* eased from the boat house and set course for Alhaja Verde.

On reaching the island, once more they hid David's boat in the cove and used Pepe's skiff, which they had left there the night before, to return to San Cristobal.

A message from Leo awaited them at the cantina. The terse note said the meeting was set for that night at eleven at the Casa Delgado de Vuente on Camino Acequia.

"I do not like it, *mi amigo*," Pepe pronounced, pacing back and forth. "The hombre who brought the note, he is *muy* bad. And that place, it is up there on the mountain, miles from nowhere. No one has lived there for years. This could be a trap."

"I know, but we'll have to chance it. At the moment we don't have any other options."

Pepe gave them directions to the remote hacienda and the loan of his pickup. He wanted to accompany them, but both Constanza and David vetoed that idea.

"If this operation goes sour and something happens to me, I want Abigail to have someone back here to turn to for help."

The explanation soothed Pepe's injured pride, as David had intended, but sent fear streaking through Abigail. She shot him an alarmed look, her face pale. Good Lord. Was he expecting serious trouble? From their own people?"

She tried to ask him on the drive up the mountain, but he waved her questions aside, saying he had to concentrate on the switchback road. After several rebuffs, Abigail gave up.

They had been climbing for almost a half hour and had not passed a structure of any kind when David pulled the pickup off the narrow dirt lane and braked to a stop behind a stand of trees. "The hacienda should be about a quarter of a mile up the road."

"Then why did you stop here?"

"You didn't think I would just drive up to the front door, did you? Before I let you get anywhere near that place I'm going to check it out." Hooking a hand around the back of Abigail's neck, he pulled her to him for a hard, very thorough kiss that left her body weak and her head whirling. "You and the mutt stay here. If I'm not back in thirty minutes, you turn this truck around and hightail it back to Pepe's. Got it?"

"But, Da—"

"No buts. You do as I say, Legs. I mean it."

Before she could argue further, he eased open the door and slipped away into the darkness.

Abigail checked the luminous dial on her wristwatch. She shifted on the sprung seat and looked around, but it was so dark she could barely see three feet beyond the truck. Chelsea padded across the seat to the driver's side and stood up on her hind legs to peek over the edge of the window. Abigail checked her watch again.

The quiet night closed in around her. Every sound seemed magnified, menacing—the dry rustle of leaves in the trees, the hoot of an owl, the insects' intermittent whir. When a small creature stirred in the underbrush beside the truck Abigail jumped and let out a squeak. Chelsea promptly bounded onto her lap and hung over the edge of the window opening, growling ferociously.

"Hush, Chelsea," Abigail ordered. Her gaze swept the darkness. She shivered and rubbed her arms. She half expected someone to leap out from behind a tree and drag her from the truck.

Abigail checked her watch again. Heavens! She'd had no idea thirty minutes was so long. She fidgeted. She drummed her fingers. She tapped her foot.

And every few seconds she checked her watch.

As anxious as she'd been for the time to pass, when it did, with no sign of David, she rued her impatience and would have wished every minute back if she could have. She gnawed on her thumbnail and searched the darkness. David, where are you?

She checked her watch again. She'd wait another five minutes.

When they were up, she waited another five...and another.

Finally Abigail scooted over behind the wheel. She reached for the ignition key, but drew her hand back at the last second and bit her thumbnail again. It had been forty-five minutes. He'd told her to leave if he wasn't back in thirty. She looked around again, her expression pained.

Darn it! She couldn't go off and leave him! She didn't care what he said, she simply couldn't do it!

Her nerves jumping, Abigail put Chelsea back into the side pocket of her purse and eased out of the truck. Out in the open, the dark night took on added menace. Her insides quivered like gelatin, and gooseflesh rippled over her arms.

Squelching the cowardly urge to climb back into the truck and do as David had instructed, she took a determined step toward the road, then halted. If he had been abducted, it might be wise to stay out of sight. A sundress and sandals were not the best attire for tramping through the woods at night, but there was no help for it.

The undergrowth among the trees scratched Abigail's legs, and low limbs and vines caught her hair and slapped her in the face. There seemed to be a thousand hazards hidden in the shadows just waiting to deal her grief. More than once, Abigail tripped on a protruding root she couldn't even see. An owl hooted, and something skittered away in the darkness. In the distance a creature screamed, and Abigail's skin crawled. Still, she kept going.

The road was off to her left. She tried to keep it in view, but between the darkness and her poor sense of direction she got off course and emerged from the woods at the back of a house set far off the road.

Light shined from two windows—in a room that Abigail guessed to be a kitchen, and from a shallow basement window.

Admonishing Chelsea to be quiet, Abigail crept across the yard, crouched low. Her heart pounded, and her mouth was so dry her tongue felt swollen.

She kept a wary eye on the back door and the lighted window beside it as she sneaked toward the basement window. When she reached the house, she pressed against the wall and dropped onto her knees. The bottom of the window was mere inches above ground level, and she had to bend over to see inside.

Abigail gasped when she did and put her hand over her mouth. David sat on the floor, leaning back against a post with his hands tied behind it. He sat with his head tilted back against the post, his eyes closed. One side of his jaw was puffy and discolored, and the cut above his eye had been reopened. Fresh blood spatters dotted the front of his shirt.

Oh, David, what have they done to you?

Anger consumed Abigail. The very idea that agents of their own government had hurt David spurred her temper to heights it had never reached before.

She had to do something to get him out of there. But what? She surveyed the only entrance available to her. The narrow casement window opened outward. It would be a tight fit, but she thought she could make it. At least the window was open and there was no screen. Abigail poked her head inside and was delighted to see there was a workbench along the wall below.

Glancing at the doorway again, she set her purse close to the opening, then got down on her hands and knees and shimmied backward through the window, feetfirst.

A soft bump brought David's eyes open, and his jaw dropped. Nothing in his life had ever surprised him—or frightened him—as much as the sight of those gorgeous legs and cute little rear end coming through the window.

He watched, too stunned to speak, as Abigail squirmed and wriggled her lower body through the opening. For a moment she hung there by her waist while she struggled to drag her purse closer. Then, after a glance over her shoulder, she pushed off.

She landed with a soft thud, and David found his voice. "Abbey, what the hell are you doing here?"

Glancing over her shoulder, she frowned. "Shhh. Do you want to get those guys down here?"

"Dammit, Abbey! I told you to leave if I didn't come back!"

Stretching up on tiptoe, Abigail managed to grip the bottom of her purse with her fingertips and pull it down. She hopped down from the workbench, hurried over to David and dropped onto her knees beside him. "That would have been rather foolish, wouldn't it?" she said, more than a little pleased with herself. "Who would have come to your rescue if I had?"

"Abbey, so help me, when we get out of this mess, I'm go—"

"Oh, shush your blustering. You don't scare me," she said blithely, and proved it by kissing him into silence. When she raised her head, her eyes were dreamy—until she focused on his injuries. "Oh, David, your poor face."

"Never mind that. Just get me untied. Quick, before those goons get back."

"Oh! Right!" Setting her purse down among a stack of crates in the shadows behind David, she ordered Chelsea to "stay" and went to work on the ropes.

No sooner had she gotten started than the door at the top of the stairs opened. Abigail jumped and looked up, and her mouth fell open as three men stepped onto the landing. "Those two are the men from the docks. The ones who ransacked my hotel room," she whispered to David incredulously.

"Yeah. I know."

"Well, well. What have we here?" the man in the lead said. David saw Abigail's shock deepen as the man's Boston accent registered. "If it isn't Miss Stewart." He looked at David and chuckled. "I wouldn't have thought a hard case like you would inspire that kind of devotion, Mr. Blaine. I expected Miss Stewart to be long gone by now."

As the men clattered down the stairs, Abigail's gaze never left them, but she muttered under her breath, "Chelsea, stay. Stay, girl. And be quiet."

"But then, what would a scum bag like you know about loyalty?" David drawled.

"You mean because I chose to throw in with my Russian comrades?"

Abigail sucked in her breath. "You mean you're a traitor to your own country?"

"Me? Of course not. Haven't you heard? There's Glasnost and Perestroika now. Why, we're all one big happy family."

"Yeah, sure," David sneered. "And Stalin was a Jesuit priest."

"Shut up, pig!" The order, issued in accented English, came from the ugly brute with the flat face, who delivered a vicious kick to David's ribs.

"Oh! You beast! You leave him alone!" Incensed, Abigail sprang to her feet and flew at the man with her fists flailing. She managed to land a sharp blow on his nose that elicited a gratifying grunt of pain before he and his partner could subdue her. Even then, she twisted and kicked and butted until Shovel-face slapped her across the face with such stunning force her eyes glazed.

"Leave her alone, dirt bag!" David lunged and strained against his bindings, spewing obscenities.

"Ahhh . . . it's like that, is it?" the American said with a sly smile.

He turned to Abigail, his eyes narrowing. "Tell me, Miss Stewart. Where is it?"

Abigail stuck her chin out in flagrant defiance, something she would not have had the nerve to do only a week before. "Where is what? I don't know what you're talking about."

Shovel-face raised his hand to slap her again, but the American stopped him. "No, Ivor. Not yet. Sergio will be here soon, and he'll want to question her himself. If you knock her silly she won't be able to answer, and he won't be pleased."

The brute did not look happy, but after a brief hesitation, he lowered his hand. Following the American's instructions he tied Abigail to another support post, six feet from where David was tied.

When done, the three men started back up the stairs. Half way to the top the American paused and looked down at David, his expression for once showing concern. "I'm warning you, Blaine. Sergio will be here soon, and he'll get his answers, one way or another. You may be able to stand anything he dishes out, but I don't think Miss Stewart can. Or that you'll be able to watch." He jerked his head toward the door at the top of the steps. Through it they could hear the other two men talking in Russian. "He'll turn Ivor loose on her. As you noticed, he enjoys hitting women. In any case, it won't be pretty. So why don't you do yourselves a favor and tell us where the list is?"

David replied with a succinct, vividly crude, two-word expression.

The other man's face tightened. "You're fools. Both of you," he snapped, and disappeared up the steps.

David lit into Abigail the minute the door closed. "*Now* do you see why I wanted to keep you out of this? Dammit,

Abbey, if you had just gone back to Pepe's like I told you to—''

"David, please. I couldn't leave you, and that's all there is to it. Instead of wasting time arguing, we should be working on getting free and getting out of here."

"Don't you think I've been trying ever since they tied me? These ropes won't budge."

"Chelsea, come," Abigail called, and the little dog dashed eagerly from the shadows. Whining and wriggling, she jumped up on Abigail and started licking her chin.

Over the top of the dog's head, Abigail's gaze sought David. "When that man hit me I was so afraid Chelsea would come after him. She's well trained and obedient, but I was praying she wouldn't pick that time to disobey."

David rolled his eyes. "Well, I'm afraid you'll have to pardon me, sweetheart," he growled, making no attempt to hide his exasperation. "At the time, that damned mutt wasn't my top priority."

"Well, she should have been. Watch this." Abigail turned her attention back to the agitated animal. "That's enough, Chels. Come on now, girl, I know you're upset. Calm down. Chelsea, sit," she commanded sharply, and the Yorkie obeyed, though she still quivered as she gazed adoringly at her mistress. "Now fetch my purse, Chelsea. Bring it to me."

"Oh, pul-leeze," David groaned as the dog trotted away. "Even if she knows what you're saying, that overgrown mouse can't drag that suitcase you call a purse. The thing must weigh five times what she does."

Ignoring him, Abigail continued to murmur encouragement. "Come on, girl, fetch the purse. You can do it. Fetch the purse. Come on, Chels, bring it here."

David snorted, but to his surprise, short scratchy sounds began to come from the shadows—the sounds of canvas scraping across concrete, inch by inch. His jaw dropped, and he stared at Abigail. "Well, I'll be damned."

The sounds drew closer. Finally Chelsea's furry rear end came into view...then the rest of her. With a Herculean effort, the purse strap clamped between her teeth, the tiny dog leaned back and strained for all she was worth and moved the bag an inch or so. Taking a step back, Chelsea set her legs again and repeated the process. Over and over.

Watching her, David strained at his ropes, unconsciously trying to help.

"That's it, Chelsea. That's my good girl. You're doing fine," Abigail crooned.

"Way to go, Chelsea. C'mon, Tiger. You can do it," David rooted. Chelsea paused just long enough to cut her eyes around at him and growl.

To Abigail's dismay, when her pet succeeded in bringing the purse to her, she couldn't get her bound hands far enough inside to grab anything.

"Aw, hell. I knew it wouldn't work." David slumped back against the post, muttering a string of curses. He had to do something. Fast. He couldn't let Ivor get his hands on Abbey.

"Keys, Chelsea," Abigail commanded. "Fetch the keys."

David's head snapped around, a surge of renewed hope swelling his chest. "The pocketknife! Of course! Your key ring has a pocketknife attached to it! Now if the little fur ball just knew what you were—"

To David's surprise, the dog burrowed into the purse. Seconds later she emerged with the key ring in her mouth.

"Good girl, Chelsea! Good girl! Now take it to David. Go on, take it to David."

Hesitating, Chelsea looked at David and growled.

"Go on, Chels. Take it to David," Abigail said with more force, and the little dog reluctantly obeyed. "Put it in his hand, Chels. Give it to him. That's it, that's my good girl." The instant her mission was completed, Chelsea raced back to her mistress.

David's fingers pried open the blade of the knife and went to work on the ropes. He sawed back and forth, gritting his teeth. Dammit. Trust a woman to have a pocketknife and not keep it sharpened.

One by one, though, the twisted strands of hemp gave way beneath the blade. Just as the last one popped, the door at the top of the steps opened again.

David stilled.

"Hide, Chelsea. Hide," Abigail whispered, and the dog darted out of sight into the shadows.

This time the American was alone. He sauntered down the steps with a cocky grin. "Ivor and Vladimir were worried that you might try to escape, so I volunteered to stand guard. Not that I think you could get free." Sprawling out in a threadbare upholstered chair, he propped his feet on a trunk. He glanced at Abigail and fixed David with a goading look. "I just thought it best to keep Ivor away from Miss Stewart. For now."

Behind the post, David's hands balled into fists. Rage boiled inside him. He had an almost overpowering urge to go for the guy's throat, but he restrained himself—barely—and met the taunting look with a hard stare that revealed nothing.

"In the meantime, while we're waiting for Sergio, I'm going to grab a little snooze." Lacing his fingers behind his head, he leaned back against the tattered cushion and closed his eyes.

David forced himself to wait. He marked time as he flexed his hands and searched the basement for something to use as a weapon. One minute. Two. Three.

At the end of the fourth he sprang. Like an uncoiling spring he bounded to his feet. The guard awoke with a start, but before he could move, David snatched up a broken ax handle and smashed it down on the man's head. With a groan, he collapsed and slid from the chair into a limp heap on the floor.

"Oh, David, you did it! You got him!" Abigail crowed as he lifted the man's gun and hurried over to cut her loose.

He pressed a swift kiss on her lips. "Don't get too excited yet, sweetheart. We've still got to get by those gorillas upstairs." The man on the floor moaned, and David cursed. "But first it looks like we're going to have to tie and gag our friend here. I don't suppose you'd have any cord in that purse of yours? The ropes they used on us aren't long enough, now that I've cut them."

Abigail dug through her purse and pulled out a silk scarf. "Will this do?"

"As a gag, but I still need something to bind his hands."

A quick search of the basement turned up nothing usable. When the man began to stir, David picked up the ax handle to deal him another blow.

"Wait! I've got an idea. Pull him over to that post. Hurry, before he wakes up." David complied while Abigail rummaged through her purse again. When she pulled out a small tube and held it up he scowled.

"What's that?"

"Krazy Glue. It bonds anything together instantly. Here, help me sit him up so that he's straddling the post."

David was skeptical, but he did as she asked. He expected her to glue the man's clothing to the post or the floor, but Abigail looped the unconscious man's arms around the post, squeezed a squiggle of glue onto each of his palms and slapped them together.

"There. He won't be going anywhere anytime soon." Standing, Abigail dropped the tube back into her purse and dusted off her palms in an age-old gesture of triumph.

David stared at the unconscious man, looked at Abigail's audacious grin and shook his head. *This* was the meek little female who had stowed away on his boat just a few days ago? The same one who had called *him* a hooligan?

Slowly his grin grew to match hers. "Sweetheart, you're some kind of woman. And I take back everything I ever said about that purse of yours. About the mutt, too."

He gave her a hard kiss, and with his hand still cupping her nape, he looked into her eyes. "We're going to have to deal with those two goons up there, too, you know. I'm too big to get through that window. Are you up to it?"

Abigail lifted her chin. "Lead on, McDuff."

"That's my girl."

With Chelsea once more riding in Abigail's purse, they crept up the stairs, David in the lead, the gun held ready at his shoulder. On the landing he looked at Abigail and mouthed, "Ready?" She drew a deep breath and gave a determined nod, and David eased the door open a crack.

The two men were sitting at the kitchen table, eating. One had his back to them. The other, the brute named Ivor, sat facing in their direction but he was too busy shoveling food into his face to notice anything amiss.

David squeezed Abigail's hand and flung the door open so hard it crashed against the wall. The two at the table jumped up, toppling their chairs as David stepped into the kitchen.

"Freeze! Or I'll blow your heads off!"

He stood crouched, the gun held straight out in front of him in a two-fisted grip. "Now, put your guns on the table— slow and easy. Good. Good. Now step back against the wall. And keep those hands up! Abbey, get the guns and bring them here."

Abigail did as he instructed, though she picked the automatics up by the grips with two fingers. David stuffed them both into the waistband of his jeans.

"Okay, you two, move it." He waved the barrel of the gun he was holding toward the basement door and stepped aside to let them pass.

Abigail backed toward the door to the outside. "What are you going to do with them?"

"Lock them in the basement, which is a lot less than they were going to do to us."

Something flashed in Ivor's eyes that sent alarm streaking through David an instant before Abigail shrieked. He whirled, and found himself facing the business end of a Russian-made 9 mm Makarov PM.

"Don't move, Mr. Blaine." The man with the gun had caught Abigail from behind in a choke hold, and his brawny forearm was pressed across her windpipe.

"Sergio, I presume," David said with a wry grimace.

"Correct."

Chelsea was going crazy, barking and growling and trying to get at the man, but he ignored her as though she were no more than a bothersome gnat.

"Now, drop the gun."

David hesitated, and Sergio tightened his hold on Abbey's neck. She made a choking sound, and Chelsea's barks grew hysterical. "Do it, Blaine. Now!"

Looking into her frightened eyes, David gritted his teeth and did as he was told. As Ivor grabbed the guns from his waistband David saw Abigail slip her hand inside her purse. He tensed, and Abigail didn't disappoint him.

In a flash she whipped out a small canister and sprayed it over her shoulder, straight into Sergio's face.

The man screamed. The Makarov clattered against the floor. Abigail made a dive for the stove and snatched up an iron skillet. The other two Russians scrambled for their guns, but before they could get them, David shoved the table into Ivor's groin, then whirled around and drove his shoulder into Vladimir's middle.

Both men recovered quickly, and a free-for-all ensued. David ducked, butted, gouged, kicked and threw punches, while Abigail waded through the melee swinging the skillet with both hands. Chelsea jumped from her perch in Abigail's purse and raced around the kitchen barking and biting ankles. Sergio lay on the floor writing in agony and screaming something obscene in Russian.

Abigail got lucky with one of her wild swings and conked Vladimir in the head. The skillet gave a satisfying *boing,* and the Russian went down like a poleaxed steer.

David doubled Ivor over with a two-handed blow to his midsection and finished him off with a downward chop on the back of his thick neck.

"C'mon, Legs, let's get out of here!" Whirling, he grabbed Abigail's hand, scooped up Chelsea on the run and they bolted out the door like rabbits out of a chute.

Heedless of the possible hazards, they tore down the dark road going flat out, arms and legs pumping. David's long stride ate up the ground, and he towed Abigail along with him, her sandaled feet touching earth just now and then. Mercifully the road was downhill all the way to the stand of trees where Pepe's truck was hidden.

They were almost there when behind them they heard the sound of an engine starting. "Uh-oh, here they come," David gasped.

Abigail moaned.

When they reached the truck, David tossed Abigail into the cab like a sack of grain and raced around and slid under the wheel before she had time to recover. By some miracle, the old rattletrap started on the first try. The engine roared and tires spun as David stomped on the gas. They shot forward, bumped out onto the road, made a fishtailing turn back in the direction of town and took off as though they were rocket powered. Abigail had no idea the old truck could even go that fast. She doubted that Pepe did either.

Seconds later a pair of headlights appeared behind them, bearing down fast.

"Hold on, sweetheart," David yelled over the roar of the engine as the truck slewed around a turn.

The admonition was wasted on Abigail. She held on for dear life, clutching the armrest with one hand and the edge of the seat with the other. Every time they hit a bump or chug hole, she bounced up and hit her head on the roof.

The headlights of the sedan were getting closer. Abigail gripped the seat tighter and wondered if they were about to be run off the mountain road.

She heard a distant "crack," and David swore.

"Get down, Abbey! They're shooting!"

"What!" In a reflexive action, Abigail darted a look over her shoulder through the rear window, just in time to see a streak of fire spit out of the sedan window. Something *thunked* against the truck, and she screamed and made a dive for the floor. Bullets struck the old truck in rapid succession, like a string of dull firecrackers going off. With each metallic *thunk* Abigail jumped and squeaked.

"Damn! They hit a tire!" David shouted as the truck careened out of control. They spun around and skidded off the road, and for a terrifying moment Abigail was certain they were going to turn over. David fought the steering wheel, and somehow managed to bring them to a halt. Before the truck had come to a complete stop, he grabbed Abigail's arm and hauled her out. "C'mon! Run!" he shouted, and made a dash for the woods as the sedan screeched to a halt behind them.

The Russians poured out of the car, firing. All around them bullets thudded into the earth and kicked up dirt. As they entered the mountain forest, a chip of wood flew off a tree to Abigail's left.

Among the trees Abigail couldn't see a thing, but David didn't slow the pace. His long strides and frantic speed made no concessions to the uneven ground beneath their feet or to the darkness that could have hidden obstacles in the path, not to mention any number of unpleasant things, such as snakes and predators. Abigail didn't complain because she could hear their pursuers thrashing after them.

Suddenly David stopped, and she slammed into his back. "Here. Crawl under there," he murmured, pushing her down among a clump of waist-high fern.

Abigail scrambled deep into the fronds until she came up against a tree, and David wriggled in right behind her. They lay side by side on their bellies, his arm around her shoulders, and listened as the others thrashed through the underbrush. "Don't move, no matter how close they come," David whispered in her ear. "and for God's sake, kept that dog quiet."

Abigail gave Chelsea a command, and for good measure, she clamped her hand around the dog's snout.

The rustling noises came closer. Abigail's heart beat so hard it almost suffocated her. Two men stopped to listen, then they conferred in low voices. Abigail didn't move. She didn't so much as blink. The thick fronds and the darkness gave them no visibility, but from the sounds Abigail was certain if she stretched out her hand she would touch them.

A rustle sounded among the ferns. Abigail caught her breath, remembering the snake they had encountered in these woods two days before. Something brushed against her bare arm—something slithery and cold. She bit down hard on her tongue to hold in a silent scream and shuddered from head to toe.

The men moved on, and still they waited. Abigail wanted desperately to stand up and get out of the dense fern, away from the creepy crawly things that lived on the dark forest floor. She was so tense, every muscle in her body quivered. They waited for what seemed like forever after all sound of the men had died away.

Finally David gave her arm a squeeze and murmured, "C'mon. I think we can chance it now."

Almost before the words were out of his mouth, Abigail scrambled out of the clump of fern and stood up. Shuddering, she brushed at her clothes and her hair and rubbed her forearms. It was then she noticed that David wasn't with her.

She started to call out to him just as he emerged from the ferns and stood up. "What took you so—"

He flinched as she took his arm, and Abigail sucked in her breath as her fingers encountered something wet and sticky.

"David! Oh, my stars! You've been shot!"

Chapter Twelve

"Take it easy, sweetheart. It's nothing serious."

"Nothing *serious!* How can you say that? You've been *shot!* Oh, God, there's blood all over your arm!"

"C'mon, Legs, calm down. If I were badly hurt, would I be standing here arguing with you? Hell, no. I'd be passed out or dead by now."

Abigail sucked in her breath. Instead of calming her, his words made her more frantic. "Oh, my stars! You lay on that filthy ground, bleeding all that time. You're still bleeding!" She began to paw through her purse. "God alone knows what kind of germs you picked up. If you don't expire from loss of blood you'll probably die from an infection. And did you say a word to me about it? Oh, no. Not one. Just lay there like a stump. Of all the stupid, macho things to do."

"Hey, c'mon, Abbey. Gimme a break, here. For one thing, I didn't have a chance to tell you. And even if I had, what would've been the point? You would only have worried, and there was nothing you could've done about it."

"I have a first-aid kit in my purse. I could have at least stopped the bleeding," she shot back, "which I'm going to do right now."

She pulled something from her purse, and before David realized what she was about, a small beam of light pierced the darkness.

"Holy—" He snatched the penlight out of her hand, covering the bulb end with his palm, and snapped it off. "Dammit, Abbey! Why don't you just send up a flare so Sergio and his buddies can find us?"

"It's just a penlight, for heaven's sake."

"In this darkness any kind of light can be spotted easily."

"But I have to see your wound to doctor it."

"Forget that. Just slap a pressure bandage on it and let's get the hell out of here. Sergio and his pals haven't given up. You can bet on it."

Abigail protested, but David bowed his neck obstinately and told her it was that or nothing. Feeling her way through the task, Abigail applied a thick gauze pad to the wound and anchored it with a wide strip of adhesive, fuming all the while about how quickly the loving man of the past twenty-four hours had reverted to the stubborn, bad-tempered beast she'd met four days before.

"Where are we going?" she asked when they plunged deeper into the forest.

"Back to the *Freewind*."

"You can't be serious. At night? Over this mountain? We'll never find our way."

"Don't worry. I'll find it. Besides, we have no choice. we've got to get off this island. At first light those goons are going to be on our trail."

"But, David, you've lost a lot of blood, and—"

"I can make it, Abbey. Don't worry."

He might as well have told the stars to disappear. Abbey worried every step of the way. Despite David's claim, she knew he was feeling less than chipper. He forged on, but there was a telling drag to his steps, and his labored breathing betrayed the effort it cost him to keep moving. Though she couldn't see in the darkness, Abigail was certain he was pale.

They hiked for hours, straight through the night. For all Abigail knew, they could have been going in a circle. She didn't know how anyone could tell north from south in the inky darkness. But then her sense of direction was shaky under the best of conditions. David, however, seemed confident they were headed the right way and that was good enough for her.

Chelsea, who had gotten bored with the strange night-time hike through the woods, curled up in the purse pocket and slept while the two adults trudged on.

Much to Abigail's concern, David's stamina dwindled as the night wore on. Her anxiety tripled when, after several hours, he draped his arm over her shoulder and leaned on her for support.

"David, we have to stop," she pleaded. "You can't go on like this."

"I'm fine. Just a little woozy, is all. We'll be there soon, and I can rest then."

Soon turned out to be another hour. They stumbled onto the small beach just before dawn, exhausted and gasping, and collapsed on the sand. Only after they had rested a few minutes did a horrible thought occur to Abigail.

"Oh my stars. How are we going to get to the boat? The skiff is in San Cristobal, and the life preservers are on the *Freewind*."

"We'll swim."

"Oh, sure. You know I can't swim that far, and your arm is so stiff you'd never make it, even supposing you had the strength. Which you don't."

That earned her a dark look. "You know, for such a retiring female you're sure becoming mouthy all of a sudden."

Abigail sniffed. "It's the company I've been keeping."

David grunted, but she noticed he did not deny the charge.

He looked around the beach and pointed to a big piece of driftwood. "We'll use that as a flotation device."

With Chelsea, Abigail's purse and their clothes riding on top, they held on to the chunk of wood and paddled out across the starlit cove to where the *Freewind* lay anchored.

They pulled themselves up on the deck and collapsed, winded and wrung out. With supreme indifference to their condition, Chelsea took her toy puppy from Abigail's purse, stepped daintily around the puddles of water forming around their prone bodies and disappeared below deck.

"We made it," Abigail gasped. "Oh, David, we made it."

"Damn right."

Rolling onto her back, Abigail gave a tired laugh, then suddenly pumped her arms and legs straight up in the air and let out a victorious whoop. "Wahoo! By golly, we showed them! The good guys win again! That'll teach them to mess with us!"

David made a face. "Don't get too cocky, Legs," he said dryly. "We won a skirmish, not the war. And we barely got out with our hides, don't forget."

She rolled over, coming down half on top of him, and planted smacking kisses over his face and neck and chest. "But we won! And we'll do it again!"

Grasping her shoulders, he held her away, and studied her face, a look of surprise dawning on his. "You're actually beginning to enjoy this, aren't you?"

"Well... I wouldn't say 'enjoy' exactly, but... Oh, David! I feel so... so alive! I guess this brush with danger has made me appreciate life more, has made me realize that there is more to living than playing it safe. There are all kinds of things out there to experience—good and bad. And the bad just makes you appreciate the good that much more." She cocked her head to one side. "Am I making any sense?"

"Yeah. More so than you might think."

Vaguely she heard the despondent note in his voice, but she was too keyed up to question it.

"Not that I wasn't scared, mind you. A few times I thought I was going to die of pure fright. I still shiver to think of it," she said, her voice turning somber.

With the admission, the spurt of high-spirited triumph faded, and Abigail began to tremble in earnest as the fright and the tears she had held at bay all evening came rushing to the surface. "Oh, David, for a while there I thought . . . I thought we were going to die." Her voice wobbled at the end, and at once, David's uninjured arm tightened around her.

"Aw, Abbey, baby, take it easy. It's over now. We got away. And we'll get out of this mess yet, you'll see."

Abigail believed him. She had complete faith in David. But her shivers intensified anyway. The thought of how close they'd come, of what that hulking beast, Ivor, might have done to her—to both of them—didn't bear thinking about.

"Hold me, David," she murmured against his neck. Her arms went around him as his big hand stroked her back. She clutched his strong body with all her might, unable to get close enough. She buried her face against his neck and inhaled his scent. Her lips nibbled and her tongue stroked, and she tasted the salty tang of seawater on his skin. Her fingers clutched at him, her movements becoming wild and frantic.

Catching her urgency, David crushed her to him. "Oh, God, Abbey. Abbey. It feels so damn good to hold you again."

They kissed and touched and stroked, and kissed again, both consumed by the desperate need to prove, in the most basic way, that they were, indeed, still alive, that they truly had managed to survive the terror and danger of the past few hours. They were driven to taste and touch and smell and see and hear. Both had to experience again that feeling of oneness and joy they had found only with each other.

All rational thought fled. Driven, Abigail became a purely sensual creature, acting solely on instinct, primitive instinct that demanded she reaffirm the precious life force that pulsed within her. Her breathing became raspy, her movements frenzied. Her hands slid down his back and burrowed under his bikini undershorts. Her fingers dug into his tight buttocks, squeezing, flexing. Despite the mild night,

Abigail's shivers increased, and she strained closer, greedily absorbing his warmth.

Roughly David snatched at the fasteners on her bra, jerking the hooks free. He tore the flimsy garment from her and tossed it aside as he rolled onto his back, bringing her to lie on top of him. His thumbs hooked under the elastic waistband on her panties and shoved them down around her knees. Wiggling and squirming, her mouth still fused with his, Abigail worked the scrap of cotton the rest of the way off and kicked it aside.

She smoothed her hands down his sides and encountered the narrow band of elastic at his hips. Her open mouth ran over his neck, his collarbone, the thatch of dark hair on his chest. She scooted lower and kissed and nipped her way over his hard abdomen to the band of elastic on his scandalous undershorts. She nuzzled lower, her breath warming the wet cloth and the swelling bulge that strained against it.

David's body jerked, and he groaned and clutched her shoulders. "Oh, Lord, Abbey, hurry. Hurry! I can't stand much more of this."

Abigail sat back on her heels and surveyed him through narrowed eyes—his magnificent body, his dear, battered face, that outrageous strip of leopard-print silk that stretched across his hips and molded his swollen manhood. Love filled her heart, and her chest ached with possessive pride. Her lover. Her love.

"Abbey, please."

Smiling, she peeled the leopard print down his legs and tossed it over her shoulder. Kneeling again between his thighs, she touched him intimately, her fingertips stroking with a tormenting feather-light touch that made his hips jerk.

The gentle caress pushed David over the edge, and with a low growl, he rose up, grasped her hips and brought her forward until she straddled his body. Gazing into his eyes, she obeyed the silent urging of his hands and lowered herself onto him. Slowly—oh, so slowly—their bodies achieved that perfect fit. Abigail gasped. David growled again and arched his neck.

A taut stillness. A breathless savoring. Then the movement began.

Moaning, her fingers clenching in the hair on his chest, Abigail threw her head back, lost in pleasure. David surged upward powerfully, setting the pace, driving them to the brink. Abigail's hips rocked to his rhythm, her urgency matching his.

The release came quickly, an explosion of pleasure. Abigail cried out as the exquisite convulsions overtook her. Her back arched, her head went back, her nails dug into his chest. Pushed over the edge by her ecstasy, David's hoarse cry followed hers as he reached his own completion, his hips lifting off the deck.

When it was over, Abigail collapsed limply on his chest. She lay gasping for breath, vaguely aware of David's thundering heartbeat, the strong rise and fall of his chest beneath her cheek. A moment later his moan jolted her back to reality as efficiently as a bucket of cold water in the face.

"Oh, my stars! What have I done? Your arm!" Abigail scrambled off of him and knelt at his side, wringing her hands, her expression stricken. "Oh, David, I'm so sorry. I don't know how I could have forgotten your injury. Are you all right? Did I hurt you? I don't know what came over m— That is . . . well, I do, of course, but . . . I mean . . . you're wounded and in pain and I—" She gave her hands another twist. "Oh, dear."

David chuckled. "I don't think you have to worry anymore, sweetheart. Believe me, if that didn't kill me, nothing will."

"Oh, God . . ." Abigail groaned. "I'm so sorry."

"Hell, I'm not." Raising on one elbow, he hooked a hand around her neck and brought her face down to his for a lingering kiss that set Abigail's heart to thrumming and made her forget what she was saying. When their lips parted, he grinned at her dazed look. His brown eyes sparkled with wicked delight. "But you know, baby," he whispered, "if you're gonna keep on seducing me this way, you're gonna have to get over being embarrassed about it afterward."

"*Seduce* you! Why, I did no such thing! It was—"

David chuckled and fell back on the deck, and Abigail made a face.

"Oh, you," she admonished, giving him a poke in the ribs.

Still laughing he got to his feet and extended his hand to her. "C'mon. Let's go below and get this thing bandaged so you can quit worrying and we can get the hell out of here. We left a trail even a city slicker could follow in the daylight."

Bypassing the banquette seat where Chelsea lay curled up with her toy, Abigail seated David on the bed with strict instructions not to move. After slipping into her baggy walking shorts and shirt, she scurried around gathering bandages and medicine and hot water and soap. The makeshift bandage she had applied hours earlier was streaked with dirt and grime and soaked with saltwater. When she cut it away, she sucked in her breath.

The bullet had only grazed him, but it had gouged a nasty furrow in his upper arm. The wound was deep and raw, and the flesh around it looked swollen and angry. Abigail knew from the stiff way David held his arm that it was painful, but as far as she could tell, no serious damage had been done.

Fussing over him like a mother hen, she cleansed the raw wound with soap and water first, the poured alcohol over it.

"Ow! *Ow!*" David yelped, flinching. "Dammit, that burns!"

"Oh, poor baby." Abigail patted his cheek as though he were four years old. "You men are such big hairy-chested heroes. You stand toe-to-toe and beat each other to bloody pulps without a peep, but act like crybabies over a little alcohol."

Grumbling something about a fight being different and women not understanding, David gave her a sour look as she smeared antibiotic cream on the wound.

When she'd finished applying a fresh bandage, she helped him put on a clean shirt, and as he buttoned it, she gathered up the supplies. Bending over, she picked up the dirty bandage from the floor and straightened to find David watching her.

"Nice tush," he said, wriggling his eyebrows in an exaggerated leer.

Abigail looked back at him through narrowed eyes. He grinned, waiting for her reaction. *Oh, no you don't. Not this time.* Beneath that rough exterior David was a caring man, but he was also, she was fast coming to realize, an outrageous tease. Well, if he thought he could retaliate for her crybaby remark by getting her all flustered again, he had another think coming.

She subjected him to a slow, frankly lascivious once-over that finally settled on his rear end. Her sultry gaze lifted, and she smiled. "Yours isn't so bad, either."

He looked so stunned, she had to bite the insides of her cheeks to keep from laughing as she turned and strolled out with a deliberate hip-swaying walk.

He caught up with her as she was stretching to return the first-aid kit to the overhead cabinet in the galley. Catching her chin in the V of his palm, he turned her face up and kissed her long and hotly, then straightened and looked into her eyes. "Mouthy female," he muttered.

"C'mon, the sun is coming up." Grabbing her hand, he led her toward the steps. "It's time to get out of here. And you're going to be the skipper."

"What?" Abigail hung back. "Me, drive this boat? I can't do that!"

"Steer, Legs. Steer. Not drive. And you have to. My arm is too stiff to do it, and it's throbbing like hell. Anyway, I don't think I have the strength to turn the wheel."

"Oh, my stars. Well, if your precious boat ends up wrecked on the coral reef, just don't blame me."

David paled. "Don't even say that."

The sky was turning a pearl gray as they climbed up on deck. Under David's watchful eye, Abigail weighed anchor. On the bridge he explained all the dials and gauges on the console, instructed her on how to start the engines, how to operate the throttle, how to keep the boat on a steady course. Concentrating, Abigail chewed on her bottom lip and nodded.

He turned the key and pressed the starter, and the engines rumbled to life, vibrating the deck under their feet. Abigail looked at David, looked at the array of dials, swallowed hard and grasped the wheel with one hand and the throttle with the other.

"Okay, let 'er rip," David said.

The unfortunate choice of words aptly described their roaring takeoff across the cove. The boat reared up and lunged forward like a highspirited horse that had been spurred.

"Holy shi—!"

David flew backward in a drunken stagger and would have fallen off the bridge if he hadn't grabbed the rail. Abigail would have, too, if she hadn't been clutching the steering wheel with a death grip.

"No! No! Cut back on the throttle!" he yelled.

Abigail jerked the lever back. The engine roar changed to a purr, and the prow dropped. Except for the forward drift of momentum, they were at full stop.

David stumbled forward holding his injured arm close to his side, and gripped the rail around the console with his other hand. "Dammit, Abbey! Where did you get your driver's license, out of a grab bag?"

"There's no need to be insulting. I told you I didn't know anything about driving a boat. And for your information, I happen to be an excellent driver. On land."

He made a disbelieving sound. "I think it would be best," he said in a tight voice, "if I operated the throttle. You just concentrate on steering."

That was fine with Abigail. She preferred to keep both hands on the wheel anyway. Besides, the gas pedal ought to be on the floor where it belonged.

With David controlling their speed, they eased through the water at a crawl. Because of nerves and inexperience, Abigail had a tendency to overcompensate but she did all right until they entered the narrow passageway leading out of the cove.

"A little to the right," David instructed, and Abigail gave the wheel a turn.

"No! Too much! Left! Left! Left!"

She spun the wheel left, and immediately he changed his tune.

"Not that much. Right! Right! Look out for that bank! Back to the left! Dammit, woman! What're you trying to do? Run us aground?"

"I turned the way you said every time!"

"I said a *little* to the right, for Pete's sake! A *little!*"

Through the entire passageway the boat zigged and zagged from one bank to the other, scraping overhanging limbs and bumping the sandy bottom, with David yelling directions every breath and Abigail frantically trying to follow them. When at last they hit open waters, it was a toss up who was more relieved.

David sighed and muttered a fervent "Thank God," but his relief was premature and short-lived. On the open sea Abigail skippered the boat with all the finesse and skill of a demolition derby driver. David was just grateful that there weren't many other boaters out at that hour.

He was exhausted, he was hungry, his arm hurt like hell and he would have given ten years of his life for a cigarette, but he didn't dare go below to search for one with Abigail at the helm.

He watched her, poised and tense over the wheel, gripping so tight her fingerprints were no doubt permanently imbedded in the surface. He shook his head, his feelings a mixture of exasperation and affection. How could an otherwise competent woman be such a menace behind the wheel of a boat? *His* boat, for Pete's sake!

David endured the entire trip in a state of high anxiety that overrode even the pain in his arm. Nothing in his thirty-seven years had ever looked so good to him as the island of Rincon lying peaceful and serene in the early-morning sunshine. Of course, Abigail bumped the pier several times and nearly sheared the inside ramp off the boat house before the *Freewind* was berthed, but at least they made it. When David turned off the engines, he hung his head for a minute, savoring the relief.

As they stepped off the *Freewind,* he did not let his gaze even flicker toward the hull. Between the boat getting shot to hell and gone and Abbey's Keystone Cops brand of skippering, he had already resigned himself to putting it into dry dock for repairs and paint before he left Alhaja Verde to return to work.

Work. He paused in the act of locking the boat house and thought about how strange that sounded. The high-pressure job with Telecom International, the constant travel it entailed, his carefree bachelor life-style, all seemed so remote, like part of another life. Though he'd met her only a few days ago, Abbey was the center of his world now, and he could not imagine a future that did not include her.

The trend of his thoughts startled him. *Hey, take it easy, Blaine. That's crazy. You're letting yourself get caught up in the drama of the situation. That's all.*

This was an interlude. When this business was settled, Abbey would return to Waco and her bookstore, and he'd fly to Brussels to check on the security at Telecom's operation there. In a few months this wild escapade would be just a distant memory. Why, before long neither of them would be able to recall what the other even looked like, he told himself staunchly.

He turned and found Abigail watching him, her beautiful aquamarine eyes full of concern, and a painful tightness squeezed his chest.

"You look terrible. Here, lean on me," she said, and slipped her arm around his waist as they started up the pier.

Feeling woozy again, he accepted her assistance without protest. Yes, their parting was inevitable, but it would be for the best.

The tightness in his chest increased, and he closed his eyes. Dammit! Even if he were ready to settle down—which he wasn't—it wouldn't be fair to Abbey. She was just beginning to come out of her shell and experience life. She was ripe for a little excitement. And after living with that old battle-ax for most of her life, she deserved a chance to spread her wings.

They were almost to the house when Abbey drew back, pulling David to a halt as well. "David..." Her fingers tightened on the side of his waist, and even through his exhaustion and confused thoughts he heard the apprehension in her voice. "David, someone is here."

His eyes snapped open, and his scowling gaze shot toward the house. There on the deck were two red-haired women.

David cursed, and Abigail looked at him with real alarm. "Do you think they're Sergio's agents?"

"Worse. Those are my sisters."

"Oh, dear."

"Exactly." Sighing, David urged Abigail forward. "C'mon. We might as well go face the terrible twosome. They've seen us, so it's too late to make a run for it."

Abigail's nerves twanged like a cheap guitar as they climbed the steps to the deck under the watchful eyes of the two women. She had no idea what kind of reception to expect from David's sisters. By now they would know that she and David had made use of their house, and regardless of his assurances otherwise, she felt like a trespasser.

How would they feel about their brother bringing a woman to their house? Especially one who spelled nothing but trouble? They were going to hate her, Abigail just knew it. By the time they reached the deck, she was feeling sick to her stomach. David's grumpy pessimism wasn't helping matters, either.

It was not quite seven o'clock, and the sisters were both in nightgowns and robes. One sat decorously in a padded lounger with a soft smile of welcome on her face. The other one perched on the railing, hands braced on either side of her hips, swinging her bare feet and eyeing them with undisguised curiosity.

David stopped at the top of the steps and glowered. "Great. Just what I need. What the hell are you two doing here?"

The woman sitting on the railing raised her eyebrows and answered his grumpiness with a droll, "It's wonderful to see you, too, brother dear. And we own this place. Remember?''

"That's right," her twin chimed in. "We should be asking you that question. Erin and I weren't expecting you until next week. Though, of course, you know that you're always welcome," she hastened to add.

The sisters had addressed their remarks to David, but Abigail was uncomfortably aware of their scrutiny. The woman on the lounger cast discreet glances her way, but the other one studied her with unabashed directness.

Both women had flawless skin and delicate features, and their red hair was set off by slanting brown eyes the exact shade of David's. They also shared the same stubborn jawline as their brother. In looks the twins were identical, but even if her sister hadn't called her by name, from what David had told Abigail about them, she would have known that the one with the bold stare and impudent twinkle in her eye was Erin. The other one, with her soft smile and quiet manner could only be Elise.

They were gorgeous creatures. Somehow Abigail hadn't expected that—perhaps because of David's ruggedly appealing but less than perfect looks.

Dazzled by their beauty, Abigail squirmed at David's side, uncomfortably aware that the makeup she had applied the day before was gone; that much of her hair, which was sticky and stiff from the swim across the cove, had been pulled loose from the braid by brambles and branches during their all-night trek and hung in an unkempt mess around her face; that her baggy shorts, though clean, were faded from numerous dunkings in salt water and in desperate need of ironing; that her legs and arms were covered with scratches. She didn't need a mirror to know that she looked like the wrath of God. And beside this gorgeous pair she probably looked even worse.

Chelsea poked her head over the top of the purse pocket and looked at the two women, her button eyes bright. Elise was immediately captivated. "Oh, what an adorable dog! It's a Yorkshire terrier, isn't it?"

"Yes," Abigail replied. "Her name is Chelsea."

Chelsea liked women, and in response to such enthusiasm, she jumped down and trotted over to make Elise's acquaintance, her stubby plumed tail waving like a silk pompom.

"She's precious." As Elise ooohed and ahhhed, David shot her and the dog a black look.

"I thought you weren't going to be here until next week," he growled.

"Elise and I decided to come down a few days early and open the place up. But you beat us to it. You and Miss... uh..." Erin cast a none-too-subtle glance at Abigail, then looked at her brother and waited for him to take the hint.

He did, though not graciously, making the introductions in a terse voice.

"I hope you don't mind that David brought me here uninvited?" Abigail asked worriedly. "It was... well, sort of an emergency, you see."

At once, Erin's eyes lit up, and David groaned.

"Really? What kind of emergency?"

"Uh..."

"None of your business," David snapped. "And where the devil are Max and Sam?"

"They're still in Santa Fe, tied up in some important business deal. They'll be here in a few days."

"Oh, great! That's just great! Here I thought you'd found husbands who were up to watching out for you. What were they thinking of, letting the two of you come down here alone?"

"David, for goodness' sake," Elise scolded as she stroked Chelsea's head. "We're grown women now, not children. We don't need guardians."

"C'mon. This is me you're talking to. *I know* the kind of mischief you two can get into without half trying." His eyes cut to Erin. "And some people go looking for it."

Elise hid a smile behind her hand. Erin stuck her tongue out at him and went back to grilling Abigail. "So, Abbey, how long have you known our brother?"

"Not . . . not long." She felt David begin to sag, and she tightened her hold on his waist and leaned in more to prop him up. How long she could manage, she didn't know. She was ready to drop herself.

"Oh?" Erin looked pointedly at David's arm, draped around Abigail's shoulders, and the close alignment of their bodies. "And how did you meet?"

"I . . . well . . ."

"Knock it off, Erin. Didn't Mom teach you it's rude to give a guest the third degree."

"Oh! I'm sorry." At once she switched her attention to her brother. "So how long have you and Abbey been here?"

David gave a long-suffering sigh. "We got here night before last."

"Is that right? We arrived last night. Where were you?"

"Out."

"No kidding." Erin looked them over, her lips pursed. "I'd say you were out partying except the two of you look like you've been jerked through a knothole backward. Care to explain?"

"No, I wouldn't. Now if you don't mind, we're both bushed. We're going to get some shut-eye." He took a wobbly step, but Erin hopped off the rail and blocked their path.

"Would you like for me to get another room ready?" she asked guilelessly. "I noticed the mattress in one of the guest rooms you were using has been burned."

"We'll manage with one," he ground out, much to Erin's delight. That she had ferreted out the information pleased her immensely, and she shot her sister an "I told you so" look.

Under normal circumstances Abigail would have been mortified by David's bluntness, but she felt him sag a bit more, and concern for him blocked every other consideration out of her mind. When Erin opened her mouth to ask more questions, Abigail cut her off. She knew that David was trying to keep his sisters from learning of their situation, but the time for shilly-shallying around had passed.

"I'm sorry, Erin, but I must put David to bed. He's been shot and he's lost a lot of blood. We've also been up for the past twenty-four hours."

"Shot!"

"Oh, my lord!"

Elise leaped out of the lounger and rushed over to them, and Erin quickly added her support to David's other side. Both sisters started firing questions at once.

"How was he shot? Where? What happened? Who did it? Has he seen a doctor? David Blaine, you blockhead! Why in the world didn't you say so right away?"

"Don't fuss. Look, it's not serious," David insisted. "It's just a flesh wound. All I need is a few hours sleep and a thick steak and I'll be as good as new."

"At least let us take you to Alhaja Verde to a doctor," Elise pleaded.

"No! None of us is going anywhere near Alhaja Verde. And don't either of you try to go for a doctor while I'm asleep. For that matter, if anyone—anyone at all—comes near this place, either by land or water, you're to wake me at once. Now both of you get inside and lock the doors and stay there. I mean it. And I want you both to promise you'll do as I say." Even as weak as he was, his hard look was intimidating.

The twins exchanged a worried glance. Erin grimaced but she nodded and agreed grudgingly. "Oh, all right. We'll do it. But when you wake up, you've got some serious explaining to do, brother dear."

"Abbey, wake up."

The whisper penetrated layers of sleep, but Abigail resisted it. Sighing, she wriggled her face deeper into the pillow.

"C'mon, Abbey. Time to face the music."

Abigail smiled. The male voice in her ear was familiar...pleasantly so, and it sent a tingle down her nerve endings. She blinked her eyes open and encountered laughing brown ones just inches away. David. Her heart did a flip. Dear, wonderful David.

She smiled with sleepy invitation and touched his face. He appealed to her as no man ever had, with his pugnacious jaw and his tough, rough-around-the-edges look. Even the bruises and the cut above his eye merely enhanced his vibrant maleness. His was such a strong face—and so beloved.

"Here now. None of that." He caught her hand as it stroked his jaw and carried it to his mouth. His lips were warm on her palm, and Abigail shivered when she felt the sweep of his tongue. Anticipation trembled through her, and she leaned toward him, her lips yearning. He obliged her with a hot, hard, plunging kiss that melted her bones. Then his mouth was withdrawn, and at the same instant he delivered a stinging slap to her rear end.

She jerked to a sitting position and glared at him. He grinned back. "We don't have time for you to seduce me right now," he said audaciously.

"Sedu— Why you..." Abigail whacked him in the face with a pillow, but he just laughed.

"C'mon, sweetheart. Shake a leg. It's the middle of the afternoon already. We've been asleep for six hours. That's about the limit to Erin's patience. She'll be barging in here soon if we don't come out."

"Six hours! Is that all?" Abigail groaned and held her head between her palms. She could sleep twice that long with no problem.

"Hit the shower, woman. You've got to help me convince my sisters to go back to Santa Fe. Now move it."

Abigail squinted her eyes at David. For the first time she noticed that he was clean shaven. They had both been so exhausted, they had fallen into bed as they were, barely taking the time to strip off their outer clothing. Now he smelled of soap and after-shave, his hair was combed, and he was wearing fresh jeans and a clean cotton shirt. After a mere six hours sleep he looked disgustingly chipper, all bright-eyed and energetic, and his skin bloomed with healthy color. The man's recuperative powers were amazing.

Abigail, on the other hand, felt positively grubby, which was the reason she did not take exception to his bossiness, other than to shoot him a glare as she padded to the bathroom. Thirty minutes later she felt better able to face his beautiful sisters. David refused to give her time to do her hair, and it hung down her back like a wet cape, but at least she was clean and wearing one of her new sundresses, and she had on makeup.

When they entered the living room, Elise was nervously sipping tea with Chelsea curled up in her lap, while Erin paced the floor. Both pounced the moment Abigail and David appeared.

"All right. Out with it. Who shot you and why?" Erin demanded before they could say a word.

"How do you feel, David?" Elise asked. "We've been worried sick."

"Jeez. Will you two give us a break? Couldn't we at least have a bite to eat first? We're starving, for crying out loud."

"Elise already has sandwiches made, but you'll have to eat while you talk because we're not waiting any longer," Erin commanded, herding them over to the stools at the bar as her twin hurried into the kitchen. "Now start at the beginning. And don't leave anything out."

Abigail remained silent while David related the harrowing events of the past few days. She devoured tuna sandwiches and chips, and watched his sisters' expressions run the gamut of emotions—from amusement when they heard how she and David had met, to surprise and horror over how an innocent bystander had been caught in the middle of an apparent espionage operation, to shock, then outrage over the Russian agents' violent attempts to abduct her.

"So you can see, it would be best if the two of you returned to Santa Fe on the next plane. I don't know how much time we have before they discover this place."

Elise looked uncertain, but Erin bristled. "Don't be silly. We're not going anywhere. We're your sisters. We want to help. Don't we, Elise?"

"Well . . ."

"You are *not* staying, and that's that."

"Oh, yeah! Well this is our house and you can't make us leave. So there!"

In a blink the argument escalated into a full-scale shouting match with brother and sister standing almost nose to nose.

Unused to such sibling wrangles, Abigail squirmed. To get out of the line of fire, she eased off the bar stool and wandered over to the French doors at the front of the room, pretending an interest in the ocean view. After a moment, a movement down the beach caught her attention. As she studied the bobbing dot, her eyes widened and prickles of alarm crawled over her scalp.

"Oh, my stars! David come quick! There's a man on the beach, and he'd heading this way!"

Chapter Thirteen

The heated argument ceased abruptly.

"Get away from the doors. And you two get down." David rushed across the room and pushed Abigail aside even as he issued the terse orders. Keeping her behind him, he flattened out against the adjacent wall and peered around the edge of the glass door.

The sun glared off the white sand beach, and David squinted his eyes to study the strolling figure. The man was just ambling along as though he hadn't a care in the world. He was coming from the direction of the Chapulta, the fishing village at the other end of the island where the ferryboat from Alhaja Verde called twice a day. He could be a tourist, though that was unlikely; there was only the village and a few private vacation homes on Rincon.

Slung over the man's back was a small canvas duffel. He did not appear to be carrying a weapon of any kind, but David knew that appearances could be deceiving.

"Can you tell who it is?" Erin asked from where she and Elise crouched behind one of the sofas.

"Not quite yet. Although . . . there is something familiar about . . ." David's head jutted forward, and his eyes widened as he studied the man's lanky stride. "Ah, hell, I don't believe it!"

"What? Who is it?"

"Oh, dear."

"Is it one of Sergio's men?"

"Hell, no," David muttered with utter disgust. "It's Travis."

"Travis!" Elise and Erin jumped up and rushed to the French doors.

"It is! It's him. I'd know that loose-limbed saunter anywhere," Erin whooped.

They all went out on the deck, and David's sisters waved. Spotting them, Travis waved back and jogged for the steps. He'd barely reached the deck when Elise and Erin rushed forward and threw their arms around his neck, nearly knocking him down.

"Travis! It's so good to see you."

"It's been so long! You look wonderful!"

Laughing, their cousin returned the exuberant greetings, and when the hugs and kisses were done, he turned his lazy grin on David. "Hello, Cuz. I thought I'd find you here."

"What the hell is this?" David snarled. "A family reunion? I brought Abbey here because I thought it would be a safe house, not to introduce her to my nutty relatives."

Travis chuckled, not the least put off by his cousin's ill humor. "I take it this lovely lady is Miss Stewart," he said, turning his twinkling gray eyes on Abbey. He dropped his duffel on the deck and took her hand between both of his. "I'm Travis McCall, cousin to this bad-tempered oaf. And whatever he's told you about me, it's all a lie. I swear it."

Abigail stammered some sort of greeting, though what, she couldn't have said. She was too busy staring. She had not given much thought to what David's cousin looked like. Even if she had, never in a million years would she have dreamed he'd be this wild-looking, devil-may-care charmer.

Travis McCall looked like a cross between a movie star, a pirate, and a bum. He appeared to be seven or eight years younger than David, somewhere around thirty. His thick blond hair, clipped short on the top and sides, hung below his shoulders in the back, and he wore a folded bandanna tied across his forehead like a sweatband. Reddish brown beard stubble covered the lower half of his face. A pair of disreputable sneakers, tied together by their laces, hung over one of his shoulders, the tight T-shirt that molded his chest was faded to an unrecognizable color, and beneath the holey jeans, which were rolled halfway up his calves, his legs and bare feet were coated with sand. His features were chiseled handsome, his body lean and muscled, and he moved with a hip-rolling saunter that no woman alive could watch without her thoughts straying to the bedroom. Come-hither gray eyes, a heart-stopping grin and eyelashes any female over the age of twelve would kill for, completed the rakish look. That...and the two-inch-long gold earring in the shape of a dagger dangling from his left ear.

If Abigail's notion of what an FBI man looked like had been shaken by David and turned upside down by Leo Bates, Travis McCall shattered the Eliot Ness fantasy into a million pieces.

Abigail's cheeks pinkened as the daring young man continued to hold her hand and look her up and down. "I must say, Cuz, if I had known Miss Stewart was so attractive I'd have hopped a plane and come down to help you out that first day."

"Knock it off, Travis," David growled, drilling his cousin with a hard look. "And I don't recall asking for your help. How did you find us, anyway?"

"Are we going to stand around out here all afternoon?" Erin demanded. "Why don't we go inside and get comfortable."

Elise added her own urgings, and Travis brushed the sand off his feet and legs and followed the twins through the door, grinning back over his shoulder at David. "It was a simple matter. I called Telecom headquarters and asked to speak to you. When they told me you were on vacation, I figured you'd either be on your boat or here. And you don't have to ask for my help," he said with a taunting smile.

"You're kin. I feel obligated to bail you out of whatever trouble you're in."

Chelsea stood stiff legged in the middle of the living room and growled at the newcomer, her lip lifted over sharp little teeth. Without pause, Travis squatted down and patted the dog's silky head. "Hello there, girl. My, aren't you a cutie."

David's mouth dropped when the tiny terrier instantly abandoned her ferocious stance and rolled over on her back to have her tummy rubbed. As Travis obliged, he looked up at David, his expression turning grave.

"You know, Cuz, if I could find you, others can, too. I had the advantage of being a relative and knowing about this place, so I beat them here by a day or so, but it's just a matter of time."

"I know, dammit."

Travis gave Chelsea a final pat and sprawled out on one of the sofas beside Elise. The Yorkie, not ready to be dismissed, jumped up in his lap and looked adoringly at him while he stroked her back. "So why don't you tell me what's going on and we'll put our heads together and see if we can work it out?"

David gave the dog a disgusted glare. "Damned animal tries to bite my hand off whenever I get near her," he muttered under his breath, settling on the opposite sofa.

As David filled Travis in on all that had happened, Abigail noticed the sharp intelligence in the younger man's eyes and the intent way he listened. She realized that the wild young rebel look and devil-may-care charm he exuded were excellent cover.

Not that both weren't genuine. She had a feeling that Travis McCall was hell on wheels when it came to women, and that thumbing his nose at convention probably came as naturally to him as breathing.

"So, you think Leo Bates has turned?" Travis asked when he'd heard the whole story.

"It looks that way," David replied. "Either that, or he had orders to set us up. If so, that raises the question of why?"

"Do you have any idea what Abbey has that this Sergio character wants? That's the key."

"The American working for them mentioned a list, but Abbey doesn't have anything like that on her, which means we're probably looking for a microdot. I went through her things and came up empty."

"Maybe you missed something. Why don't we have another look."

Reluctantly Abigail handed over her purse for another search. His mouth twitching with suppressed amusement, David watched his cousin's face as he upended the bag and began to empty the numerous compartments. By the time everything was heaped in a pile on the floor, Travis was as flabbergasted as David had been the first time. Even Elise and Erin looked stunned.

"Good Lord," Travis murmured.

"Amazing, isn't it?" David grinned at Abigail, who squirmed on the sofa. "Abbey likes to be prepared."

"If you'll recall," she said haughtily, "a few of those things have come in quite handy."

For the next half hour David and Travis examined every single item minutely, with no luck.

"Well, that's it. We're stymied," David said. "We've gone over everything twice and there's no—" He stopped and looked at Chelsea. The dog lay curled up in the corner of the sofa with her toy puppy. "Wait a minute. There is one thing we haven't examined."

"What?" the others asked in unison.

"That stuffed toy, that's what. It was in the side pocket of Abbey's purse along with Chelsea when she was on that plane."

"Well, c'mon, what're we waiting for?"

But not even Travis's charm was potent enough to separate Chelsea from her "puppy." When he reached for the toy, the little dog snarled and snapped. He felt the graze of sharp little teeth and jumped back, nursing his hand.

David fared no better, and in the end they had to enlist Abigail's help.

"Hurry, please," she said, holding the hysterical dog in her arms while David and Travis moved away at a safe distance to examine the stuffed animal.

Chelsea lunged and barked, straining to get at them as they poked and squeezed and inspected each seam. Her barks became even more frantic when David popped the clear plastic cover off one of the eyes. "Nutsy, neurotic fur ball," he growled back.

Then he forgot the dog as he plucked out the floating pupil. "Ah-ha! Pay dirt!" He held the round dot up to the light. "Boys and girls, I believe we've found the list that Sergio wants so bad."

"What do you think it is?" Elise asked, wringing her hands.

"Given the CIA's interest, I'd say vital government secrets. Without an enlarger, I can't read it, so I don't know what."

"Now that you've found it, what're you going to do with it?" Erin questioned.

"For now, put it back where it was." He slipped the dot back into the convex plastic cover, snapped it onto the white "eyeball," and tossed the toy back to Chelsea. "There you go, girl, as good as new."

Abigail released the dog, and after giving the two men a last warning growl, she took her toy and raced out of the room.

"What's our next move?" Travis inquired.

David's face hardened. "For starters, I'm going back to Alhaja Verde and find Leo Bates and get some answers. Even if I have to kick butt to do it."

Excitement poured through Abigail at the prospect of taking action against the little weasel who had set them up, and she jumped up out of her chair, her eyes alight. "Yeah! Let's go kick some butt!" she cheered with pugnacious relish.

"Oh, Lord," David groaned, rolling his eyes heavenward. "I've created a monster." He looked at Travis and shook his head. "Would you believe, just a few days ago she was a timid little thing who swore she could never strike a soul?''

"You're the one who told me to loosen up and go with the flow," Abigail said with a lift of her chin.

"Yeah, well, not this much. And you can forget going back to Alhaja Verde. You're staying here with Elise and Erin, where it's safe . . . at least for now."

"Whoa. Just a minute, brother of mine. Who says we're staying here? Elise and I are going with you. We can help, too."

"Aw, hell." David pulled both hands down over his face. "God, I need a cigarette," he muttered, then glared. "Look, you women aren't going, and that's that."

"Oh, yeah? Says who?" Erin bristled, and the battle was on.

Abigail and Elise joined in as well. Travis folded his arms over his chest, crossed his legs at the ankles and sat back with a grin to watch the fireworks as David tried to outshout and outargue three women.

"As usual you're being a pigheaded, overprotective chauvinistic jerk!"

"Erin is right, David. You do have a tendency to shelter us too much. We are your sisters but we're not little girls anymore. We don't need big brother hovering over us."

"Now look. We're not talking about a picnic here. This is going to be dangerous."

"Oh, really? And what we've been doing for the past few days hasn't been?" Abigail challenged.

"There was no other choice then. There is now."

"That's my point," Erin interjected, fixing him with an exasperated glare. "And if you would shut up and listen instead of bellowing orders, you'd learn that there is another choice. I have a better plan for getting the information you need, one a lot less dangerous than getting into a brawl."

"Oh, terrific. I can hardly wait to hear this." David addressed the sarcastic remark to the ceiling, his mouth turned down in a derisive grimace.

"Señor Santana is giving a party tonight at his home on Alhaja Ver—"

"A *party!* You want us to go to a *party!* Of all the stu—"

"Oh, shut up, David, and hear her out."

The sharp order, coming from Elise, stunned David so, he obeyed without thinking.

"Señor Fernando Ramón Joaquin Vega de Santana is the chief politico of the islands," Erin explained, shooting her brother a smug look. "Very little occurs on any of them that he doesn't know about. If approached carefully, it's possible that we could persuade him to shed some light on this situation."

"You know . . . that's not bad," Travis said.

David frowned. "What kind of man is this Señor Santana? Can we trust him?"

"That depends," Erin answered. "He's ambitious, shrewd and manipulative. His loyalties are questionable, his ethics even more so. But . . . he is quite interested in working a deal with Max and Sam to export local arts and crafts though Global Imports, skimming his cut off the top, of course. I would think that would be incentive enough for him to help us."

"Mmm, maybe. It depends on what the other side has to offer. But it might be worth a shot."

"If it doesn't work out, we can always go back to Plan A and wring the information out of Leo," Travis drawled.

"Okay, we'll do it. But I still don't think it's safe to take Abbey back to Alhaja Verde, so you women will stay here while Travis and I will go to the party."

"Oh, no, I'm afraid you're wrong there, David," Elise informed him sweetly. "You see, the invitation is for the Lawfords and the Delanys. Security is very tight at these affairs. Without Erin and me, you couldn't get through the front gate. So like it or not, we're coming with you."

David cursed, but Erin pretended not to hear him. "Good. Then it's settled. You men can wear Sam's and Max's tuxedos, and I'm sure that between us, Elise and I can find something for Abbey."

"Of course we can," Elise agreed. "How about that slinky aqua sheath of yours. It would look wonderful with her eyes."

"You're right. It would be perfect. She's shorter than we are, so we'll have to hem it up, but otherwise it should fit."

"Oh, I don't know," Abigail protested as the two women hustled her toward one of the bedroom wings. "I just wouldn't feel right about borrowing—"

"Nonsense. We insist. And we'll do your makeup and hair, too. Elise gives a marvelous haircut." Erin lifted a handful of the long, still-damp tresses that hung down past Abigail's hips. "What do you think about cutting it to shoulder length, Elise?"

"Hold it right there!" The barked order brought the three women to a halt at the entrance to the right bedroom wing. They turned and found themselves facing David's wrathful glare. "Don't you cut so much as an inch off Abbey's hair. You got that? You do, and you'll wish you'd gone back to Santa Fe when you had the chance."

Abigail turned the color of a ripe tomato, and Travis struggled not to laugh. The twins blinked in surprise. They exchanged a quick glance, and identical slow grins tilted their lips. "Whatever you say, brother dear," Erin said wickedly, and slipped her arm through Abigail's. On Abigail's other side, Elise did the same.

As she walked down the hall between the sisters, she could feel their gazes on her pink face.

"Well, well, well," Erin drawled.

"Whew! You've got it bad, don't you, Cuz," Travis observed with a grin the moment the women disappeared from sight.

"Shut up, Travis."

David stomped to the bar and snatched up the telephone. He punched out a series of numbers as though he were driving nails with his fingertips.

"Who are you calling?"

David ignored him, and after a moment he barked into the mouthpiece, "I want to speak to either Max Delany or

Sam Lawford." A pause, then, "Look, lady, I don't give a rat's behind if they're in conference with the Prime Minister of Great Britain! This is their brother-in-law, and I'm calling about an emergency concerning their wives."

Swirling the champagne in his glass, David ground his teeth as he watched Señor Santana take Abbey's hand and pat it . . . again. Dammit, the man had been salivating over her like a dog with a meaty bone from the moment they walked through the door.

Santana was a smooth operator, he'd give the oily bastard that. He had cleverly managed to separate Abbey from their party and was standing talking with her, a few feet away.

Their host smiled into Abbey's eyes and touched her bare shoulder. David's eyes narrowed. His fingers tightened around the stem of the glass, and the hand in his pocket balled into a fist. The urge to knock the Latin Lothario's pearly teeth down his throat was becoming more irresistible by the second.

A light touch on David's arm caused him to start and drew his attention to his sister. He looked down into brown eyes that sparkled with wicked amusement, and his own narrowed even more.

"Did I forget to mention that Señor Santana is something of a ladies' man?" Erin asked a shade too innocently.

Elise giggled, and Travis rocked back on his heels, grinning.

David glared at the three of them. "Funny. Real funny."

When he looked at things objectively, he supposed he couldn't blame Señor Santana for being smitten. From the moment he'd first gotten a look at Abbey in that dress he'd been knocked for a loop himself . . . and he was *still* reeling.

That aqua sequined number fit that luscious body like a glove. It glittered and sparkled and clung to every dip and curve as faithfully as a lover's touch. He'd wanted to peel the thing off of her and make love to her on the spot the instant she'd walked into his sisters' living room.

But it was more than just the dress. Erin and Elise had redone her makeup to accentuate her best features, bringing out those beautiful eyes and high cheekbones. They'd styled her hair in a fancy upsweep, with part of it hanging down her back in a mass of soft curls that made his fingers itch to run through them. The way Abbey looked now, he couldn't believe that he had ever thought of her as just attractive. Hell, she was flat-out gorgeous.

Yes, from a purely objective view, he could understand Santana's fascination with Abbey.

But, dammit, he wasn't interested in looking at the situation objectively. Abbey was *his!* And he didn't want any Latin lover touching her—with his eyes or his hands.

David deposited his empty glass on the tray of a passing waiter and pulled a cigarette from the plastic bag in his inside pocket. He ignored the amused looks his sisters and cousin gave him. On the trip over from Rincon, when they had learned why he was searching the boat, they had all thought it hilarious that Abbey had hidden his cigarettes. Laughed like a pack of hyenas, the lot of them, he thought sourly, cupping a match to the end of the cigarette.

The stash in his pocket, which he'd found taped to the underside of the galley sink, was all he had. When they'd stopped by Pepe's to get him to keep an eye on the *Freewind* and Chelsea, the damned cigarette machine had been on the fritz. Or at least, that's what Pepe had claimed, but David was beginning to suspect that Abbey or his sisters had put a bug in his ear.

David drew on the cigarette, his gaze boring a hole through Señor Fernando Ramón Joaquin Vega de Santana. He was considering marching over there and yanking Abbey away from the lech—and to hell with asking for his help—when he happened to notice a man across the room who looked familiar. Where had he seen that guy recently? Then it hit him: it was the man he'd noticed in the lobby of Abbey's hotel—the one he'd known but couldn't place. He still couldn't, but he was more positive than ever that he knew him.

"Travis, see that guy over there standing by the pillar?" he said, not taking his eyes from the man. "Does he look familiar to you?"

Casually, Travis's gaze drifted in that direction. "Well, I'll be damned. That's Charley Higgins."

"Charley Higgins? Of course! That's the guy who left the Bureau to work for the CIA?"

"That's him. I'd heard scuttlebutt before I left D.C. that he was heading up a top-secret operation, but I didn't think about it being here."

David stubbed out his cigarette in a nearby ashtray. "C'mon. You and I are going to have a little talk with good ol' Charley."

"Hey! What about us?" Erin asked.

"Stay out of trouble. And keep an eye on Abigail for me," David said, and began to make his way around the dance floor.

Abigail's smile felt frozen. She murmured something noncommittal in reply to Señor Santana's latest suggestive remark and edged away a step. He, of course, edged right along with her. She was going to murder David Blaine. With her bare hands. Slowly. She had been expecting him to come to her rescue, but instead the clod had left her alone with this lecherous Latin. Now he and Travis were leaving the ballroom with another man.

At first, Señor Santana's attention had been flattering. She had been thrilled with Erin and Elise's handiwork, but David's stony silence when he'd seen her had been deflating. Señor Santana's interest had been a balm to her wounded ego. His slick charm had quickly lost its appeal, however.

Abigail was racking her brain for a way to escape their host without insulting him, when another man approached.

"Fernando, my friend," he said, addressing Señor Santana. "You have monopolized this lovely creature all evening. I must insist that you give the rest of us a chance." The men shook hands and greeted each other heartily. Fernando was not pleased, but only the hard glint in his eyes betrayed him as he performed the introduction with his usual effusive charm. He identified the man as Nathan Sumner, a businessman and yachtsman who vacationed often on Alhaja Verde.

Mr. Sumner was a tall, slender man of perhaps forty-five. His smooth good looks were set off by what appeared to be a perpetual tan and a thick shock of black hair, gone silver at the temples, which gave him a distinguished appearance. There was an air of power and wealth about him that was unmistakable.

Scarcely had Senor Sañtana finished the introduction than the band began a slow tune. Nathan Sumner turned to Abigail with a suave smile and took her hand. "Would you care to dance, Miss Stewart?"

Abigail accepted the invitation with the avidity of a drowning victim grabbing a lifeline. Excusing herself, she went into Nathan Sumner's arms and gave a sigh of relief as he whirled her across the dance floor.

"Correct me if I'm wrong, but I get the impression that you are . . . shall we say . . . not unhappy to leave Fernando's company," he said, smiling at her with wry amusement.

She grimaced. "Does it show that much?"

"Frankly, yes. But don't worry, Fernando is so confident he is irresistible, I'm sure he didn't notice."

"You're probably right. Anyway, I want to thank you for coming to my rescue."

"Believe me, I was delighted to do so." His ironic smile did not reach his eyes, and Abigail experienced a sudden chill as he maneuvered her through the other dancers. This man, she realized, was as cold as Señor Santana was smarmy. Falling silent, she looked over his shoulder and wondered if she had not jumped from the proverbial frying pan into the fire.

They reached the edge of the dance floor beside the open terrace doors. To Abigail's surprise, he stopped and took her elbow in firm grip.

"What are you—?"

"You are coming with me, Miss Stewart. Quietly," he added, smiling at her with chilling menace. "Please do not try to resist me or call for help. Two of my men have their guns trained on you right now. If you oppose me in any way, they will shoot you."

Shocked, Abigail stared at him, her heart hammering. "Who are—?" Her eyes widened as her gaze touched the silver at his temples. "Oh, my stars," she gasped. This was the man from the yacht.

"Smile, Miss Stewart," he ordered. "We want everyone to think you're merely stepping out on the terrace with me for a breath of fresh air, now don't we?"

He propelled her through the doors. Several couples were on the terrace enjoying the balmy night, but none paid them any mind. Coolly, without the least sign of tension or haste, Nathan Sumner escorted her across the flagstones and down the steps.

Glancing back over her shoulder Abigail saw Erin silhouetted in the doorway, and hope leaped inside her. Had Erin seen them? If she had she would find David and he would come after her.

When they entered the shadows, Nathan picked up the pace, and though Abigail tried to hang back, he hustled her along the path toward the gate at the back of the garden. Halfway there, two shapes materialized out of the darkness on either side and one grasped her other arm as they closed ranks around them.

"Where are you taking me?" she asked as she stumbled along in her borrowed high heels and long gown.

"Somewhere where we can . . . talk. About a certain item that you have that belongs to me. Somewhere private, where we won't be interrupted."

Abigail swallowed hard. She wished she hadn't asked.

On the other side of the gate a dark sedan waited. Abigail was stuffed into the back seat and, to her horror, when she straightened up she found herself wedged in between Nathan Sumner and Ivor, who grinned at her evilly.

Fear clawed at her. It was her fault. All her fault. Oh, God, how could she have been so stupid? When she noticed his silver temples, why hadn't she made the connection right away? She'd been so anxious to escape Fernando Santana, she hadn't given a thought to anything else. Now she was going to pay for the stupid mistake with her life.

Oh, David, help me. Please help me.

Chapter Fourteen

David slammed Charley Higgins up against the paneled wall of Fernando Santana's study and held him there with a fist balled in his shirtfront. Travis lounged back against the door, arms folded over his chest, feet crossed at the ankles, watching the action with an amused smile.

"Now, listen up, Charley, because I'm only going to say this one more time," David snarled into the CIA man's face. "What kind of operation are you heading up here? You spooks over at Langley must know about the microdot, otherwise you wouldn't be so damned interested in Abbey. So why haven't you picked her up?"

"Look, I told you," Charley Higgins croaked. "I don't know what you're talking about. I'm just here on vacation."

"All right! That does it!"

David drew back his fist, but a sudden pounding on the door stayed the blow and had Travis jumping away from the wooden panel as though he'd been touched by a cattle prod.

"What the—"

"David? David, are you in there?"

The frantic note in Elise's voice was unmistakable. The cousins exchanged a wary glance. Releasing Charley Higgins, David signaled to Travis to let her in.

Elise rushed into the study wringing her hands. "Oh, David! Travis! Thank God you're both here! You've got to come quick! Erin and I saw some men taking Abbey through the back garden."

"What? When was this?"

"Just a minute ago."

"Where is Erin now?"

"She's following them. Señor Santana's garage opens onto the alley." Elise looked at her brother apprehensively and wrung her hands. "She broke in and hot-wired the houseboy's motor scooter." At David's groan she rushed on. "I tried to stop her, but she wouldn't listen. Oh, David, you've got to do something!"

It was a toss-up as to who cursed more colorfully, David or Charley Higgins.

"Damn you hotshots!" the CIA man raged, striding for the door. "If you hadn't dragged me out of there I would have seen who took her and I'd be trailing them right now. If you two have bungled this assignment with your interference—"

"Wait a minute." David grabbed him by the collar and jerked him to a halt. "On vacation, were you? You lying scum. Why, I ought to—"

"C'mon, Cuz, we don't have time for this right now!" Travis urged, pulling David away from Charley. "We've got to find Abbey before it's too late."

"Where do we start? We don't know who the guys were or where they're headed."

"I . . . I know who one of the men was."

The hesitant statement brought three heads swiveling toward Elise with a barrage of demands.

"Who?"

"What's his name?"

"Tell us, quick!"

"I-it's Nathan Sumner. He's a wealthy industrialist."

"C'mon," Charley Higgins barked. "Sumner has a yacht docked at Pier One. My guess is he's headed for the harbor."

The black sedan glided to a stop across the quayside road from where Pepe's dilapidated truck was parked. Abigail did not dare even glance in that direction for fear of drawing Nathan or his cohorts' attention to the vehicle ... and Pepe.

Nathan Sumner reached for the door handle, then paused and looked at her. "You know, you could make this easy on yourself and tell us what we want to know. You will eventually anyway." He smiled his cold smile and ran the backs of his knuckles down her cheek. "Tell us where the toy dog is, Miss Stewart," he said in his soft-as-velvet voice. "And I promise your death will be quick and painless."

Abigail could not help it; she shuddered violently. Nathan smiled.

"Wh—" She stopped and cleared her throat. "What toy dog? I don't know what you're talking about."

The smile vanished, and Nathan's face tightened. "Very well, if that's the way you want it." He opened the door and stepped out into the road. Ivor shoved her across the seat. Hampered by the long gown and high heels, she almost stumbled to her knees as she left the car.

Nathan and his two thugs formed a phalanx around Abigail, and as they crossed the quayside road she sent up a silent prayer that Pepe would stay out of sight and not try to be a hero. David had told him to just watch the boat and report anything suspicious, but with Pepe you never knew.

All hope of them passing the truck by ended when a furious spate of high-pitched barking erupted within the cab. Oh, Lord, Abigail groaned silently. Chelsea had spotted her. Gritting her teeth, she stared straight ahead and kept going, hoping that Nathan would pay no attention to the frantic yips.

She should have known it was a forlorn hope at best. They had taken only a few steps when the din drew her captor's attention.

"Wait a minute," Nathan said, halting. He gazed back at the truck, where a furry little head bobbed into view every few seconds through the rear window. He looked back at Abigail with a smug smile. "Why, I believe that's your little dog, isn't it, Miss Stewart? And as I recall Patrice's message, the toy belongs to your pet."

Abigail answered with a lift of her chin and a glare, which merely amused him.

Fear for Pepe nearly choked Abigail as they led her to the truck, but to her surprise—and relief—he was not there; only Chelsea. Beside the terrier on the seat lay the ever-present stuffed puppy.

Nathan jerked open the door, and the Yorkie's yips of delight over seeing Abigail turned to warning barks. She backed away, snarling and growling low in her throat, and stood over the toy with all the ferocity of a mother protecting her young. When Nathan made a grab for the stuffed animal, Chelsea bit him twice before he could yank his hand back. She'd had her baby taken from her once that day already; she wasn't about to let it happen again.

Cursing, Nathan cradled his injured hand and stared at the puncture wounds. He glared at Abigail and barked, "Get that damned toy, Miss Stewart. Now. Or I'll have Ivor shoot that vicious little mutt."

Her expression pained, Abigail hesitated. She couldn't just hand government secrets over to an enemy agent. But she couldn't let them kill Chelsea, either. If they did, they'd get the toy anyway, she reasoned, so she had to do it. "There, Chels. Take it easy, girl," she crooned as she reluctantly reached inside the truck. Chelsea whined and pranced, but she did not resist.

Abigail's fingertips touched the fuzzy cloth, but before her hand could close around the toy, Erin came flying out of the darkness and rammed her shoulder into Ivor's back.

Abigail let out a squeak and jumped. With a grunt, Ivor staggered forward and slammed into Nathan, and both men went sprawling. The third man was so stunned he just stared, unable to move for an instant. Recovering her senses, Abigail kicked out and caught him square in the groin. He doubled over and hit the ground rolled up in a ball like an armadillo, moaning.

"C'mon!" Erin grabbed Abigail's arm. "Let's get out of here!"

Abigail hiked up the sequined gown, and they took off down the pier toward the *Freewind,* running full tilt. Chelsea, her beloved toy clamped between her teeth, raced right at their heels.

In a matter of seconds, Nathan and Ivor were pounding after them. Abigail lost a shoe. She kicked off the other one in midstride and poured on more speed.

When they reached the boat, she scooped up Chelsea and tossed her on board. "Get the other line," she yelled to Erin as she tackled the rear mooring. Working frantically, their gazes darting every few seconds to the men bearing down on them, they cast off the lines and jumped aboard.

"Grab a gaff and push us off. I'll start the engines." Abigail was already climbing the ladder to the bridge as she shouted the instructions. Nathan and Ivor were less than ten yards away.

Erin ran along the side, pushing the gaff handle against the dock. The strip of water between the side of the boat and the pier grew wider with painful slowness—three feet, four feet, five . . .

The engines cranked and sputtered, then fired to life. Erin staggered back and fell hard on her rump as the *Freewind* surged away from the pier, and the two men giving chase came to a teetering halt at the edge, arms flailing like windmill blades.

Up on the road tires squealed and car doors slammed. Running footsteps thundered down the pier, and David shouted, "No, Abbey! Not the boat! For God sake, not my boat! Come back!"

Abigail didn't hear him over the roar of the engines. Neither did Nathan and Ivor. The two men quickly commandeered a speedboat and went zooming out into the harbor after the women.

David, with Travis and Charley Higgins and a half dozen or so of his men following, raced down the pier. At the

Freewind's empty berth he staggered to a halt and stared, appalled, as Abbey steered a drunken course across the wide harbor. Behind the *Freewind,* the speedboat bounced and pounded over the bigger craft's wake.

Caught in the speedboat's searchlight, Abbey stood at the wheel, the aqua sequined dress a glittering beacon in the darkness.

"Ho-ly hell," Travis muttered beside David. "That lady is one *ba-aad* sailor."

"You got that right," David groaned.

Abbey was trying desperately to get out of the harbor, but the speedboat was quicker and more maneuverable and kept cutting her off. David moaned and winced when she made a sharp turn and missed an anchored sailboat by a hair. "God, help us. If she doesn't crash it'll be a miracle."

More car doors slammed back on the road. "David! David!" Elise ran toward them with Sam and Max.

"Great. *Now* they get here," David muttered.

"Ha…have you found…them?" Elise gasped as the trio skidded to a halt.

"We chartered a plane as soon as you called," Sam said. "You were just leaving when we arrived at Santana's. What the devil is going on? Elise is so upset she's not making sense."

"She said something about the KGB and a kidnapping, and my wife following the ones who did it," Max put in, looking around anxiously. "Where is Erin?"

David slanted him a sour look and pointed. "Out there."

In unison three pairs of eyes turned seaward to the two boats racing around the harbor, and three mouths dropped. For once, even Sam appeared thunderstruck.

"Apparently she got Abbey away from the men who snatched her, but the KGB don't give up easily."

"Dammit! Are you telling me that my wife is out there being chased by foreign agents?" Max exploded.

Before David could answer, a gasp went up from the others as the powerboat sheared a dinghy off the stern of a yacht.

David turned pale and cursed.

Max almost came unspooled. "Holy—! Who the hell is the maniac skippering the *Freewind,* for God's sake?"

"That's Abbey. And the answer to your first question is, yes, those are KGB agents."

"Well, isn't anyone going to *do* something?"

"What do you suggest, Max? There isn't another boat in the harbor that can catch that jet boat. Hell, if I could do something, I'd be doing it. That's my sister and my lady out there."

"Everyone just stay calm," Charley Higgins ordered. "My men are rousting out the harbor patrol now. They'll go out with them and pick up Sumner and his henchmen. We already have the one they left on the dock. One of those women gave the guy a shot that'll have him singing soprano for a month."

"You mean all we can do is stand here helpless and *watch!*" Max demanded.

"Only if you've got a strong heart," Travis drawled.

The *Freewind* careened around the harbor. Abbey's carefully coiffed hair streamed out behind her, straight once again. The borrowed sequined dress molded her body and whipped around her legs. Her feet, which were bare except for the shredded stockings, were braced wide. She gripped the wheel tight with both hands and concentrated fiercely on avoiding the sailboats and other pleasure craft that dotted the harbor and on escaping the pesky speedboat that darted around the *Freewind* like a gnat around a sweaty brow.

"Abbey! Abbey!" Erin called to her, struggling up the ladder. She gained the bridge and tottered toward Abbey. "I found... Oh! *Ohhhhhh!*" she shrieked, and staggered sideways, flailing her arms as Abbey spun the wheel hard to the left, and the boat went into a tight turn heeled over almost on its side.

Erin barely managed to grab the rail and save herself from being pitched overboard. When Abigail righted the boat, she lurched back across the deck to her and latched on to the brass rail that surrounded the control console. "I found Pepe tied up below deck!" she yelled to Abbey.

"What!" Abigail shot her an alarmed glance and yelled back, "Is he all right?"

"Yes! But the cabin has been trashed! The cushions and the bed are all slashed! Everything is in shambles! They must've been searching for the toy!"

Abigail spun the wheel to the right, then to the left and fishtailed between two sailboats. Erin closed her eyes, and her lips moved in what looked to be a silent prayer.

"Where is Pepe now?" Abigail shouted.

"Now?" Erin craned her neck and looked over the rail to the deck below. "Right now he's down on his knees praying! By the way!" Erin hollered in her ear. "Have you ever operated a boat before?"

"Just once!"

Erin rolled her eyes.

The speedboat pulled up alongside, and Nathan Sumner's disembodied voice blared through a horn. "Give up, Miss Stewart. You can't outrun us."

"He's right, we can't!" Erin yelled. "And every time we get near the mouth of the harbor he cuts us off! So what do we do?"

Abigail chewed on her bottom lip for a few seconds. Then she set her jaw and swung the *Freewind* to the right, away from the speedboat and toward the harbor entrance. The smaller craft dropped back and turned to head her off.

The speedboat raced past them and cut across their path. Abigail firmed her mouth and took a tighter grip on the wheel. "Hang on!" she yelled to Erin.

"What're you going to do?"

Instead of veering off, as she had every other time the smaller boat blocked their way, this time the *Freewind* bore down on the vessel at full throttle. The faces of the two men on the boat were at first scornful, then disbelieving, then panic-stricken.

Erin's eyes widened. *"Oh—my—God!"*

"Oh, my God! I don't believe it. She wouldn't! She couldn't! Oh, hell, she's going to!" David yelled. "She's going to ram them!"

Nathan Sumner and his henchman came to the same conclusion. The terrified men dived for safety seconds before the *Freewind's* prow hit the fiberglass boat and sent it sailing skyward, smashed into a hundred pieces.

Elise screamed, and a storm of shocked curses and exclamations erupted from those watching from the dock. As the furor raged, David stood like a man turned to stone, his heart clubbing his rib cage, his eyes fixed on the *Freewind*.

Travis laid a hand on his shoulder. "Take it easy. They're okay. I can see them both on the deck," he murmured.

The Harbor Patrol boats, which had already left the dock, moved out to fish the men out of the water. Reducing speed, Abigail turned the *Freewind* around and headed back to the docks.

David and Max waited anxiously at the side of the pier, watching the sleek power cruiser cut an erratic path through the water at what seemed like a snail's pace after the hair-raising chase. When the boat drew near enough, both men jumped aboard. At the same time, Pepe jumped off, fell to his knees and kissed the pier.

"Max! Darling!" Erin scrambled down from the bridge, her face alight.

David dashed past his sister with barely a nod as she threw herself into her husband's arm. He took the bridge ladder in two leaps, not even wincing as the hull banged against the pier and scraped the side.

"Abbey! God, Abbey, are you all right?" He leaped across the bridge and snatched her into his arms before she could shut off the engines. "Oh, Abbey," he groaned against the side of her neck, rocking her in his tight embrace. "I have never been so scared in my life."

He kissed her then, long and hungrily, with the wild passion of a man who has been pushed too far. Hands clutched and stroked, slanted mouths rocked and tongues swirled as their bodies strained together.

When the need for air ended the kiss, he ran his hands over her—her back, her hips, her arms, finally sinking his fingers into her tangled hair and cradling her head. "Oh, baby. Are you sure you're okay? Those bastards didn't hurt you, did they?''

She touched his cheek and smiled, her eyes glowing at the concern she saw in his. ''I'm fine. Really. And, David...I'm sorry about your boat. I—''

''Don't worry about the boat. It's insured.''

He could not have stunned her more if he had suddenly taken off and flown around the harbor. Nothing he could have said would have convinced her more that he truly cared for her. She was touched and elated and so swamped with emotions she could not speak, and she looked at him with misty eyes, her soft mouth trembling.

He pressed a firm kiss on those quivering lips, and when he straightened, her knees were wobbly. He smiled into her eyes and slipped his arm around her shoulder. ''C'mon. There's a whole raft of CIA guys down on the pier. Let's go give them the microdot and find out what the devil we almost got ourselves killed for.''

Abigail's face lit up. ''The microdot! I'd almost forgotten about it!''

Below deck she held Chelsea, who snarled and snapped, while David removed the film from the toy's eye. On shore, minutes later, Abigail handed the microdot over to Agent Higgins, flush with triumphant pride over her part in keeping the information from enemy hands.

''There you are, Mr. Higgins. I'm sure you're as relieved to have this back—whatever it is—as I am to be rid of it.''

Charley Higgins stared at the tiny dot of film, his mouth set in a grim line. After a moment he sighed and slipped it into his shirt pocket as though it were of no more importance than a grocery list. ''Yeah, sure. Thanks,'' he said with an annoyed edge to his voice.

''Hey, wait a minute!'' David barked. ''That's it? A lousy 'thanks'?''

''Whadda you want, a medal? Get off my case, Blaine. You've given me enough grief already. From now on, just keep your nose out of things that don't concern you.''

''What the—?''

Puzzled, David and Travis looked at each other, and slowly their faces hardened as the truth struck them simultaneously.

"Why you sorry scuzball," David growled. "You *wanted* that information to fall into Russian hands, didn't you? Which means only one thing, whatever is on that film is phony. We risked our lives for nothing. It was all a setup, wasn't it? *Wasn't it?*"

"All right, all right. It was phony. But the operation was important."

David made a low sound and lunged for the man, but Travis and Sam pulled him back before he could get his hands around Charley's throat. "You scum! You dirt bag! I'm gonna tear you apart!"

"Easy, easy, Cuz. He isn't worth it."

"Travis is right," Sam added. "Cool down, David."

"Look, Blaine, we had to put out false information," Charley insisted. "We've got a high-ranking mole in the Company and we were trying to flush him out. We'd narrowed the suspects down to five men. So we gave each one a different set of false information. We would have known who our mole was by which information surfaced."

The explanation did nothing to cool David's anger. He stared at the agent through narrowed eyes. "It won't wash, Charley. All you had to do was pick up Abbey and the microdot. You'll know who your man is as soon as you examine the film. You *wanted* the other side to have that information," he accused. "Why? What is it?"

"Look, I don't have to tell y—"

"Charley, if you value your hide, you'll spit it out. Now!"

"All right, all right." Charley heaved a sigh and raked a hand through his thinning hair. "The microdot contains a short list of double agents—Russians supposedly working for our side. The men on the list are actually loyal KGB men. The plan was to have had a twofold benefit. It would get the other side to take out their own men and, depending on which enemy agents suddenly disappeared, we would have the identity of our mole."

David lunged toward Charley again, but Travis and Sam held him back. "You risk our lives to trick the other side into snuffing out their own men! Why you sick bas—"

"What's the big deal?" Charley spread his hands, truly perplexed. "Miss Stewart was never in any real danger. One of my men penetrated Sergio's group months ago. He was looking out for her safety."

Charley frowned and turned a hard look on Abigail. "By the way, that reminds me. Peterson wasn't too happy about having his hands glued together. We had to saw that post apart to get him free. He's in the hospital now, waiting for the company that manufactured the stuff to send a solvent that'll unstick his hands."

His chastisement of Abigail enraged David all over again. "The American with Sergio's group is one of you guys? *That's* your idea of protection? Hell, that's a laugh. Abbey and I know firsthand just how effective that jackass is as a guard."

The wail of several sirens interrupted the confrontation. Within moments a caravan of police cars screeched to a halt on the quayside road, and the local police poured onto the pier.

They all spent the next three hours at police headquarters explaining things. Nathan Sumner and his men were charged with kidnapping and attempted murder but, because they were in Mexican territory, the espionage charges had to be handled through the state department.

It was almost dawn when the tired group left the San Cristobal police station. By the time they reached the beach house on Rincon Island, Abigail's earlier elation and high spirits had dissipated. In their place was a gnawing worry and apprehension.

Since entering the police station David had been quiet and distant. He barely looked at her, and he spoke to her only when forced to. Abigail could almost feel him withdrawing.

As they trailed into the living room of the beach house, Erin stretched. "I don't know about you guys, but I'm going to bed," she said over a huge yawn. A chorus of muttered good-nights followed, and the two couples drifted away to their respective bedrooms, leaving Abigail and David standing alone in awkward silence.

Abigail shifted from one foot to the other. She stared down at her toes, poking out of the shredded stockings, suddenly conscious of what a fright she must look in the bedraggled gown with her hair all wild and tangled and what was left of her glamorous makeup smudged.

"Well, uh ... good night, Abbey," David said.

Her head snapped up as he took a step toward the left wing. Panic streaked through her, and before she thought, she blurted, "Aren't you going to sleep with me?" Immediately hot color flooded her face, and she could have bitten off her tongue.

Sighing, David turned back. "Look, Abbey, I've been thinking about ... well ... about us, and ... I think it would be best if we ended it now."

Excruciating pain stabbed Abigail's heart. Her chin wobbled, but she fought to control it. "I see."

"No. I don't think you do," David said with gruff tenderness. He stepped close and cupped her face.

Battling the terrible ache in her chest and the need to cry, Abigail stared at the ruffled front of his formal shirt.

"I care about you, Abbey—more than you know—but I just don't see us having a future together."

"I understand. You don't have to—"

"Abbey, listen to me. I'm a jaded, worn-out ex-agent. I've had my fill of adventure and excitement—more than enough to last me a lifetime. If I didn't know that before, this little episode has driven the fact home. I'm ready to settle down to a quiet, ordinary life."

She looked up then, a spark of hope in her eyes, but his next words doused it. "You, on the other hand, are just beginning to try your wings." She opened her mouth to argue, but he placed his forefinger across her lips, silencing her. "Abbey, honey, in the short time we've been together, I've watched you change from a frightened little mouse who jumped at her own shadow to a vibrant, self-assured woman. Don't you see? You're just now ready to experience life. To explore the possibilities. You deserve the chance to have a little fun, to have a taste of excitement and adventure.''

With a sigh, he rubbed her chin with his thumb and gazed at her with longing and regret. ''No matter what we feel, our lives just don't mesh, Abbey. We've reached different turning points. We have different needs.''

Gathering her pride around her like a cloak, Abigail gave him a wavering smile. ''I hadn't thought of it that way, but of course, you're probably right,'' she said in a stilted voice. ''And as you said, the wisest thing would be to part now, before either of us gets hurt.''

She stepped back, away from his touch, desperate to end the painful conversation before her brave front collapsed and she made a complete fool of herself. ''Well, I guess there's nothing left to say. Except . . . good night.'' Turning away, she started for the right wing on shaky legs.

''Abbey, are you all right?''

She stopped, got control of her wobbly chin, and looked back over her shoulder. Her throat ached as though she'd swallowed an apple whole, but she managed a quiet, ''I'm fine,'' and marched on without looking back.

In the room they had shared the night before she locked the door, then collapsed onto the bed and pulled a pillow over her head to muffle the cries that spilled forth like water through a broken dam. Oh, God, she loved him so.

The sobs tore from her, long, agonizing sounds straight from her soul. She cried over her foolish hopefulness. She cried over the loss of her dreams. Most of all, she cried over the future that stretched out endless and lonely, for Abigail knew that she would never love again. Not as she loved David.

What she had felt for Ted all those years ago was paltry by comparison to what she felt for David. He had made her feel, for the first time in her life, like a real woman—a vibrant, exciting, desirable woman. David, with his rough edges, his blunt manner, his tender heart and chivalrous soul, had freed her spirit, and in doing so, had captured her heart.

Of course, she didn't believe a word of his explanation, but even that had made her love him all the more. He had warned her in the beginning that their love affair might not last and that he wasn't sure he was the marrying kind. He wasn't obligated to give her any reasons for ending things between them. The truth was he did not love her. But despite his rough exterior, David was a gentle man. He had offered the explanation to let her down easy and allow her to save face.

Abigail cried until she was thoroughly spent and there were no tears left. Still curled in a ball, she lay on her side and gazed at the far wall. She had no right to be upset, she told herself. Hadn't she known from the beginning that this was merely a brief interlude that could not possibly last? She'd told him that she would settle for what she could have, and that was what she would do. No matter how much it hurt.

Chapter Fifteen

David's sisters lit into him that afternoon the instant he showed his face. He'd been so miserable and sick at heart at the thought of losing Abigail, he'd managed only a few hours sleep all day. He walked into the living room with dark circles under his eyes, a knot in his stomach and a giant ache where his heart should be, and came face-to-face with two irate woman.

"Well, it's about time you woke up," Erin declared with her hands on her hips.

"Something wrong?" He glanced at his brothers-in-law, who sat sprawled in the whicker chairs, but Sam merely shrugged, and Max spread his hands wide.

"You bet something's wrong. What did you do to Abbey?"

"What?"

"Abbey just told us that she's leaving today on the last ferry," Elise explained. "She's in her room getting ready."

The pain in David's chest sharpened. He experienced a strong urge to march into Abbey's room and tell her that she wasn't going anywhere—ever—but he squelched it. He was doing the right thing in letting her go. The right thing for her, at any rate, and that was what mattered. He'd been telling himself the same thing all day, but it didn't make the pain any less.

Carefully keeping his face impassive, he sauntered into the kitchen and poured himself a mug of coffee. "There's no reason for her to take the ferry to Alhaja Verde. I'll take her back on the *Freewind*."

"She shouldn't be going at all," Erin declared. "Now, I want to know what happened between you two. And don't give me any of that tight-lipped silence, either, David Blaine. I'm going to pester you until you tell me, so you might as well give up."

"And if she doesn't, I will," Elise declared.

David aimed a sour look at Max and Sam. "Can't you control these two?"

"Nope," Max conceded with a cheerful grin.

"You were never able to," Sam drawled. "Why expect miracles from us?"

"Out with it, David," Erin ordered, tapping her sandaled foot on the wood floor. Elise sat on the arm of the sofa, swinging he leg, her arms crossed beneath her breasts.

"Oh, all right. If you must know, I told her that I thought we should end things between us."

"Oh, David, why?" Elise wailed.

"Why, you pigheaded idiot! Any fool could see that you're in love with her. What on earth did you do that for?"

Knowing they would not rest until they'd gotten the whole story, David explained. When he had finished, his sisters stared at him as though he'd taken leave of his senses.

"That's it? You're throwing over the love of your life for a flimsy reason like that?"

"Dammit, Erin. It's not a flimsy reason. And I never said that I loved her," David retorted.

"But you do, don't you?"

David glared, and she raised her eyebrows imperiously.

"Don't you?"

"All right, dammit! Yes, I love her. There, are you satisfied? But it still wouldn't be right for me to marry her."

"You want to know what I think?" Erin asked.

"No, I don't."

"I think this business about her needing to spread her wings is just a smoke screen. *I* think you're just plain old scared of making a commitment. You've played the footloose bachelor so long the thought of hearth and home and family scares the hell out of you. Doesn't it, you big, tough ex-G-man?"

"Just butt out, Erin. Okay?" David slammed his coffee mug down on the counter and stomped toward the door. "I need a cigarette. If anyone wants me I'll be on the *Freewind*. And you can tell Abbey I'll be ready to shove off anytime she is."

"Well!" Erin huffed, watching him through the windows as he stomped across the deck and disappeared down the steps. "Butt out, indeed. Ha! Fat chance." She tugged her sister off the sofa. "Come on, Elise. If we put our heads together we can come up with an answer to this problem."

"Whoa. Wait a minute, sweetheart," Max cautioned. "You're not really going to interfere are you?"

"Don't be silly, darling. Of course we are."

For the trip home Abigail put on the floral sundress with the coordinating jade jacket. She had just placed the rest of her meager wardrobe into the shopping bag Elise had given her when the twins tapped on her door.

"David told us what he did," Erin said, getting right to the point. "Well, Elise and I aren't going to just sit back and let that pigheaded brother of ours ruin both his life and yours."

"Oh, no, please, you mustn't interfere. Look, I appreciate what you're trying to do, but I don't want to put David on the spot. He can't help it if he doesn't love me."

"Doesn't love you!" Erin hooted. "That idiot is so in love with you, he can't see straight—much less think straight."

"Oh, no, you're wrong. He couldn't possibly..." Abigail bit her bottom lip and looked back and forth between the two women. "Do...do you really think so?"

"Yes, we do," Elise said, and hope soared in Abigail's heart. "He's just being his usual overprotective self, is all. We simply have to do something to bring him to his senses."

"Elise and I have come up with a plan, and Travis has agreed to help. Now here's what we'll do..."

"Have you seen Abbey?" David asked the four people sitting on the deck an hour later. "I'd like to get going before it gets too late."

Erin took a sip of her lemonade and looked at her sister. Elise smiled. "She went for a walk on the beach with Travis."

David's eyebrows shot downward. "With Travis! What the hell is she doing with Travis?" Shading his eyes, he looked down the beach. A hundred yards or so away, two figures stood close together, deep in conversation. "Why the devil did you let her go with Travis? Abbey is vulnerable right now, and you both know his reputation with women."

"Oh, relax, David," Erin said. "There's no romance brewing between those two. They went for a stroll to discuss business. Abbey is talking to Travis about becoming a government agent."

"*What!*" David whirled around, his eyes wild. "You're kidding, right? Tell me you're kidding."

Erin shrugged. "All I know is she said she wanted to become an agent."

"Over my dead body!"

He swung around and galloped down the steps. The group on the deck did not move until he reached the bottom and stormed away down the beach. "Quick! Where did you hide the binoculars?" Erin demanded as she and her sister scrambled off the loungers.

"Over there behind the flowerpots."

"Good Lord! Don't tell me you're going to spy on them?"

"Of course we are." Snatching up the field glasses, Erin ignored her husband and hurried over to the rail with her twin and focused on David's striding figure.

"Can you see him clearly?"

"Oh, yeah. And hot damn, is he ever mad. I can almost see smoke coming out of his ears."

"Let me look," Elise begged, doing an excited jig. "Come on, Erin, don't hog the glasses. Give me a turn."

Max looked at Sam. Both men shook their heads and heaved beleaguered sighs.

"Uh-oh. Get set. Here he comes," Travis warned in a low murmur. "No! No, don't turn around. Remember what I told you—stay calm and play it cool. And follow my lead."

"All right. Oh, Travis, I'm so nervous. Do you really think this will work?"

"Honey, from the look on my cousin's face I'd say it was a lead pipe cinch. He looks angry enough to chew nails. Brace yourself now, he's almost here."

"Travis! What the devil is going on here?" David roared.

"Hi ya, Cuz. Hey, you're just in time to help. Abbey was just talking to me about becoming an agent."

"Then it's true. I didn't believe it when Erin first told me." He glared at Travis. "And just what the hell do you think you're doing, encouraging her in this madness? And as for you," he raged, turning on Abigail. "You can just get this crazy idea right out of your head. You are *not* joining the Bureau! Do you hear me? It's out of the question!"

Abigail was elated by his reaction. Excitement and hope skittered through her, and her nerves began to flutter, but somehow she managed a guileless smile. "Why, David, why are you so upset? I'm just following your advice. After all, you did say that I needed excitement and adventure in my life," she said reasonably, which to her delight, incensed him even more. "Working as an agent seems to me the perfect way to do that."

"You are not joining the FBI," David reiterated between gritted teeth.

"Hey, no problem, Cuz. I'm not going to help her get in the Bureau," Travis assured him. "Shoot. After the way Abbey handled herself with Sumner and his bunch, I figure she's more suited to be CIA. When I get back to D.C., I'm going to set up a meeting for her with Charley Higgins's superiors."

David looked ready to explode. He stared at his cousin, speechless. His jaw bulged. His nostrils whitened. His throat worked. Then he blew.

"Like hell you will!" he roared. "*My* woman is not joining that bunch of spooks over at Langley!"

Startled by the bellowed ultimatum, Abigail jumped and let out a little squeak. The next breath she let out another as David hoisted her over his shoulder in a fireman's lift and stalked back toward the house with long, angry strides.

Dangling over his shoulder Abigail raised her head and looked back at Travis. A huge grin split his handsome face, and he lifted his fist in a thumbs-up sign.

All the blood rushed to Abigail's head. She bounced with every jarring step, her French braid hanging down and whipping against David's jean-covered rump. She quickly discovered that viewing the world upside down while being jostled did unpleasant things to her tummy.

"David, I—"

"Shut up, Legs," he snapped. "I'll deal with you at the house."

The jostling grew worse when he pounded up the steps. On the deck he stomped past Elise and Erin without a word.

They stood close together, looking suspiciously innocent, hiding a pair of binoculars behind their backs. Both women grinned at Abbey and winked, and Erin muttered cheerfully, "Well, so much for noble self-sacrifice."

Inside, David marched through the living room, past Max and Sam, ignoring their startled looks. Without pausing, he stomped down the hall to the bedroom he and Abbey had shared, strode inside and kicked the door shut behind them.

Abigail shrieked when David tossed her onto the bed. She bounced twice, and when the world righted itself and her spinning head cleared, David was bent over her, a hand on either side of her hips, his face like a thundercloud.

"Now," he pronounced in a gritty voice. "You and I are going to get a few things straight. First of all, you are *not*—I repeat—*not* going to join the FBI or the CIA or any other government agency. You got that?"

"Yes, David."

"What you are going to do is marry me. Immediately."

"Yes, David."

"And don't give me any argument about it, because it won't do any good."

"I won't. I promise."

He straightened and began to pace. "It's obvious to me that left on your own you'll just end up in one scrape after another," he ranted. "Well, I'm not going to stand by and let that happen. You hear me?"

"Yes, David," Abigail said softly, but he was so caught up in his tirade, her meek, slightly smug acquiescence did not register.

"I know you're anxious to live a little, experience new things, and that's fine. But from now on, if you want excitement, I'll provide you with all you'll ever need. Understand?"

"Perfectly."

"And what's more, you . . ." He stopped and scowled at her. "What did you say?"

A languid, purely feminine smile curved her lips. She reached for his hand and pulled him down until he was bent over her again. "I said, yes," she whispered, cupping her hands around the back of his neck.

He sucked in his breath and gazed at her, as though afraid he hadn't heard her right.

"Yes," she whispered again. "Yes. Yes. Yes."

She felt the tension leave him, saw the flame leap in his eyes, and her smile widened.

"Aw, Abbey." He surrendered to the gentle tug of her hands, and as their lips met he stretched out on top of her.

They kissed rapaciously at first, their mouths rocking, open and hungry, as each sought confirmation of the love they had yet to declare. Wet tongues dueled in a rough caress, speaking of need, of the anguish just past, of the joy that lay ahead. The kiss went on and on, their lips clinging, devouring with greedy passion as hearts thudded and their blood surged hotly through their veins. David nipped Abigail's lower lip, then drew it into his mouth and sucked gently. She moaned, a low, throaty sound, and stroked the back of his neck, telling him without words the depth of her feelings.

But soon it wasn't enough. Their love was too new, their hearts too unsure; they needed the words.

"Abbey," David murmured against her lips. "Are you sure this is what you want?"

She framed his face between her hands and pushed him away until she could look into his eyes. "Yes, I'm very sure. I love you, David. I think I have since that second night, when you held me while I cried."

"Aw, sweetheart, I love you, too. But—"

"Shh." She placed her hand over his mouth. "I know what you're going to say, but it isn't so. Believe me, I've had enough adventure and excitement these past few days to last forever."

"You're sure?"

"Very." She smiled tenderly and stroked his face. "I came to Alhaja Verde for a once in a lifetime vacation. Instead, I found my once in a lifetime love."

The soft declaration banished the last of his doubts. With a low moan, David kissed her again. Like a spark to tinder, at the first touch of their lips passion exploded between them.

Urgently, a little roughly, as their lips clung and their yearning bodies pressed and rubbed, David's fingers worked at the buttons on the front of her dress.

"David, your family! They're—"

"Very discreet," he finished for her, freeing her breasts to his avid gaze. "By now they've all gone for a long walk on the beach. I guarantee it," he mumbled, rubbing his lips against her milky skin, and Abigail could only moan and arch her back as his mouth surrounded her velvety hard nipple.

"Y-you're sure," she gasped, reaching for the snap on his jeans.

"Mmm." His tongue stroked a raspy caress, and his warm breath feathered over her wet flesh. "I'm sure. Now come here, woman, and love me."

They worked feverishly to divest each other of their clothes, but progress was hindered by shaking hands and the need to touch and caress. Finally, between lingering kisses and whispered words of love, buttons, hooks and zippers were dealt with, and they were tumbling together on the wide bed, lips fused, eager hands touching, stroking, learning anew lovers' secrets.

Neither could wait. The painful time apart had built their desire to a fever pitch. Wrapped in each other's arms, they kissed deeply, and as David rolled her to her back Abigail's legs wrapped around his hips in a movement as old as time, as instinctive as breathing.

Together they soared. Each seeking and giving pleasure, sharing the special rapture that only true love brings. The sweet tension stretched tighter and tighter. David's face was flushed and contorted with fierce gladness as he watched Abigail's aquamarine eyes go smoky with pleasure.

Abigail threw her head back on the pillow and clutched David's back. Then his name ripped from her throat as again they shared that shattering explosion that rocked them to the depths of their being.

As thundering hearts calmed, as breathing returned to normal, they drifted back to reality with a sigh of satisfaction. Abigail stroked David's slick back, a soft smile on her face.

"Mmm. I like that," he mumbled drowsily.

Rousing himself, he braced up on his forearms and smiled down at her. He dropped a quick kiss on the end of her nose and rolled away from her. Abigail expected him to take her in his arms and cuddle, but instead he bounded from the bed, stretched, then reached for her hand.

"David! What are you doing?" she squealed when he yanked her from the bed.

"C'mon, woman, we haven't got time to dawdle," he said, towing her toward the bathroom. "We've got to hurry."

"Why? Where are we going?"

He stopped and gave her a hard kiss. "To Alhaja Verde to get married."

"Tonight?" she squeaked.

He grinned and kissed her again. "Tonight."

Epilogue

David let himself into the apartment. He listened for a moment and smiled as he heard a faint sound from the bedroom. Perfect.

He eased down the hall and came to a halt in the doorway, smiling when he spotted Abbey, dressed in a pink satin slip, sitting at the dressing table, brushing her hair. It shimmered down her back in a golden brown cascade that fell below her hips.

"Happy Anniversary, Legs."

Abigail twisted around on the bench, her face lighting up, and David's heart contracted. Lord, she grew lovelier every day.

Chelsea, curled up in her favorite spot at the foot of the bed, looked up and lifted her lip at him.

"You remembered."

"Of course. What kind of husband would I be if I forgot our first-month anniversary?" He crossed to where she sat, caught her chin in his hand and tilted her face up for his kiss.

"I've got a present for you," he murmured when their lips parted, and placed a small box on the dressing table.

"Darling, you shouldn't have. It's present enough just knowing that you've finally quit smoking."

"Don't argue, woman. Just open it."

"Oh, David, they're lovely," Abigail exclaimed as she lifted the pearl earrings from the bed of green velvet.

"I brought Chelsea a present, too."

Abigail blinked up at him. "You brought Chelsea a present?"

"Yeah. I'm tired of that little fuzz ball growling at me every time I get near you, so..." He reached into the deep inside pocket of his suit coat and pulled out a bundle of fur.

"Oh, David! He's adorable!"

"He's five years old, he weighs four pounds, and got a pedigree as long as your arm," he explained as he set the male Yorkshire terrier on the floor. "His owner died, and he needed a home. I thought if Chels had her own love interest, maybe she wouldn't be so jealous of me."

The tiny dog scampered over to Chelsea at once, his tasseled tail waving. Chelsea lay with her snout on her paws, her eyes half closed, the picture of disinterest. Her suitor danced around her, yipping enthusiastically, but she ignored him, except to snap when he dared get too close.

Laughing, Abbey shook her head. "Nice try, darling, but I'm afraid it won't work."

"Don't be too sure. Give him a little time." Bending from the waist, David urged, "Come on, boy. Turn on the charm. I'm counting on you, fella."

Abigail giggled and teased that Chelsea was too virtuous and levelheaded to fall for such an obvious Don Juan.

But to her surprise, before long Chelsea began to coyly tolerate the smitten male's attention. After a while the canine pair trotted from the room—Chelsea with regal disdain and the feisty male cavorting around her like a lovesick swain.

David closed the door behind them and shot his wife a smug look. "Never underestimate a determined male."

"So I'm learning. By the way, does your little friend have a name?"

An unholy grin spread across David's face. "Yeah. It's Hooligan."

"You're kidding."

"Nope." Bending, he scooped his wife up in his arms and headed for the bed. "As soon as I heard his name, I knew he was the man for the job."

"Mmm. Yes, I think maybe you're right." Abigail wrapped her arms around his neck and smiled—a slow, suggestive smile rife with sensual secrets. She touched the top of his ear and combed her fingers through the hair at his nape, her nails lightly raking his scalp. "Every female should have a hooligan in her life."

* * * * *

Oh, what a tangled web we weave . . .

*Although elusive David Blaine is now happily
"tied down," not all the plot threads spun
two years ago in FOOLS RUSH IN (#416) and
WHERE ANGELS FEAR (#468) are wrapped up
yet! In the coming months, expect to be enmeshed
again with this warm, adventurous family as
Ginna Gray continues weaving their delightful
tapestry . . . only in Silhouette* **Special Edition.**

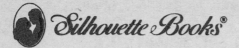 *Silhouette Books*®

SILHOUETTE BOOKS ARE NOW AVAILABLE IN STORES AT THESE CONVENIENT TIMES EACH MONTH

Silhouette Desire and Silhouette Romance

May titles: April 10
June titles: May 8
July titles: June 5
August titles: July 10

Silhouette Intimate Moments and Silhouette Special Edition

May titles: April 24
June titles: May 22
July titles: June 19
August titles: July 24

We hope this new schedule is convenient for you. With only two trips each month to your local bookseller, you will always be sure not to miss any of your favorite authors!

Happy reading!

*Please note: There may be slight variations in on-sale dates in your area due to differences in shipping and handling.

SDATES-R

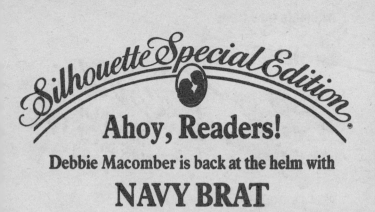

Silhouette Special Edition

Ahoy, Readers!

Debbie Macomber is back at the helm with

NAVY BRAT

Navy brat Erin McNamara planned to pass adulthood joyfully embracing the landlubber's life—even if it meant steering clear of Lt. Commander Brandon Davis, the navy man who set her heart racing at twenty knots per minute! But Brandon was equally determined not to give up his *seafaring* ways. And although the outlook was stormy, he simply had to navigate irrepressible Erin into becoming his navy bride!

This April, drop anchor with NAVY BRAT (Special Edition #662), Debbie Macomber's follow-up to NAVY WIFE (Special Edition #494) and NAVY BLUES (Special Edition #518)—and set your sights on future navy stories—only in *Silhouette Special Edition!*

IT'S A CELEBRATION OF MOTHERHOOD!

Following the success of BIRDS, BEES and BABIES, we are proud to announce our second collection of Mother's Day stories.

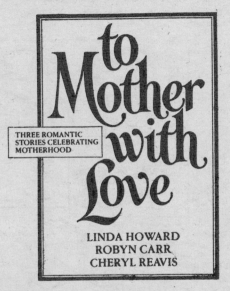

to
Mother
with
Love

THREE ROMANTIC
STORIES CELEBRATING
MOTHERHOOD

LINDA HOWARD
ROBYN CARR
CHERYL REAVIS

Three stories in one volume, all by award-winning authors—stories especially selected to reflect the love all families share.

Available in May, TO MOTHER WITH LOVE is a perfect gift for yourself or a loved one to celebrate the joy of motherhood.

Silhouette Books®